FIRST

AWAKENED

A FIRST BORN BOOK

FROM

THE GUARDIANS OF DARE CHRONICLES

Janelle Gabay

FIRST BORN

FIRST AWAKENED

LAST CHANCE

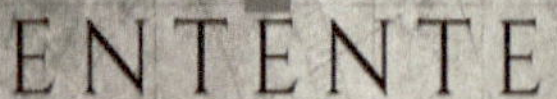

ENTENTE
RAIN'S GATE
ANGEL FALLS PORTAL
LAVENDER WITCHES COVEN
MANAUS
LAUTARO'S CASTLE
TEMPLE OF THE SUN PORTAL
IGUAZU FALLS PORTAL
CARRERA LAKE PORTAL
CAVE OF HANDS PORTAL

WAKER

A Waker is a Guardian immortal injected with Death Serum and then awakened with a serum that is missing the key ingredient. These Awakeneds act and look as they always had except for the whole black eyes. All Awakeneds, regardless of which serum is used to wake them, have black eyes. However, the Guardian awakened by the deficient serum slowly deteriorates physically and mentally. Over time, they turn from Awakened to Waker. A Waker has an uncontrollable craving for blood and an urge to kill.

The Waker is a new creature. Only with further study and more time will we truly understand the range of their capabilities and capacity for evil.

—From Joe Prescott's notes on the James and Tracy experiment dated March 31 to September 19, 2121.

ONE

GUARDIAN VILLAGE

SEPTEMBER 17, 2121

Tarian Prescott stepped from the shadows and thrust the needle into the back of the Waker's neck. She spun around. The realization of her fate swept over her face. She looked at him, the Awakened Hunter, with her infinite black eyes, then crumpled to the cobbled street.

Tarian hoisted her limp body over his shoulder and lumbered down Rue de la Magie. The woman, Victoria Spade, marked his eighth kill, and it wasn't getting any easier. It had been seven months since the Guardians had blown up Zachary Eastwood's warehouse full of hundreds of immortal offspring, crippling his plans for an immortal army. On that day, Tarian thought he had avenged his father's death, but instead, he'd only cracked the surface of a layered nightmare.

Though the injection contained Death Serum, it didn't fully extinguish the life of the immortal. To finish the kill required incinerating the body. Tarian strode straight to the bonfire passing boarded up abandoned shops one after the other. He kept his eyes down fixed on the street. Every store held a fond memory for him that was now tainted by the blood and destruction of a Waker's wrath.

He walked past Café de la Nouvelle Natuche and swallowed hard, unsuccessfully suppressing the memories that infused the location. He steeled his mind, but it was no use. The memories were everywhere like wisps of air floating and touching every inch of him. The Café would forever remain the place where Audrey had given him his test results confirming he had special gifts. The place where the embers of his love for her first lit. All those months ago, he could never have predicted his current life. He was the most gifted immortal Guardian. A man hunting immortals stabbed with Death Serum only to be awakened as monstrous Wakers. A man in love with Audrey, the woman who captivated every cell in his body. No, he preferred to keep his eyes focused on the rough stones beneath his feet and not on the lost magnificence of the village.

Tarian rounded the corner to find the fire blazing stronger than ever. The flames lurched upwards toward the starless sky like arms outstretched to grab hold of the dead. He heaved Victoria's body into the hungry flames. The bonfire of his past had burned gently to keep lovers warm while the bonfire that burned in front of him now blazed viciously to kill the Wakers.

Tarian held his brown eyes wide, fighting every instinct to shut them and not witness the horror of flesh burning. He kept his body forward, feeling the warmth blanket him. He endured the rank stench of burning organs because he was the Awakened Hunter. He'd vowed to himself and the entire village that he'd find and kill the twenty bloodthirsty Wakers that Zachary had created.

As he gazed upon the hell before him, he thought of Zachary: the immortal man, his father's best friend and murderer, Audrey's friend and betrayer. Zachary had injected his father with Death Serum. He'd devised an antidote of sorts to the Death Serum and administered it to victims, but those he awakened were not restored. Instead, they became vicious monsters that roamed amid villagers and Guardians as normal people. But they were anything but normal, and now these Wakers hungered for flesh and blood. At night, they destroyed the village and hunted the innocent.

Each recollection of the past, each crackle of hair scorching, each pop of bone disintegrating further enraged Tarian. His hands curled into fists, his eyes focused, and he rushed back out away from the hot breeze into the cool night. His adrenaline wouldn't be quenched until he had all the Wakers sizzling in the fire.

Three hours of sweat-filled tracking had passed and led to nothing. One kill wasn't good enough, but soon the sun would rise and his body required sleep for maximum performance so he turned toward his apartment inside Guardian Headquarters. Like an angry child, he stomped his way home daring a Waker to approach.

"Come on," he said under his breath, voice hoarse from fatigue. "I dare you." He knew they lurked in the shadows. He hoped they heard him, but his only response was chatter from insects.

Plodding on, he spotted a dark lump lying in the middle of the street. Suddenly, the pile of ragged cloth moved. It jerked to life, dragging itself in the opposite direction.

A small boy tried to move his mangled legs. "Get away! I have a knife. Don't come any closer!" His words clipped with panic as he continued his pitiful crawl.

In a voice he used on his youngest sister, Chloe, Tarian said, "It's okay. I'm not the Waker. I hunt the Wakers." Tarian stepped cautiously.

The boy stilled.

Tarian drew nearer. The hair he had mistaken for brown was blood-soaked. Dark red covered his blonde locks and glinted in the moonlight.

"Be careful, he's out there." The boy's eyes grew wide with a prey's terror.

A swish of movement in the shadows captured their attention. They looked at one another knowing it was the beast. It wanted to feed on the boy but didn't dare encounter the Awakened Hunter. Tarian scooped his small body into his arms.

"Don't let him get me." He clutched Tarian's jacket and buried his head into his chest.

"It's okay. I won't let anything happen to you." Tarian's spine stiffened with predatory instincts calling him to the hunt.

The Waker lurked among the bushes, veiled in the darkness, testing them.

Tarian's gifted night vision cleared a path through the darkness. He stared down the bloodthirsty Waker that stood several feet away. It was a male. Panic seized Tarian. He lived in dread that one night he'd see the face of his father on a Waker. After all, Joe had been injected with Death Serum, but he'd been cremated so Tarian's fear was foolish. He hesitated. The Waker's skewed features didn't match the symmetry of his father's. Relieved he could freely attack this monster, he prepared to lunge.

The small boy's body melted into Tarian's arms. His eyelids fluttered shut. Red and yellow fluid oozed from the gouges on his legs. Tarian ran, choosing to save the boy rather than kill the Waker.

Yards away from the entrance to Guardian Headquarters, Tarian hurdled over a wooden fence, cutting a direct path to the doors. He bound up the glass staircase to the second level and burst through the infirmary doors.

Tarian yelled, "Victim! Hurry, he's fading!" Tarian placed his body onto a bed, stroked his matted, sticky head. "Fight, come on."

The boy didn't answer.

"Look at me!"

With much effort, the boy turned his head.

"Fight! Don't give up. You got away."

"I did." His voice gurgled, but his smile shined in triumph.

Tarian's cinched, worried eyes assessed the nurse as she cleaned the boy's wounds. He bent toward her and whispered, "Will he be okay?"

The nurse nodded, but her eyes mirrored his concern, and her lips remained stiff with only a forced curl on one end.

Tarian turned back to the boy. "I think after this I'm going to make you an honorary hunter."

The boy struggled to find his voice while he vigorously shook his head. "I never want to see another Waker again." Tears swelled in his bright blue eyes then streamed down his cheeks.

"Okay." Tarian wiped the tears away with a finger. "What's your name?"

"Thomas."

"Hi Thomas, I'm Tarian."

"I know."

Tarian wanted to ask him several questions about the attack and his attacker, but instead, he smiled and patted his head until the doctors took him into the operating room.

Tarian left the infirmary and ambled through Headquarters' maze of stairwells and hallways to return to his apartment. Exhausted he lobbed his gore-drenched clothes into the laundry machine, shuffled into the shower, and let the water wash away the smell of smoke and perspiration. Warm steam crept over him relaxing his overworked muscles. Finally, he slipped his clean body under the covers, but sleep wouldn't come.

Several long minutes of tossing and turning passed before he ditched his apartment, took four steps down the hall and stood in front of the closed adjacent apartment door. On the other side of the door his girlfriend slept peacefully in her bed as he fidgeted half naked in the hallway like an idiot. He paced, debating whether to enter her residence at this late hour. He could enter, that wasn't the problem. The access control system of her place had been programmed to recognize him as his would recognize her, but would she be upset with him? He'd already slept over three nights this week. Tonight would violate her three-night maximum rule. But he missed her and never saw her during the days. He didn't know where her daily duties as Chancellor took her, and not for lack of trying. She simply disappeared inside the labyrinth of Headquarters.

"This is ridiculous. I should've moved in with her a long time ago," he growled as he remembered their last argument concerning their separate living conditions. She'd explained that she simply wasn't ready to fully commit to him yet. He paced some more, running his hands through his chestnut brown hair.

"What the heck," he mumbled and opened the door. The entrance and living room were pitch dark, but he knew the path to her bedroom even without night vision and silently cut across the rug. Once inside her bedchamber, he whispered, "It's just me. Don't shoot."

She made a grunting acknowledgment, and he slid in next to her, encircling his beautiful girlfriend with his entire body. His rugged leg rubbed the smooth skin of hers as he inhaled the sweet red clover fragrance of her straight, burnt honey hair.

Audrey stirred slightly, pulling his arms tighter around her waist and letting her hips find the curve of his.

Together, they fell into a deep sleep.

TWO

EARLIER THAT DAY

Audrey slumped in a chair, arms crossed, concentrating on the sheen covered stonewall inside the cavernous chamber. The hidden laboratory dwelled several stories below Guardian Headquarters. The room held fourteen sleeping immortals lovingly termed Sleepers. They'd been the first to be stung by a Death Serum filled needle and were supposed to have been cremated a long time ago. Instead, they lay still as corpses in a strange hibernation state.

Audrey had inherited this reclusive rabbit hole from her predecessor, Eleanor Dare. Audrey had been appointed Chancellor to the Guardians of Dare after Eleanor's death, or, as she now knew, sleep. Within a week of taking the position, she found herself neck deep in a sticky beehive of secrets.

Audrey shivered and tucked her hands deeper under her armpits. This chilled room made her realize just how often she relied on her gift of temperature control. She'd always labeled it an insignificant ability compared to her fellow Guardians who could shape-shift or turn invisible, but as she sat in her chair miserable and cold, she realized just how valuable it was.

Bang! Rattle!

One of her two test subjects, Tracy, the Sleeper turned Waker, shook the steel bars of her cage with the ferocity of a mother bear. The rattling noise echoed off the stone and roused Audrey from her misery. "Stop it!" She turned to face Joe, "Can we sedate her yet?"

"Audrey, she just woke up from sedation and now she's hungry. Give her a minute. She'll calm down," Joe said.

Rattle! Bang!

Audrey grunted. She glanced at the other test subject, James, expecting to see it asleep but instead found its black eyes staring at her. A shiver ran down her spine contrasting the heat beginning to slick her palms with sweat. While Tracy had been hers and Joe's failed attempt at awakening a Sleeper, James had been one of Zachary's Wakers. Audrey had discovered James was a Waker months ago and secretly injected him with Death Serum snatching him off the streets of the village, before Tarian had become so adept an Awakened Hunter.

Bang! Rattle!

Audrey hissed.

Joe asked, "Teresa, will you please go upstairs and grab some rare steak? That will calm her down." He placed the order without lifting his head from his work. Books piled high on his desk, discarded balls of white paper overflowed in his wastebasket, screens glowed with many open links, while an impressive display of other devices lay splayed out like a deck of playing cards. These items competed for space against beakers, syringes, microscopes, and more. The desk Joe worked upon was an intricately carved piece of burl walnut, but no one ever got the chance to appreciate its beauty under all of his mad scientist materials.

"Sure Dad." Teresa hopped off the stool with elflike grace and headed for the door. She paused and glanced over her shoulder. "You know, Chef Richard is asking a lot of questions. And my new nickname is The Cannibal," she sighed and rolled her eyes. "It's gross. I don't even eat meat."

Audrey's bad mood lifted at their bantering. Teresa inherited her narrow face from her father, but Tarian resembled Joe more, the broad shoulders and chestnut hair. Tarian's hair always lay perfectly in place whether tousled or combed, while his father's hair disobeyed and fell into a messy nest atop his head. Joe was thinner and older while Tarian's muscles were prominent and well-defined, but they shared the same height.

Audrey watched Teresa prance out of the secluded den. "You love having her down here, don't you?"

"Yes," he said, and a smile ran away with his face. He broke from his work to look into Audrey's eyes. "But she's growing up too fast."

"Yeah." Audrey dropped her gaze.

"She has her mother's eyes," he said in a whisper as if talking to himself.

Teresa's seventeenth birthday was a little more than a month away, the day before Halloween. All Audrey wanted was to give Teresa her father back, which simultaneously gave Tarian his father back. She had to figure out how to awaken the Sleepers without turning them into monstrous Wakers. She and Joe had tried and failed with Tracy. They couldn't afford another mistake like that. Until they could master the Awaken Serum, Joe had to remain in hiding, and Tracy and James had to remain behind bars. If the villagers knew Wakers lived inside Headquarters, they'd get their pitchforks and come running. And if the High Council knew Joe was alive as an awakened, they may consider him a Waker and sentence him to death. Audrey wouldn't risk that chance.

She and Joe hadn't replicated the Awaken Serum that had so successfully revived Joe after he was declared dead from a Death Serum injection, nor had they been able to find a drug to stop the aggressive blood lusting behavior of those awakened improperly by Zachary's antidote.

Rattle! Bang!

"Shut up!" Audrey hissed, the anger inside her seeping out through her voice and rising temperature. She radiated heat. Her chilled body turned into an inferno.

Joe strolled over to the Waker's cage. "It's okay Tracy. Here." Joe handed her a plastic sleeve of chicken giblets. "Eat these. Your steak is on the way."

She uncurled her fingers and took the skinny package from Joe. Once the food was in her grip, she scampered to the back of her cage, hunched into a deformed ball, and ripped open the packaging like a wild animal. She fiercely devoured the treat. Her transformation from peaceful awakened Sleeper to monstrous Waker took only ten days, not the estimated ninety. Like the immortal Guardians, the Wakers came in all shapes, sizes, physical ages, and temperaments, making it that much more difficult to categorize them, predict their behaviors, and form definite conclusions.

Audrey gagged as bits of liver and spit sprayed from the woman's mouth. Her smacking lips grated on Audrey's nerves worse than the rattling cage bars had. She watched Joe as Joe watched Tracy. A warm tenderness suffused his face. "Why do you call her Tracy?"

"Because that's her name." He squinted his eyes as if to say, *that's a stupid question.*

"I know, but she's not the Tracy she used to be. With every passing day she becomes less and less human. That's not the Tracy I knew." Even as the words spilled from Audrey's mouth, she knew they weren't completely true.

Every day as her friend dipped deeper into the depths of monstrosity, she had witnessed small glimpses of the Guardian that was once her friend and comrade. But for Audrey to maintain her sanity, she had to separate her memories of Guardian Tracy from the behavior of the beast she'd created and imprisoned. She couldn't curl up in her cozy bed wrapped in the protective arms of her loving Tarian, if she thought of her old friend rotting away behind steel bars tucked underground. She had to protect her sanity with nameless pronouns. "It's been turned into this monster creature. It's … she's a Waker now."

"So am I, Audrey. So am I." His words trailed off.

Aching pain pulsed through her heart. She'd not meant to

insult him, and she sure as hell didn't equate Joe with the beasts that wandered the streets of the village at night clawing the flesh of the innocent and feeding on their blood. "You've been awakened but you're not a Waker. You're different, Joe."

"I'm only different by sheer luck."

"No, because unlike Zachary, you cared enough to do more research. Zachary intended to make monsters."

"Zach thought he'd be able to control them," Joe said.

"Well, he's dead, and now we have to deal with them, and none of them can be controlled," she said. *And I've failed*, she thought. Her head fell into her hands with a thwap. She grabbed handfuls of her hair, yanking it as hard as she could. Failure didn't suit her. Her competitiveness shredded all her kindheartedness. She did love these ghoulish Wakers, or she had loved them. They were her fellow immortals, the same people she'd shared so many experiences with, the same friends who'd lived by her side for centuries.

"I have one last idea. If it doesn't extremely diminish the bloodlust in James or reverse the transformation of Tracy, we'll have to visit the Xias," he said.

Audrey let out a long sigh, fearing she should have gone straight to the Xias in the first place. Maybe if she had, Tracy wouldn't be a Waker, maybe she'd be awake and behaving normally like Joe. As a soldier and a leader, she knew the dangers of admitting weakness. Soliciting help outside of the village made the Guardians vulnerable. The Guardians always solved their own problems. Again, the option to bring in outside help versus the two failures rotting away in cages underground weighed her down like a wet wool rug.

Joe gingerly held a syringe between his fingers. He placed the needlepoint inside a glass beaker filled with a thick, pale pink liquid and sucked the substance into the syringe. He put the filled syringe on a sterilized metal dish. "While Tracy eats, I'll inject this."

Audrey stood up and took two steps toward the door.

"Where are you going?" he asked.

"To church to pray for solid test results. To pray I don't have to turn our Sleepers over to the Xia Preta. That Tarian doesn't leave me when he finds out I've been harboring his father in the basement. To pray that I'm not damned for turning Tracy into a monster," she sighed, "The list goes on."

"It's all going to work out," Joe said.

His voice sounded so sure and confident, and Audrey wanted desperately to believe him, but the shimmers of guilt tickled her skin and dug their way into her bones. "Yes, but how much longer? I've been hiding you since March. Your son is never going to forgive us for this. I lied! I told him Eleanor cremated your body! He's going to hate me … us," she paused. "God knows I would."

"Tarian will be okay," he said with brevity and calm as if it was an afterthought.

Audrey's throat tightened at his nonchalance. Their lies would catch up to them soon. And Tarian would be furious. But they had scarier people to worry about, as she reminded Joe. "If this doesn't work. If we have to reveal our weaknesses to Roman

Feng's Xia cousins and cut a deal and it fails, the High Council will have our heads … or worse."

THREE

THE NEXT MORNING

Tarian awoke to an empty bed and the gurgling of brewing coffee. He stumbled toward the aroma and poured a cup. Evidence of his girlfriend surrounded him, but Audrey wasn't there. She had left hours earlier and set the auto brew. He missed her but didn't complain. Her job as the Chancellor to the Guardians of Dare was all-consuming.

He cupped his giant mug of morning java and smirked. *How incredibly cliché have our lives become? Two ships passing in the night.* He laughed for a second then his heart sank into the hollowed out shell of his stomach. He swigged the last sip and vowed to take her to lunch that day.

Before lunch, he had to prepare for his meeting with the High Council. They required a debriefing after each kill. He left the apartment, rushed down three flights of stairs, and jogged through a maze of hallways.

"Good morning, Tarian." "Good morning, Tarian!" "Good morning, Tarian." His fellow Guardians whirred by him in the crooked corridors. They passed in blurs of purple and green, dressed according to their gifted abilities. He wore the sleek black uniform of an Awakened Hunter.

"Good morning, Bro." Teresa hooked her elbow around his, bringing him to an abrupt halt. "Where're ya off to so fast?"

He smiled at the sight of his little sister. Her transformation into a mature young woman always caught him off guard. There were times when he'd walked straight past her without recognizing her. In his mind's eye, she remained the fawnlike, gangly girl, all legs with big doe eyes peeking through a mane of amber locks. "Hi Sis, I'm late. Meeting with the High Council."

"Yikes."

"How are Mom and everyone?" He tried to take a step toward his destination, but Teresa held tight to his arm.

"That's why I caught you. Mom insists you and Audrey come over for dinner tonight."

"Not sure." Tarian pretended to search his memory for plans, but the truth was he didn't want to miss a night of hunting. When someone died or got maimed because he hadn't killed a Waker, he bore the boulder-sized weight of responsibility.

"Ha! You thought this was an offer? It's a command. Dinner. Seven. Be there!" Teresa released him and strolled away.

"Uh, well."

"Shut up, Tarian. You're coming." She walked backward pointing at him. "There are other hunters. You don't have to kill them all."

But he did have to kill them all. He was the most skilled. None of the other hunters had killed a Waker yet. He'd evolved into an ideal tracker with his exceptional night vision and acute hearing. He injected many Wakers with Death Serum because of his superior speed and strength. His ability to touch the flesh of another person and read their past gave him an advantage when loved ones attempted to protect and hide these bloodthirsty immortals.

Tarian stepped into the chilly High Council Court still thinking about his sister's request/order. He took his position at one of the two open seats at the massive round rosewood table. He sat and waited, relieved that the meeting hadn't commenced.

The dark room curved into an oval. Thick, black velvet curtains draped the windows giving the illusion that the area dwelled deep below the surface of the earth. It didn't. If the curtains blew open, bright beams of sunlight would shine through along with a view of the jagged village rooftops.

The four council members didn't acknowledge his entrance. They sat spread far around the table, engrossed in their work.

Tarian cleared his throat, still no acknowledgment. He hated these meetings. He despised these people. That wasn't entirely true, he liked Councilor Elizabeth. At least she smiled. Like the others, her skin seemed without pigment, white as ivory and noticeably centuries old, but hers was smooth and pulled tight to her high hairline, making her oddly elegant in her blackberry, hooded coat.

"Ahem," Tarian cleared his throat again. Nothing. "As if I have nothing better to do," he murmured under his breath and leaned back in his chair. He plopped his feet on the table. No reaction. He waited.

Audrey waltzed in wearing her well-tailored deep purple suit befitting her role as the Guardians of Dare Chancellor. She took the chair next to Tarian and pushed his feet down. "Honestly, Tarian! This antique table is priceless. It's older than all of us." She placed the two-inch pile of papers she carried onto the table.

"Hi beautiful, I didn't know you were coming," he said.

"You're not going to like what I have to say." She glanced at him then cleared her throat to get the Councilors' attention.

They begrudgingly lifted their beady eyes on their parchment faces and acknowledged Audrey. Councilor George said, "This meeting will commence! What do you have for us Chancellor?"

"Good day High Councilor George, Elizabeth, Harry, and William. I'm here to put a stop to the murder of Guardians. I know these Wakers are destructive but—"

"What? No! They suck the blood of innocent people after they've gouged them open. You've seen the victims. I just brought a boy in last night!" Tarian stood and glared at Audrey. *What the hell is she talking about?*

"Tarian these are our family. You're too young to remember them as they were. They fought with us and struggled with us for hundreds of years."

"And now they're killing innocent mortals … children."

"Yes, the Death Serum has turned them into monsters, but what if we can turn them back?"

He searched her face for answers. So this was why she left his bed so early in the mornings that he stayed with her, to go behind his back. He saw red then the pit of darkness engulfed him. Swirling nausea forced him back to his seat. Haunting thoughts of his father drifted to the forefront of his brain. Many a night he'd lain awake wondering if his dad's body had truly been destroyed by fire. Years ago, Eleanor had ordered his father's body cremated, but his recurring dream left him feeling otherwise. The night terror began with his blade plunged into the heart of a Waker, then as he peered over his victim, he recognized his dad's face, mangled, worn, and monstrous.

"Let me see your papers," Councilor George asked.

She slid the stack of papers over and watched as each member took the information.

"What's going on?" Tarian whispered through gritted teeth.

"Like I've told you many times, they're not evil. They're just a byproduct of the Death Serum. It's like a disease," Audrey whispered back.

"And like I've told you that doesn't matter. They kill children, or have you forgotten little Catherine?" Tarian's chocolate eyes bore into hers. Catherine was only nine and her death had been the catalyst for the villagers to board up their stores, retreat into their homes, guard their babies, and look to the Guardians as both protector and enemy.

"I didn't say stop tracking them. Yes, get them off of the streets, but we have to try everything to save them."

Councilor Harry spoke, ending their bickering. "You have not succeeded Chancellor. Your test subject still craves blood and shows no sign of remorse."

"What test subject?" Tarian asked.

Audrey ignored Tarian's question. "Yes, but we've made progress. Give me more time. Capture the other Wakers and let me do more tests on them."

"What test subject?" Confusion and anger pinched his eyes and thinned lips.

"Not good enough." Councilor Harry shoved her papers aside and focused on Tarian. "What have you got?"

Tarian looked from Audrey to the council members and back, but no one spoke. He let out a long, harsh sigh, then offered Victoria Spade's information. "The Waker's been destroyed."

"Good work. And her husband, Guardian Ethan?"

"He's innocent. He wasn't helping her. I found her in the woods," Tarian lied. Ethan had been harboring his wife, but the two men had come to an understanding. Tarian promised Ethan that in exchange for his wife's location she wouldn't suffer, and he wouldn't be punished for aiding a Waker.

"Only twelve more at large. We must hurry before any more lives are lost," Councilor Elizabeth said. "Keep trying Audrey. I do understand your need to save the Wakers. It is a terrible situation all the way around. Do realize that we want to save as many lives as possible, but we can't have villagers' children dying on our watch."

"We've received word that another Waker has been seen on the outskirts of the village, near Battlefield Park," Councilor George informed Tarian.

"I'll check it out."

"Meeting adjourned," George pounded the table with a gavel.

Audrey left the room.

"Audrey, wait!" Tarian called.

She strode furiously down the hall and spoke loud, deliberate words. "Did you know Victoria and I rode into battle side by side? We came over on the same ship five hundred and thirty-four years ago. Together we negotiated treaties with Native Americans. Together we scoured the nation for every last mind control ring. She was a good woman!" Audrey's silver blue eyes moistened but remained stern and focused.

"What am I supposed to say? I've said I'm sorry a thousand times. I can't go back in time to stop Zachary from creating an immortal army and Dad from making a Death Serum to counter that army then stop Zachary from finding a way to wake up Death Serum victims and use them as some sort of zombie weapon," Tarian paused and inhaled a long breath. It was a tired, old argument. He was doing what was right, what had to be done to save the villagers. Once calm he continued, "I can do a lot of special things Audrey, but time travel isn't one of them. Victoria killed two people and almost killed Hope. That little girl's only alive because of Teresa's healing ability. I have to stop them. It's my job."

"I know." She aggressively swiped away the tears that rolled down her face.

"And what about me? Don't I deserve an apology? You have a Waker test subject?"

Audrey remained stubbornly silent. She'd stopped marching and stood what seemed like miles away from him.

Tarian's anger continued burning, but he didn't want to fight anymore about the Wakers. With soft shoulders and a small smile, he crept toward her. Sometimes she accepted his affections, and other times she pushed him away. To his relief, she didn't move as he put his arms around her and squeezed.

"I love you." He kissed the top of her head, the angles of her cheeks and the tip of her nose.

"Stop that," she said, but her lips betrayed her as they lifted into a smile.

He pulled her into him. Seconds passed but neither wanted to release the other. Their lives had tumbled out of control but for this one minute, nothing mattered except the union of their two heartbeats.

"We've been ordered to dinner tonight by Mom."

"But ... I ..."

Tarian peered down at her, raised an eyebrow, and shook his head.

"Okay," she said.

"We need it. It'll be good for us to forget about work for just one night."

"You're right." She entwined her fingers in his and smiled.

The day had taken an unpredictable turn. The romantic lunch with his girlfriend had turned into an unexpected dinner at Mom's. Now, he needed to spend several hours trying to find the Waker hovering near the village border. A tricky situation since Wakers slept in hiding during the day.

FOUR

TERESA'S SECRET

Teresa bounded up three flights of stairs to the residences. She scanned the hallway, found it empty, and proceeded to Patrick's apartment. The door recognized her and let her inside.

"Good morning," she called out as she rounded the corner to enter the kitchen.

"What are you doing here?" Patrick looked up from where he sat at the bar, sipping coffee, and browsing the news. "Teresa, we have to be careful."

"Relax, no one was in the hall, and I just ran into my brother downstairs. He's in a council meeting. Can't I surprise my boyfriend?" She wrapped her arms around him.

"Of course." He returned her hug then slipped away into the bathroom.

"You don't have to do that!" Teresa called after him. "I love your black irises."

"You're weird. They're enormous and soulless." Patrick emerged from the bathroom with evergreen irises and brilliant white scleras. He grabbed her and kissed her. "Council meeting, huh?"

"That's right. Should give us thirty minutes." Teresa kissed him with teenage lust and dug her hands under his shirt.

"No, baby." Patrick tucked his shirt back into his pants and pushed her gently away. "You're too young."

"In a month, I'll be seventeen." She tempted him again with a nibble on his neck.

"You're killing me, but I've waited centuries so what's another couple of—"

"If you say years, I swear I'll," she sighed, "I don't have centuries like you do." Her head dropped as her mood shifted.

"I was going to say months, maybe *a* year, but not years." He lifted her chin up with the tips of his fingers then lightly kissed her. "Plus, we still don't know if I'm completely safe from the disease. If I ever hurt you, I'd never forgive myself."

"You're fine! It's been forever since Dad woke you up." She heard the whine in her voice and hated when she sounded her age, but she longed to be with him. Just looking at his youthful face and muscular chest made her stomach twist, her heart pound, and her body melt.

"Forty months and …" he paused to add in his head, "Eighteen days since your father tricked me, to be exact."

"Still a little bitter, are we?" She tugged his belt loops inching him closer to her.

He smirked. "You know I love your dad, but he injected me with Death Serum."

"Yea, but then he woke you up."

He laughed. "A week later, then made up a false story about a strange illness I supposedly contracted in the lab."

"You're fine." She kissed him to stop this conversation. He loved to tell the story, over and over again, just to tease her and guilt her father.

"Most likely, I'm fine. I agree," he said.

"You're not like the other Wakers." She snuck another kiss behind his ear. "And Dad needed to test his theory on someone."

"Luckily, his experiment on me was successful. I feel normal but awakening sleeping immortals is still new territory. I could change," he paused to look at her then continued. "Let's not talk about your father while I kiss you." He smoothly took her in his arms, holding her tightly, and kissing her softly.

Their romantic embrace lasted several long minutes. Her desire for him rose to uncontrollable, and her hands wandered until he lifted them from his waist and placed them on her own.

He winked. "Nice try." He walked to the coffee pot. "Coffee?"

She sneered at his ability to restrain himself, forced her raging hormones deep down into her gut, and cursed.

"Coffee?" he asked again.

She nodded. "Why can't Dad replicate that same serum he made back then?"

"I'm not sure. We've tried everything. Something the Xias used in the original two vials of serum is missing. I'm guessing this ingredient wasn't revealed to Joe on purpose."

"Why?" Teresa asked.

"Leverage, maybe. I've told him we need to go to the Xias to find out why we can't duplicate their Awaken Serum, but he's stubborn and it's dangerous to deal with outsiders."

He added honey and cream to her coffee then put a lid on it. "Let's go."

"Chamber or infirmary?" she asked.

He tucked an amber strand of hair behind her ear. "Let's check on Hope."

She smiled up at him. He was achingly beautiful, and although he was centuries old, he had the body of a nineteen-year-old. Stone shoulders of a Roman statue, eyes set symmetrically across a bone structure that angled and leveled along sharp cheekbones and a chiseled jawline.

She'd met him during her work as an apprentice for Eleanor. Teresa and the rest of her family had fled to the Guardian village after Tarian's life had been threatened at the Entente Military Academy (EMA). The EMA had been attacked. Her father had died a couple of years before, and they'd only just learned of Tarian's immortality. Her life had been uprooted. As a teenager in high school, it had been the end of the world. No more cute boys, no more friends, no more Salem High. But Eleanor sensed she was special and quickly put her to work in the lab alongside Patrick. It was the best thing that ever happened to her, the beginning of her destiny as a healer.

When they reached the infirmary, Patrick held the door open for her. The once empty space now overflowed with patients.

Beds lined the walls separated by barriers to give adequate privacy and prevent the spread of disease.

"I can't believe this is the place where I fell in love with you," Patrick whispered.

Teresa winked at him, "Such a romantic." She'd already told him that she'd fallen head over heels for him the first day she saw him.

The patients requested her by name as she trod down the aisles, quickly assessing each one and leaving Patrick behind at his station. Delia used to be the only patient Teresa came to visit. Now a busy day lay ahead, and as much as she wanted to help them all, she itched to be in the Chamber where the real work awaited.

She trotted into Hope Appleton's section, delighted to see her sitting up and scarfing down pancakes dripping with syrup.

"Wow, you look well," Teresa said. When Hope's treatment had begun several weeks before, she was an unconscious mess.

"I feel great. Whatever that goo was that you rubbed on my wound healed it, and I slept all night without hurting in my chest." Hope shoved a heaping fork of food into her mouth.

Teresa's herbal concoction and healing touch elicited miracles, especially with the young. She didn't know how or why. She simply had the gift. Eleanor had schooled Teresa in many areas of medicine, but Teresa's ability to heal came naturally. It hurt to think of her mentor, so she shook off the pain and delved into her work.

"And I see your appetite is back." Teresa reviewed Hope's

charts. "Where's your mother?"

"She has a surprise for you. She left to get it after I woke up. I told her how much you miss her apple pie, so she went to the bakery to bake one for you."

"She didn't have to do that."

"She wanted to. She misses it. Ever since she closed the bakery, she's been miserable. I think she may open it back up for just a couple of hours a day. Other people have said the attacks only happen after sunset." Hope spoke between bites.

"Yes, that's true," Teresa said.

"I wish them all dead. I want your brother to get all of them. I heard there's only twelve left."

"He's doing his best." Teresa smiled at Hope. It wasn't genuine, but it looked as if it was. She hoped that Audrey and her father would soon figure out how to prevent the Sleepers from turning into bloodthirsty Wakers. Perhaps it wouldn't be too late to change the villagers' opinions of the Death Serum victims.

"He's so cute," Hope teased, after catching Teresa gaze at Patrick, who stood on the opposite side of the room.

"Who? Patrick?" Teresa blushed as she turned to face Hope, butterflies fluttering up from her gut and choking her throat at the mention of his name.

"Yea." Hope rolled her eyes and huffed. "It's so obvious that he likes you."

"No." Teresa shook her head, but realized she wasn't fooling this young girl.

How many other people had seen her casual flirting?

Patrick was right. Her foolish behavior had to stop. She promised herself to avoid watching his every move, hard as it would be to keep that promise, Patrick showed no signs of violence like the others. If the High Council ever learned that he was a Waker and ordered him eliminated, Teresa would be heartbroken, and life as she knew it would be over.

FIVE

BEFORE FAMILY DINNER

"I'm going to see *your wife* at dinner tonight!" Audrey scowled at Joe, but he paid her no attention. "How am I supposed to look Carolyn in the eye and lie to her?" Audrey paced the Chamber floor in her wool-lined boots.

Joe hastily scribbled notes. "There's nothing to lie about. I won't be the topic of conversation." His wife, Carolyn, had been led to believe he'd died years before.

"You know what I mean!"

"Just a little while longer. If Teresa can do it, you can too."

"Your daughter's a brick wall, a fifty-year-old woman trapped in a sixteen-year-old girl's body. I know why Eleanor recruited her. They're identical. Plus, she's a teenager. Teenagers always lie to their mothers."

"Are the plans set?" Joe changed the subject.

She stopped pacing and crossed her arms. "Yes, I made all the arrangements today after the High Council meeting. I mentioned the test subject in the meeting and Tarian wasn't happy about it. He let me off the hook this morning, but his composure won't last. He's going to press me on it. He's going to want to know who it is and where it is."

"Then you need to get across the Entente to the Xias as soon as possible."

"I know. Roman and I leave tomorrow, and he's asking too many questions."

"And once you're on the plane, you can tell him every detail."

"I hope this works. This is our last alternative." Audrey ran her hands along a sleeping immortal. She had a habit of petting each one like an absurd doll collection.

"It has to be the key. The Xias put an ingredient into the serum that I don't know about." Joe shook his head and stared blankly, lost in thought. "That has to be the reason Patrick and I haven't lost our minds like the others. Other than that, the only difference between my serum and Zach's is the ichor he stole from the Cavern System, but I've accounted for that."

"We'll find out. Roman has a meeting scheduled with his aunt. Let's keep our fingers crossed." Audrey slipped off her boots, trading them for her two-inch, blackberry pumps. She'd taken to wearing heels after becoming Chancellor, attempting to look as professional as her predecessor, Eleanor. She had big shoes to fill. Eleanor was a born leader and beloved by all, now her body lay still among the other Sleepers.

"Good night, Joe." She kissed him on the cheek.

"Good night, Audrey. I wish I could go with you." He

lowered his gaze to the cold gray floor. He'd been trapped inside this dungeon for far too long.

As the door slammed shut behind Audrey, Joe grew quiet and introspective. This dungeon was his penance, but looking back on all he'd done, all the secrets he'd kept from everyone, he knew he'd done his best, what he thought was right at the time.

He chuckled. It was almost comical reminiscing about his radical decisions. He'd discovered Tarian's immortality at age nine when his son was the sole survivor of a school bus accident. For years he, Zachary, and Audrey had studied Tarian's DNA, watched his every move, and analyzed his behavior but couldn't discern what accounted for his immortality. In their five hundred plus years, none of them had had an immortal child before.

His mind shifted into that dark place he dreaded remembering. *How did my best friend, the wonderful man I knew, become a tyrannical despot?* He'd never understand why Zachary did what he did, why he wanted to turn Tarian's miracle birth into a way to produce thousands of immortals to create an army. Joe had told no one of his suspicions about his friend, not even Audrey.

He shook his head now, sitting alone in the cold chamber. *I should've told Audrey,* he sighed. But he knew why he hadn't confided. He'd lied to himself, couldn't bring himself to believe such evil could exist inside his best friend's heart. Zachary's many long years of living had hardened his soul. Watching mortal loved ones die, watching mortals start war after war and destroy each other was too much for Zachary's sanity to endure.

Joe huffed as he thought back to his idea to concoct a

Death Serum to counter his friend's crazy idea. "My idea was just as crazy," he said to himself. "And then I tested it on Patrick without his permission. Patrick's a good man to still talk to me after what I did."

Once Joe was awake and cognizant, Patrick confessed he had told Eleanor about the week of his life that he couldn't remember, the supposed illness that had turned his green eyes to black. Eleanor didn't believe Joe had told the truth and thus began Patrick and Eleanor's tedious puzzle piecing of all of his secrets.

Now that Joe had so much time alone, he often wondered what would've happened if Eleanor hadn't been suspicious and ingenious as to dig up his body and keep it along with all the other Death Serum victims. Or if Audrey hadn't deduced from his Will that the mementos he'd left to his children were not random. He'd hidden the only remaining vial of Awaken Serum inside his youngest daughter's teddy bear. One of only two he'd received from the Xias years before as an antidote to the Death Serum.

He leaned back in his chair and looked to the ceiling, pondering whether to shape-shift into his hawk persona and go for a soar in the clouds. After Audrey had woken him up, he had often ventured out and flown high and far, but he had to stop when his flights risked revealing his renewed existence. A Guardian friend of his had recognized him as his alter ego and gone to Audrey with questions. Audrey wouldn't risk anyone revealing him to the High Council and had insisted he remain inside.

Joe stopped reminiscing and talking to himself. It didn't do any good to linger on his past mistakes. He sat upright in his chair, leaned over his desk, and continued dabbling with his compounds.

SIX

FAMILY DINNER

Tarian sat down to a table covered with platters of breaded pork chops, steamed vegetables, garden salad, and piping hot dinner rolls. His stomach growled. He immediately grabbed a roll.

Audrey scooted her chair next to Tarian's and glared at him.

"What?" he said, barely audible through the mouthful of bread.

"Why don't you pass them around?" Audrey asked, but it wasn't a question.

"I was going to." He sent the basket in the opposite direction.

"Tarian!" She crinkled her face.

"Oh, sorry! Did you want a roll?" He smirked, gave her his best puppy dog eyes, and tickled her knee under the table.

Soon everyone ate, and no one spoke until Teresa said, "Audrey, remind me tomorrow, I have a few things to tell you before you leave on your trip."

Audrey shot her a look of warning.

"Trip? What trip?" Tarian spun toward Audrey, causing the salad dressing he poured to splash over the plate.

"Oh, nothing. It just came up."

"So why does Teresa know about it?" Tarian's sharp tone sliced the joy out of the air.

"Well, because she was in the lab when I finalized my plans," Audrey bit back.

"Where are you going?" Carolyn asked.

"Los Angeles."

"The Technology District, Roman's hometown?" Carolyn asked.

"Yes," Audrey said.

"Is Roman going?" The razor-edge still lingered on Tarian's tongue.

"Yes. I need to establish better diplomatic relations with the Xias in the Technology and Bar Districts. The western border remains porous, and Congress wants to reinforce it with more troops and drones. If I can convince the Xias to work with us, we'll have a much better chance of success." Audrey stabbed a carrot.

Tarian grew suspicious of the obviously well-rehearsed explanation. "Roman has agreed to this?"

"Yea," Teresa responded for Audrey. "He has family connections to the appropriate people."

"That's valiant of him." Tarian stared suspiciously at both of them. He wanted to touch them, steal their thoughts; but Audrey would never forgive him, and he couldn't read Teresa since she shared his blood.

Tarian's relationship with Roman was complicated. Roman had stolen Delia, his former girlfriend, away from him. Well, not really. Tarian's immortality scared her away. She'd chosen Roman. It hurt not being accepted for what he was, but at the same time, he'd been falling for Audrey. Since Delia's death, Roman had been nothing but an excellent asset to the Guardians and a friend to Tarian, but jealousy still coursed through Tarian's veins.

"Yes, we're lucky to have him," Audrey said.

"Enough talk of politics. I heard from Charlie today. He got the classes and instructors he wanted at Harvard." Carolyn glanced at Audrey, "Thank you."

Audrey shrugged. "I really didn't do much."

"Well, it helped. I want to take the kids and go see him."

"Oh Mom, I'm so busy … school … work … I can't go," Teresa stammered, shaking her head.

Carolyn sighed, "I figured you'd say that. I guess we'll wait and go another time."

Chloe's fists pounded the table in protest. "I want to see my brother!" Half chewed food garbled her speech.

Carolyn's stare shot to her youngest daughter. "Chloe, swallow your food first."

"Mom, go." Teresa drew her words out like a typical teenager hell bent on being independent.

"I'm not leaving you here alone."

"I'm never here anyway."

"Yes, but I can't leave you home alone with those horrible

things roaming the streets at night." Carolyn spoke sharply.

"Why would I go out at night?"

"I don't know," Carolyn said.

"Exactly. Go. Have fun! The Inn is protected, and I never go in to work until the sun's up." Teresa popped a piece of bread into her mouth.

"We'll see."

"Road trip!" Chloe yelled raising her arms over her head.

Tarian smiled at his littlest sister. "Mom, I can stay here while you're gone."

"Thanks, hon."

"A lot of good that does, you're out all night hunting." Teresa rolled her caramel brown eyes.

After dinner, Joe Jr. pounded his drums, and Chloe strummed her guitar. The two youngest Prescotts performed enthusiastically. Everyone politely clapped at each pause, hoping the cacophonous performance had concluded, but Joe Jr. had one last drum solo that climaxed with an ear-cringing clash of cymbals.

"Did you like it? We're awesome right?" Chloe jumped into Tarian's lap.

"The best," Tarian lied, his oversensitive ears still ringing. "Don't they have an autonomous function?"

"That's not fun." Chloe frowned.

He squeezed his little princess. The pound of her healthy heart thumped against his chest. His guilt bubbled, and he itched to hunt, to save the vulnerable village children and avenge those whose hearts no longer beat.

"Thomas wanted me to say hi to you tonight," Teresa told her brother.

"He's doing well?"

"We couldn't save his leg." A reflexive smile, the kind that covers uneasy sadness, crossed her face.

"I'll visit him in the morning."

Teresa nodded. "He'd like that. He wouldn't shut up about you."

Tarian covered Chloe's ears. "It snatched him right out of his bed."

"How awful!" Carolyn winced and shut her eyes.

"Stop it." Chloe clawed at Tarian's hands prying them away from her ears. "I know all about the creepers in the dark. I'm not a baby!"

"I know you're not." Tarian hugged her.

"But you do crawl into my bed every night with nightmares about them." Carolyn tapped Chloe's button nose as she walked by on her way to the kitchen. "Dessert time!"

SEVEN

SOME TRUTH REVEALED

When the aircraft had leveled off at fifty thousand feet, Audrey turned to face Roman. "Joe's alive," she blurted out then sighed with regret. That wasn't how she meant to start this intense conversation.

"Excuse me?" Roman shook his head, entirely confused.

"We're not going to Los Angeles for border control."

"You just said Joe's alive! Joe Prescott?"

"Yes, he is."

"He's a Waker!" Fear flashed in Roman's eyes.

"No, no, he's fine. I used a proper antidote, so he woke up without bloodlust or aggressive tendencies."

"Where is he? I thought he'd been cremated."

"No, Eleanor told everyone he was cremated as a cover story—"

"What about the other Guardians? Not the Wakers, but the others, the ones that died after Joe but before Zachary was discovered as the traitor?"

Audrey sighed, "They're in a state of hibernation in an underground chamber. Eleanor didn't want the High Council interfering in her studies of these sleeping immortals, so she kept them hidden. As for me, when I became Chancellor I decided against notifying the High Council for fear they'd consider Joe to be a Waker and sentence him to death at the hands of his own son."

Roman blinked slow and deliberate. "After everything Tarian's been through that would be horrific."

"He doesn't know."

"What?"

"I don't know what stopped me from including him. I was uncovering so many of Eleanor's secrets. I was scared and didn't want to impose my nightmarish responsibilities on him. When Joe awoke he demanded I tell no one, especially in the beginning when we had no idea if he'd transition into a Waker or not." She stopped herself before she let slip, *I was almost certain he'd be fine since Patrick has been awake for over three and a half years now from the same batch of Awaken Serum.*

"Why is he fine and everyone else isn't?" Roman asked.

"Because the Awaken Serum I used on him came from your family."

"What?" Roman attempted to stand, but the seatbelt snagged him. He unbuckled it and paced.

"I know about your cousins, and why your mother hasn't spoken with her sister in over a decade."

Dense silence fell over the cabin as Roman stared at

Audrey. He searched her face, mouth agape then closed again. Raising one eyebrow, he said, "Really. Joe's alive. Huh!" More silence as Roman let a small smile creep across his face at the memory of his dear friend and mentor. Then in an even tone, he continued, "He's the only one that knows the truth about my family."

"I know." She mirrored his smile, relieved at his amicable response.

"Who else has been awakened successfully?"

"Nobody." The word cracked out of her mouth like a whip and Roman's smile faded. She kept her eyes focused on his yellow irises. She couldn't tell if he believed her or not, but she wouldn't give up Patrick's secret just yet.

"How? How did you figure all of this out? You had to have had help." His questions shot out in bursts as he grappled with everything Audrey told him.

"I had a note from Eleanor. In the years after Joe's death, when the other Guardians also mysteriously showed up dead, and since we had no idea what caused deathlike symptoms in immortals, Eleanor shrewdly decided to keep all of the victims in a special chamber. Remember at that time, Death Serum was only a theory. We didn't know what was killing us. After that, all I know is she knew the Sleepers could be woken up, but she hadn't been able to figure out how. The note she'd left me at her gravesite explained that Zachary had found a way and that his Wakers walked among us. Since I had seen the black eyes on Zachary, and all the sleeping bodies in the chamber had black eyes, I assumed Zachary had managed to wake himself up from this hibernation state. With his body burned to ash, I had no proof and no idea how to transition the bodies. I did have clues though. A vial of Awakened Serum was hidden inside Chloe's teddy bear, and with it, I was able to bring Joe back to life." She paused. Roman's eyes grew with questions, and she hoped he wouldn't inquire too deeply. So much of what Eleanor had learned came from Patrick, not shrewd perception.

Finally, Roman asked, "How did you know to look inside her stuffed bear?"

Audrey's shoulders fell—relieved she could safely answer this question. "Actually, some things Tarian had said to me. Remember the mementos Joe left to his kids?"

"Yeah, of course. I delivered them."

"That wasn't random and somehow I made the connection. Intuition, I guess. Anyway, the vial worked. Joe woke up, but then the attacks started. It wasn't until a Waker attacked a villager that we realized the dire results of waking immortals, that we had an impossible task ahead of us. Joe and I calculated that the transition period from awoken Death Serum victim to blood-lusting Waker is approximately ninety days. Unlike a vampire, the blood lusting starts out minor then escalates. They can usually manage their bestial nature for a while before it takes over completely. However, each Waker is different." Audrey's heart ached with regret. "They were walking among us and we had no idea."

"And Joe has been awake and hiding for over ninety days?"

"Yes, about one hundred and eighty days, give or take. Ever since he awoke, he and I have been attempting to duplicate the serum he received from your cousins."

"I don't believe that my murderous cousins can make an antidote. How can two corrupt bar owners do that? How do they even know about the creature world?"

"Joe hired you for a reason, Roman. He knew what your mother had neglected to tell you. Your cousins are preta."

Roman went silent. His face drained of all color, and he turned away to stare out the window.

EIGHT

WHILE AUDREY IS AWAY

Tarian opened the door to the library. Chilly air brushed his face. *The cold must help to keep the ancient books in pristine condition,* he thought. He hoped anyway. He wanted those old books. He sought their ancient secrets.

"Tarian!" Piper wrapped her arms around him. "How are you? Coffee?" And she vanished without waiting for an answer.

Accustomed to her unique gift of travel and her inconsistent thought patterns, he waited for her reappearance. He walked down the corridor and sat in the pillowy chair next to the fireplace to await her return.

"So how are you?" Piper asked as she handed him the mug of coffee.

"Okay." Tarian took a sip of his perfectly prepared brew.

"Where's Audrey?" she asked.

"She went with Roman to the Technology District."

"Oh, that's right." Piper twitched one shoulder and nodded.

Did she know about the trip? When he first met her, he dismissed her as an over-excited junior. Her hyperactive personality combined with her wrinkle-free face, petite stature, and pixie-cut pale gold hair streaked with purple made her appear sixteen, but Tarian had since come to suspect she possessed extreme intelligence and power.

"I heard that a Waker managed to escape from the village," Piper said.

"Yes, I captured him before he did any harm to an outsider."

"You've killed nine then?"

"Yes." Tarian didn't want to discuss his job. He wanted to discuss Audrey and Roman's trip. "Do you have any books on the history of the Xias?"

"Of course." Piper zipped past him and then disappeared. She returned with three books. "Here."

"Great, thanks."

"You're welcome." She vanished again.

She'd be back. Meanwhile, he skimmed through the books and drank his coffee. The generic books only had superficial histories, but they did have bibliographies. He ventured deeper into the stacks of the library and found what he sought. His eyes roamed over the titles on the spines. One grabbed his attention. *Xia Preta.* He pulled the tiny book from the shelf. Dust had settled on the top, and he blew it away.

The book was old and fragile, short and narrow. Its original sports car red had faded to a muted blush. Hints of the vibrant red stuck to the corners and spine while the gold inlay still glowed vividly. If the title hadn't been printed in the glinting gold ink, Tarian would've missed it hiding between the other, larger books.

"Tarian!"

He dropped the book, startled by Piper as she materialized next to him. "Piper, you scared me!"

"Sorry, but Margaret's looking for you. She wants you in her office straight away." She picked up the book from off the floor and guided him out the library.

"I'd like to check that book out," he said.

She gripped it tighter. "Absolutely, come back after your meeting."

Tarian leveled his gaze at her. She merely smiled, her lavender eyes looking as innocent as a child's. Children could be good liars.

From the doorway, he glanced over his shoulder one last time. "Don't put that book away. I don't want someone else checking it out."

"I know. You told me. Now go, Margaret doesn't like to wait."

Tarian hesitated, unaccustomed to being rushed out of the library. "Hmmph," he snorted, then gave up and navigated the crooked halls to Margaret's office. He knocked on her door.

"Enter," Margaret's high-pitched voice responded.

Tarian strode into her office. She wore an evergreen uniform and sat behind an antique desk, painted white with a marble top. "Good afternoon, Vice-Chancellor."

"Hello, Tarian. Good work with the Waker, Mr. Netherbee. Do you have the report on how he managed to escape the village border? Did he have an accomplice?" Margaret's jowls flapped as she spat the questions, one after the other.

"Yes, I sent you all the information. You should have everything you need to secure the village and prosecute his girlfriend for her involvement," Tarian said.

"How's Chancellor Audrey's work in the Technology District going?" Margaret's forced smile conveyed no warmth.

"Actually, I haven't talked to her since she left this morning."

"Yes, it's a highly secret mission, isn't it? She ordered all the crew off the jet. Unmanned except for her and Roman. Very unsafe."

Even though Audrey had failed to mention this fact, he wouldn't rattle. "Yeah, that's right," he said, forcing a chuckle and a nod to hide his shock. "You know Audrey, she's very independent, thinks she can do it all. And she's a great pilot."

This confirmed his suspicions. Audrey was hiding something, and Margaret was fishing for information. Why?

"I know our autonomous aircrafts are the best but …" she huffed and sighed, "It's just … still not … It's ridiculous."

Tarian shrugged his shoulders and kept his mouth shut.

"Well, if you ask me …"

I didn't.

But she went on anyway. "I think she's spreading herself

too thin. I have a stack of Guardian files stuffed with everything from magical secret service license renewals to Congress requests that she hasn't even read yet. Some of these are six weeks old, and I have to deal with the complaints."

"I'll remind her, Margaret."

"Do you think she wants to be Chancellor?"

"Of course."

Margaret shook her head, and with it, the folds of loose skin on her neck. "I'm just not so sure. But then, who could possibly take her place?"

Margaret baited him for information or admission that Audrey was overloaded, or worse, incapable. He remained quiet and kept his opinions to himself, knowing she'd twist anything he said and use it against him and Audrey. It was no secret that Margaret didn't agree with the High Council's decision to replace Eleanor with Audrey. She felt the position of Chancellor deserved a democratic vote, probably because she would've liked the opportunity to run for the job.

"I don't know, Margaret, I don't know. But I have a lot to do, so as long as you don't need me anymore." Tarian eased his way toward the door.

"No, you're free to go."

Tarian bolted from her office.

An hour before midnight, Tarian received contact from Audrey.

"Hi, Beautiful," he answered, happy to see her gorgeous face.

"Hi, honey, are you getting ready to hunt?" Audrey asked.

"Yep, you know me so well. Just about to walk out the door. What about you? I heard you flew unmanned?"

"Yes, I wanted to discuss a few things with Roman and didn't need anyone else listening in."

"What sort of things?"

"Mainly insight into the history of the Xias. Some personal stuff, and I just didn't think Roman would appreciate eavesdropping."

"Very considerate of you." He clipped his words.

"What's that's supposed to mean?" She parroted his tone.

"Nothing."

"It *is* nothing. Don't read more into this than there is."

"Well, I hope you find what you're looking for." A sting fringed his statement. Bitterness quickened his blood rushing it through his veins and spiking his suspicions.

"Me too." Her tone even, not rising to the bait.

"I have to go. Rumor has it that the Waker, Sally Hemsworth, has been seen lingering around the shoe shop."

"Sally?" Her voice broke as she said her friend's name.

"Yes. Sorry, Audrey," he paused. He paced out of view, hiding his reddening face. The silence lengthened. With each heavy footfall his anger neared resentment. "This would be a lot easier if you'd fight the Wakers with me."

She ignored the barb. "That makes no sense. You're being

childish."

Her calm irritated him, and he hated it when she threw his young age in his face. "No, I'm not. You're a decorated soldier. The Wakers would be extinct, and the village would be safe again if we did this together."

"Don't talk to me off-grid," she complained.

He moved the camera, so his entire apartment was now on display.

"Thank you," she said curtly then in a softer tone she continued. "You know I can't do that. I voted to capture them not murder them, remember?"

"Well, the High Council wants them eradicated, and so do I."

Neither spoke for seconds. Audrey let out a long exhalation. "I don't want to argue. Be safe. I love you."

"You too. Love you." He ended the connection before he said something he'd regret, but his anger continued to swell. His thoughts tunneled into a very dark place as he recalled Delia's last words: *Don't trust her, don't trust her, don't trust her.*

"No." He *did* trust her. If she was hiding something, it must be worth hiding. He'd get the truth out of her as soon as she returned home.

Four o'clock in the morning and Tarian sat on the bench under the buttery yellow light of the streetlamp. Tired and miserable at his inability to find Sally, his muscles ached, and his eyes burned.

She stood mere feet away hidden behind the thicket of tree branches and camouflaged by darkness.

Tufts of his body hair rippled with the sensation of her presence, his skin prickled from her stare, but his concentration shifted back to the secret Audrey kept from him. Threads of doubt and uneasiness had rendered him senseless.

"Enough!" He inhaled several deep breaths to clear his mind. Once focused on the hunt, he stared Sally down. He pounced, propelling his tall body across the street in less than a second. His foot found the Waker's ribs.

Crack!

She crumbled to the ground gasping for breath. Finished!

Tarian let the bonfire flames lick his arms as he watched the tenth Waker burn to ash. Satisfaction didn't find him tonight as it had all the nights before. With knitted brows and slumped shoulders, he lolled back to Headquarters.

By the time he arrived, confusion, anger, and exhaustion swirled like an emotional tornado. He decided to climb seven flights of stairs instead of ride the elevator. He hoped the rush of endorphins would flush his mind clean. He needed to sleep.

As the door shut behind him, he heard his sister's voice. He listened from inside his apartment. With his advanced hearing he heard her footsteps.

"One, two, three … fifty-five," Tarian counted. The steps stopped, a door opened, two more steps, the door shut, silence. "Patrick's place?"

Tarian padded from his apartment and stood in front of Patrick's door. His little sister had just sneaked into Patrick's apartment at four forty-five in the morning. Violence rose inside him. *What was she doing sneaking into Patrick's apartment at this hour?* He paced the hall then returned to his apartment to lay in wait.

Thirty minutes later, Patrick and Teresa left the apartment and headed to the elevator. When the elevator doors shut, Tarian bolted from his apartment and flew down the stairs to the lab, stole inside, hid behind a divider, and waited. Several minutes passed, then Tarian realized he'd misjudged. He raced into the hall. He paced the corridors, checked the stairwell, the eatery, the infirmary. They'd disappeared.

Once more, fatigue overtook him. He needed rest more than answers right now. He reasoned his little sister was fooling around with Patrick. He didn't like it, in fact, he hated it, but he'd talk to her later.

Falling into bed with a thud and still dressed in dirty clothes, he slept for hours.

NINE

THEY MEET

Audrey followed Roman up the weed-filled stone steps of his aunt's house. The yard needed tending, but the elegant, ranch-style home sprawled like a fierce lioness atop the cliff. Giant panes of glass rose high and stretched wide across the front and back of the building. Audrey peered inside to see modern furniture interspersed with pre-Entente War Asian pieces.

Roman placed his hand on the screen shielding the front entrance, and the door opened. "This place hasn't changed." He glanced back at Audrey, the ends of his lips curling.

They both stepped inside and waited only a few seconds before Qui floated into the foyer. She looked devilish dressed in red silk, the fabric cascading behind her. She was tall and pale.

"Roman." Her wide smile displayed perfect teeth as she enfolded him into her arms. "I haven't seen you in fifteen years. You look wonderful."

"Thank you Aunt Qui, as do you."

"Thank you, dear. And you must be Chancellor

Gualtiero." Qui extended a long, slender hand with manicured burgundy nails.

"Please call me Audrey." She shook her hand.

"Come in, I've made tea. If you don't mind, I'd like to catch up with my nephew a little before we get down to business."

"Not at all." Audrey followed Qui into the next room. Audrey sipped her tea and listened as the two family members exchanged stories about the last decade and a half.

"I can't believe how old you really are, and that we're separated by several generations. You were always just Aunt Qui. My favorite aunt who lived in the crystal palace." Roman's eyes crinkled with overflowing fond childhood memories.

"You used to love coming here. The twins will be so happy to see you again. Do you remember how you used to pester them? They thought of you as a little brother."

"I remember the day Mom said you were very sick, and we could no longer come to visit you." Roman turned to Audrey. "Mom sent me to live with Aunt Marybeth, my dad's sister, in Berkeley. She made me switch schools. I had no friends." He took a long drink of tea then resumed his story. "I asked about you, Jun, and Hu many times, but Mom always had a reason why I could never see you again. Honestly, I assumed you died."

"When she found out about our true nature, she was devastated."

"Why? It's weird, to say the least, but we were all so close."

"She never fully believed the story that I was her half-sister from China, but the Xia Preta frown upon you if you don't attempt relations with your blood relatives. She was determined to find the truth and she did," Qui paused and gave Roman a soft smile. "Fear does strange things to people. As a mother, she wanted to protect you. I understand that. She still won't accept my calls. I warn you; she may never speak to you if she knows of your involvement with us."

"I know. I won't lie to her. I'm just not going to tell her unless she asks. When that day comes, I'll accept her decision. But I want to know what happened to you. Audrey has told me about pretas and the elusive preta community here in Los Angeles, but I need to know your story," Roman said.

"Where do I begin?" Qui pondered with a long sigh then a pause of inner reflection. "I was a modern Chinese woman back in 1940. I didn't marry the man I was told to marry. Instead, I fell in love with an Australian archeologist. We had two wonderful children. Life was all I had hoped it would be until that infamous dig in China. The curse took the twins and me and killed my husband. Turned us into a mutant version of hungry ghosts." Her voice trembled so she paused again and took a sip of her tea. Her composure seemed as fragile as the fine porcelain teacup in her hand. With a straightening of her spine and lift of her nose, she went on bravely. "I was a cursed creature with two kids and no husband. With no family to take me in, I had to find a new community, and I did. I found others like me, even a few within my own bloodline. Unfortunately, some of my Chinese family will not accept those who are cursed while others will."

"Mom wouldn't accept it," Roman shook his head.

Qui nodded. Her face struggled to remain composed and brave.

"I understand. I too have kept secrets from her because I know she won't understand. She'd never accept my life now, living and working with the Guardians. I don't blame you Qui. You were young and curious about the world then you fell in love. I know what it's like to fall in love with someone you're not supposed to." Roman closed his eyes, but his yellow irises glistened once his lids lifted.

"What was her name?" Qui said.

"Delia. She was much younger than I and already in a relationship with a friend of mine. She became very ill. I tried everything to save her. I wish I'd known about your gifts."

"Me too," Qui said.

"So what do we do now?" Roman asked.

"Tonight we'll go to the bar. Jun and Hu are expecting us. If you would like to rest, I have set up your rooms." Qui escorted them to their living quarters.

"Thank you," Audrey said as she stood in the doorway of her room.

Qui took Audrey's hands in hers. "You are welcome my dear. You are a pretty one with a strong lure. Be on guard tonight."

Audrey scoffed, "Don't worry about me."

"Do not be a fool. Never forget what we truly are." Qui gripped Audrey's hands confirming the seriousness of her words.

Audrey watched her glide away. She puzzled over Qui's warning since no feelings of danger or uneasiness lingered inside her. She'd dealt with creatures like Qui in the past, but it had been over a century. She strolled to the other side of the room to gaze out the glass wall. The spectacular view of the valley took her breath away. "What mysteries lay in this beautiful city?" she murmured.

The dark of night hid the trash that littered the streets of the Bar District, but the smell of sin puddled in the corners. Blood, urine, and alcohol blended with exotic perfumes infusing the air with a fragrance that was neither pleasant nor foul. A hint of fall chilled the otherwise warm breeze, but most patrons still dressed skimpily in garments exposing young, tanned flesh.

Audrey, Roman, and Qui entered through a back door. They walked down a narrow passageway that throbbed with loud music blaring on the other side of the wall. Once the door at the end of the hall pushed open, the full force of the beat rushed to greet them. They now stood on a ledge with a railing. Audrey leaned over and watched thousands of young people thrusting and swaying, their faces stress-free, and their bodies falling victim to the rising energy.

"This place is very …" Audrey didn't have the word to describe the vibe that pulsed through her.

"Hot," Roman yelled above the music.

"It is the most popular bar on the strip." Qui smiled. "My twins have a knack for making people feel their best."

Audrey wondered how many of the adolescents below were mortal and how many might be enjoying more than just music. What exactly were the twins selling here? Sex, drugs, and rock and roll had attracted the youth forever.

Qui held a door open for Audrey and Roman. Audrey welcomed the muffling of the pounding beat when the closed door absorbed the majority of the noise. Hu and Jun stood waiting for them. The twins were tall, slender, and dressed in black leather, one female the other male. Audrey immediately felt trapped in the small office as the twins stared at her.

"Cuz, how ya doin'?" The female twin said to Roman.

She didn't have her mother's regality. Instead, she emanated a brash, threatening air. Lean muscle set on a spindly frame like a spider. Her eyes and lips lined black with makeup. Her image and tight leather clothing suited the bar business well.

"Hey Jun," Roman said.

They hugged then the male twin joined in—a threesome of teenage teammates grunting and patting each other's backs.

Hu was a thicker version of his sister. Audrey took note that Jun had a scar above her left eye, and Hu had a red rim that encircled his yellow irises. Both had black, short, spiked hair, hers shaped into a mohawk with eight peaks whereas his shot straight up. Both had honey-colored skin and taut, angular bodies, but the male twin carried himself with his mother's fluid grace.

Audrey soon realized she knew them. She'd dealt with them in the past. Not directly, as they were on opposite sides of mortal law enforcement back then, but she recognized them and wondered if they'd remember her.

"Hello lovely," Hu drawled, his prowling eyes roaming all over her.

"I'm Audrey, Chancellor of the Guardians of Dare, nice to meet you," she said and waited for a response. None. *Had they forgotten her?* Hu's eyes drew her in against her will. She found herself completely out of control. She would've done whatever he asked.

"Hu, that's quite enough," Qui said.

"What?" Hu smirked innocently with raised eyebrows.

Audrey shook off the strange tractor beam that pulled her toward him. She didn't remember that ability from the past, but then again, she'd never gotten this close to him before. Regaining her authority, she began the meeting. "My fellow Guardian, Joe Prescott, met with you a little over four years ago. At that time, you provided him the means to awaken an immortal injected with Death Serum. It seems an immortal injected with Death Serum enters a state similar to that of a mortal drained of hunpo by a preta or blood by a vampire. The high amount of antibodies and heat energy inside your preta plasma helps awaken immortals or so you told Joe. However, if that's the case then why can I not duplicate this in my lab?"

"Because my lovely, I lied to Joe. No preta plasma was put into those vials." He smiled and purred as he spoke. "The Bruja Blanca created Joe's mixture, and she wasn't happy to send her product outside of her home."

He'd moved to her side so quickly she hadn't noticed until

he was caressing her cheek with the back of his hand.

"What?" Her sharp tone conveyed her annoyance, but she couldn't manage to step away.

Qui leveled a harsh glare on her son, and he moved away from Audrey.

"The Bruja Blanca won't tell you. She guards her recipes with her life. She trusts no one." Jun huffed and smirked.

"Smart woman," Audrey said.

"We need her to make enough serum to awaken over twenty infected immortals," Roman said.

"Twenty?" Audrey asked.

"Yes, we need extra to help save those already suffering the bloodlust."

"It's worth a try, but I'm afraid it's too late for them," she finally admitted to herself

"But you said in the jet that you argued to the High Council otherwise." Roman's brow furrowed.

"I know, but in truth, Tarian's right. They can't be saved. I'm being foolish. I need to put all of my efforts into the fourteen Sleepers. They have a chance."

"Ha! Good luck Chancellor," Jun laughed.

"Why?" Audrey asked.

"Because my lovely, the Bruja Blanca doesn't give her product away for free," Hu said.

"Fine, I'll pay her. I'll fly her to our village. We have a top rate facility. I'll put her up in the most luxurious of apartments. Anything." Audrey's desperation dripped from her every word.

"Oh my Timber Wolf." Hu flew to her side, attracted to her anxiety.

Audrey squirmed in his presence but her instincts longed for his touch, his security. She pressed her eyes shut trying to prevent the flood of unwelcome feelings.

"The Bruja Blanca won't leave Los Angeles." Hu took Audrey's hand.

"But I can …" She pulled her hand loose from his, but again her feet refused to step away.

"No," Hu interrupted. "You can do nothing." He stroked her unbending hair and leaned in to whisper in her ear. "Bring your Sleepers to us."

"No." Roman placed a hand on Audrey's arm and pulled her away from his cousin.

"You want your friends back or not, Cuz," Jun said.

"You need to control your brother," Roman ordered.

"It's instinct nothing more. Her scent is strong." Jun sniffed the air. "Red clover. Not my favorite, but my brother and I differ on a lot of things. You're lucky. He's restraining himself." Jun strode her leather legs to her brother's side.

Roman threw his arms in the air and began to pace the room. "How in the hell am I supposed to smuggle fourteen corpses into the Technology District?"

"We'll do it three at a time," Audrey said. "She needs to prove she can recreate her miracle Awaken Serum before I'll bring all of them here anyway."

"Good, then it's settled," Jun said. "We'll arrange the

treatment. You arrange the transportation."

"Agreed." Audrey shook Jun's hand then darted out of the room.

"Audrey!" Roman rushed to catch up with her.

She ran the length of the ledge not looking at the party below this time. She wanted to get as far away as possible from the bar. Roman raced after her down the narrow corridor. Audrey burst through the exterior door and inhaled deeply, sucking in the sickly sweet fragrant stench of the alley.

"You can't do this. You can't come back here," Roman said.

"Yes, I can and I will. I have to. I have to save them. Roman, I've handled a lot in my centuries of living. I can handle Hu."

"Maybe you can, but what about Tarian?"

Audrey couldn't sleep. She got out of bed and strolled over to the window. The glow from the city lights below piqued her curiosity. The bar called to her. Roman's warning haunted her. She had a strong will, but Roman was right, she couldn't come back here until she broke Hu's trap.

She didn't trust the creatures' bar. The twins had been key players in the cocaine industry during the late 1970s, early 1980s. What side of the law were they on now? She slipped unnoticed out of Qui's house then called for a district car to take her into the city. She wanted to see what lay beneath the loud music, so she entered as a patron. Dressed in all black clothes, nothing that would stand out, she stepped past the doorman and into the haze of undulating lights and sweating youth. She let herself be swept up by their dancing and joy. The sorcery of the music thumped her blood and skipped through her veins until it consumed her entire body.

As she mingled through the crowd in her state of bliss, she caught the eyes of the young clientele. Eyes of every shape and color, but all looked harmless. The fear she'd felt earlier that day had vanished. Yes, there were many creatures mixing with mortal humans, but like Qui had said, it was just one giant party.

In the past, the creatures adhered to strict rules, which forbade fraternizing with humans. But that was a long time ago, before the destruction of the outside world, the Entente War, and the erection of the border. Life had changed. The rules bent. Audrey was proud of that change, knowing that the Guardians had helped to save the nation. This party going on around her proved the result of that hard work.

Convinced the bar was merely an entertainment establishment, she suddenly felt tired. She twirled on her heels and headed up to face Hu. She'd discovered in her many lifetimes that each problem had a solution that just needed to be found.

The exit eluded her as she walked the maze of partiers. She could see the horizon, but due to the endless sea of people, it escaped her. She jogged, then sprinted and ran. Her exhausted limbs collapsed. She lay on the floor at the feet of the masses crushed and helpless.

A strange forest grew up around her. Damp, cool air kissed her skin while giant trees hovered over her, and a dirt path wove to a distant light. She slowly got to her feet. The luminous shimmer drew her forward inch by inch. Certainty flowed in her blood where fear should be. The deep dark forest felt like home until a tiger rushed past in a blur.

"Who's there?" Audrey called into blackness. No response—the ripple of a graceful tail as the body of orange and black stripes zigzagged through the trees. The tiger teased. She refused to play its game and stood still.

"Aww," the voice growled from the darkness. "You don't want to play?"

"No."

"But I do."

The tiger stood. Tiger face to woman face. Sharp fangs to dull teeth.

Audrey didn't flinch. "You're not a real tiger."

"But you are my Timber Wolf."

"Dogs don't like cats."

"I beg to differ." The large mouth curled open and bit her.

"You bastard." Her hand shot to her neck. Blood wormed through her fingers as she held the spot where teeth had punctured her skin.

"I said I wanted to play," Hu purred, no longer in tiger form. Drops of her blood stained his lips. He pulled her into him and sealed his mouth around the wound and sucked out her blood.

He had trapped her. As he sucked, pleasure filled her tissue. She couldn't battle the overwhelming sense of euphoria. Her body felt sheer, like fine silk, a slippery fabric with no substance that rippled around him. Her mind finally grabbed hold of reality, unsure of how much time had passed, and gathered the strength to pry him off. She stumbled backward gasping for air.

Hu bared his teeth in pure satisfaction. "You are a fighter."

"Yes, and I have a boyfriend. I need you to stop this demonic illusion!" She hated him for his ability to make her lose her self-control. His powers were great, and she knew it, but she couldn't let him know it. She wouldn't give in.

Hu slinked forward. He wanted her to run. The flight instinct was his drug. She was the mouse with which the tiger wanted to play. But she was the wolf. She wouldn't give him what he wanted even as fear traveled through her like fire. She stood her ground until his body touched hers. He slipped his arms around her waist, and they spun. He moved with perfection. The forest disappeared, and they danced in the club among the crowd, whirling and twirling, moving smoothly as one. People surrounded them, but as he led her in the dance, they were the only couple on the floor.

Once again, he'd found a way to control her. Anger boiled in her gut, and soon Hu felt her gift. The heat emanating from her skin burned into him. He released her and stepped away. She'd found the key to resisting his seduction.

The red rim of his yellow eyes thickened, and she feared he'd pounce on her, but his tension drifted away, replaced with a wicked smile.

"You are fun, a worthy opponent. See you soon, Timber Wolf." Hu gently kissed her cheek then strutted away.

She stood dumbfounded. What had she gotten herself into? She remembered how elusive he'd been during the cocaine wars, and it worried her. She and the Guardians had helped the Drug Enforcement Agency put an end to the trade. Did he remember? Would he hold her accountable?

TEN

TRICKERY

Tarian sat in his usual spot reading the *Xia Preta* book he'd come across yesterday morning. It was late afternoon, and Audrey had just informed him she needed another night in Los Angeles.

"What are you reading?" Piper materialized in the chair next to him.

"*Xia Preta.*" He watched for a reaction.

"Oh," she said without expression.

Tarian's suspicions rose. Piper's stillness warranted concern. As he studied her, a smile crept across her face. She'd forced it, and he continued to stare at her hoping she'd break.

"Coffee?" she asked.

"No!" he yelled so loud and fast she jumped. "Sorry, you just disappear so quickly, I wanted to catch you before you evaporated again."

"Oh, sorry."

"I have a question. Are preta and hungry ghosts the same

thing?"

"Yes."

"Okay. If you think about it, Death Serum is like a bite to an immortal. Like a vampire bite or a bite from a Xia Preta to a human."

"I guess, but Xia Preta are quite different from other preta or hungry ghosts. They all have a link to the Xia Dynasty bloodline and have been cursed by their forgotten ancestors. They're more like cursed creatures. Cursed with an insatiable need for something, blood usually, but it could be anything. And some are considered mutants because they have special abilities. Not all Xias are preta though."

"Okay. I'm reading here where after the bite there's a hibernating period and then an awakening period. This awakening period is very tricky and determines the nature of the Xia Preta. If the process is done correctly, then the ghost has a healthy appetite for blood but can control his desires and live a suitable life among mortals, but if the process fails the ghost has bloodlust and must be destroyed before he hurts the mortals." Tarian paused waiting for Piper to agree.

"Bite? Hmm? Xia Preta can't make other preta. They're not like vampires. I think you mean after they're cursed," Piper said.

"Maybe?" Tarian flipped back through the book totally lost by the confusing descriptions he'd been trying to decipher.

"If that's what you read, then I guess it's true. But I also think they feed off of some sort of energy like auras." She rocked rapidly. "So, they do bite other people and can kill them but don't usually. I also know their community follows the creature code set by the Esurient Eternals."

"Who?"

"The Esurient Eternals are like our High Council. It's like law enforcement for the creature world."

"The preta need policing?"

"Coffee?"

Tarian's eyebrows lifted. He leveled his gaze on her and concentrated. His gut told him she no longer wanted to talk about this. Why? He needed to up the ante if he expected any information on Audrey's dealings with these people. He could lie or guess and see how she responded, but he needed more time to think.

Piper fidgeted and continued to rock in her chair, then she asked again, "Coffee?"

"No, I'm good. Maybe in a little while."

"Okay," she vanished.

Tarian put the book down and paced. His mind sorted through his memories until it created a linear list of facts. First, Audrey had been sneaking off at four in the morning for months. Second, Teresa sneaked into Patrick's room at four in the morning while Audrey was away. Third, Audrey was testing on a Waker, and the High Council knew about it. Fourth, he just realized he didn't know who the test subject was. Fifth, Audrey, Teresa, and Patrick were always gone from the lab when he stopped by to visit. Sixth, Teresa's healing powers had intensified.

Tarian fell back into his chair. He'd just thought of six highly concerning things. More ideas jammed his head. Seven, eight, nine, ten, and more.

No, I'm exaggerating. I'm becoming paranoid. "Piper!"

She appeared looking frazzled. "Are you okay?"

Tarian masked his unease with the calmest expression he could muster. "I miss Audrey."

"Me too."

"But I know she needs to help the … what does she call them?" He attempted to sound sincere.

"Sleepers?" she asked, genuinely trying to help but falling straight into his trap.

"Yes, Sleepers. The Xia Preta can help with the Sleepers," Tarian paused and again hoped Piper would interject some information.

"It worked on Patrick."

"Who?" Tarian's mouth gaped and his brows furrowed. Regret fell over him. He'd dropped his mask and blown his shot of gathering more intelligence.

Piper said nothing.

He cleared his throat. "Oh, yes, Patrick. He's been a success."

She swayed in her chair, lavender eyes wide and serious.

Teresa must know this. Teresa is harboring a Waker. His insides burned as if drenched with acid while his outside tried to remain cool. "Well, it's getting late. I better get some work done." Tarian stood to leave.

"Bye." Piper disappeared in a flash, taking the *Xia Preta* book with her.

Tarian marched toward the exit, feeling guilty. He hoped she didn't realize he'd been manipulating her. He hadn't wanted to betray her trust, but people were dying, and he feared whatever Audrey was mixed up with could get her killed.

ELEVEN

Teresa awoke at three thirty in the morning. She slammed her hand down on the alarm twice, then forced her body out of bed at four o'clock. She stumbled into the bathroom, tripping over the rug, stubbing her toe. "Damn!" Luckily, she didn't have to worry about being quiet since her mother had taken her younger siblings to visit Charlie in college, and if Tarian was there, which he hadn't been the night before, he slept like a rock. Once clean and ready, Teresa sneaked downstairs to leave the Inn and head over to Headquarters.

"Where have you been straying off to the past couple of mornings?" The innkeeper asked.

Teresa jumped with shock. "Ms. Emma, you scared me. You're up early."

"I'm up this early every morning. You just don't see me. But I see you."

"Oh," Teresa said, the bite of sweat pierced her armpits.

Ms. Emma's implication had fangs.

"Be careful my dear."

"Always. See you later Ms. Emma."

"Hold up." The old witch grabbed something from behind the counter and handed it to her.

Teresa took it. "A wand?"

"A weapon worthy of those horrid beasts. Just point, flick, and say 'ignis.' The shots of fire will keep a Waker away, but it won't kill them."

"Thank you, I'm not going far. Just have to run into the infirmary to see a patient," she lied, and by the devious wink Ms. Emma gave her, she'd swear that she didn't believe her.

Teresa rushed into the street, her heart pumping like a jackhammer. She prayed for Audrey's quick return. She wouldn't be able to keep up this façade for much longer. At least one person had already noticed her strange behavior and venturing out before dawn was too risky for her taste. She preferred healing to fighting. Patrick had also given her a weapon. It sat in her pocket next to the wand.

The short walk from the Inn to Headquarters seemed to lengthen with each footfall. Beads of perspiration formed across her forehead as shivers slithered down her spine. She stopped and whipped around; certain she'd find a Waker standing behind her.

"Damn it, Teresa," she cursed as the wand flew out of her hand. It clanked on the cobblestone a good distance away. She fumbled to get out the weapon Patrick had given her. She thrust the stunner device straight out and held it firmly walking in circles toward the wand, scared to turn her back in any direction. She got close to the wand when she heard a rustling in the bushes.

Swoosh.

She pulled the trigger but hit nothing. A vague image rushed like a shadow between buildings and shrubbery. Then it came for her. Her finger wrapped around the trigger one more time. This time she hit the monster square in the chest. It stumbled back giving her just enough space and a few seconds to bolt in the opposite direction and reach the entrance to Headquarters.

She forced the glass doors shut quickly, sheltering inside. She stepped away from them but kept her focus on the creature lurking outside. It looked through the glass, appraising her with its frightful black eyes. She stared back at it. Was she safe? The thing paced the length of the entrance doors, then it stepped forward. Teresa almost screamed fearing it would attempt to break the security of Headquarters, but it didn't. It stopped, growled like a wild animal, then sprinted into the night.

Teresa had backed herself into a corner. She crept into the foyer and closer to the glass door to watch the Waker run away. She'd seen enough and smashed her eyes shut but the deformed, inhuman image remained. She hyperventilated as tears streamed down her cheeks. She fell to the floor to collect herself. She knew she'd faint unless she lay down and stopped panting.

"Get yourself together." She fiercely wiped the tears from her face. She patted her skin in the hopes that it would calm down and erase any clue that she'd almost been attacked. No one could know about this. No one. She'd been foolish. She knew better now. She was just inexperienced. But she'd gotten away. No need to worry anyone.

Feeling her panic subside and confidence surface, she rose to stand on wobbly legs. It was the right choice to keep this a secret. Two deep breaths gave her the strength she needed. With each step up the seven flights of stairs, she conquered her shaky nerves, and when she finally reached the residences, she felt secure.

Her foot hit the hallway carpet and she smiled. "I did it. I'm okay. Everything's okay," she said in a long, exhausted breath.

She stood in front of Patrick's door waiting for recognition, but it wasn't her hand that opened it. A man's body forced the door wide. She screamed, all her fear racing back into her heart as it nearly pounded out of her chest.

Someone pushed past her and barreled inside.

"Tarian?" She regained her composure and followed on his heels. "What are you doing here?"

"Me? What are you doing sneaking around with a Waker?"

His words stunned her silent, but her face remained neutral, disguising her guilt. She closed the door to the apartment in the hopes that no one else heard them.

"What's going on?" Patrick came around the corner, then flinched at the sight of Tarian. He hadn't put in his green contacts.

"Black eyes." Tarian charged.

Tarian sliced through the air. His fists pummeled Patrick's

face, cracking jawbone. Patrick kneed Tarian's gut. The two men stumbled in separate directions. The fight slowed as both men stalked and circled each other.

"Stop it!" Teresa said through clenched teeth. A kaleidoscope of emotions blurred her vision, and she couldn't get her bearings to intervene in their fight.

Neither man looked at her, glaring only at each other, moving slowly with their legs bent in a panther's crouch. Tarian thrust forward and Patrick vaulted over his shoulders. He slipped his landing and rolled, giving Tarian the opportunity to pounce. Patrick pushed to his feet preventing Tarian's pin down. Both men hurtled through the apartment knocking over furniture. Tarian reached for his weapon.

"No," screamed Teresa.

Tarian paused hearing his sister's plea. Patrick stood on wobbly legs as his chest heaved and he held his arm in pain. Tarian regained his focus, gathered his powerful immortal strength, and shoved Patrick to the floor. Patrick swung his unharmed arm, fingers stretched and clawed Tarian's face. But Tarian's strength outmatched Patrick's. He held him down and reached for a glass full of water sitting on the end table. Tarian thrust the glass towards Patrick's head.

Teresa screamed again as she saw her brother's fist with the glass plunge downward then it stopped, water and glass hung in mid-air, one millimeter from Patrick's face.

"I'll take that." Piper strolled over to the two men fixed in time. She grabbed the glass from Tarian's hand then released them from her spell.

First the water crashed down onto Patrick's face. Second, Tarian's body followed. Patrick pushed him off.

"You were going to kill me!"

"What are you doing to my sister?"

Teresa dashed to Patrick's side. "He's not doing anything to me." She saw the rabid rage in her brother and knew he still posed a threat to her boyfriend. She stepped between them to shield Patrick with her lanky teenage body. "I love him. He's not a danger."

"How do you know for sure?" Tarian yelled.

"He's gentle and kind," Teresa said. "He's nothing like those monsters out there." Her voice broke as she recalled the ghastly memory of her recent encounter with the Waker.

"You don't realize how brutal they are. You've never been attacked," Tarian said.

She bit her quivering lips as more tears spilled from her eyes, but she didn't move from Patrick's side.

"No, Teresa, Tarian's right. I don't know for sure if I'm okay," Patrick said.

That was all the answer Tarian needed. He lunged again, grabbed Teresa, and flung her out of his way.

"Stop!" Piper yelled, barricading everyone inside their bodies.

Teresa hit an invisible force that froze her in place. Every muscle in her body tightened. She pushed against the magic, but this caused only agonizing pain. She relaxed and the spell lifted. She looked at Piper. She'd never seen her perform any magic other than to dematerialize. Now she appreciated the full range of her powers.

"I'm sorry," Piper said in her sweet voice. Her face blanketed with concern, her hand trembling.

"Thank you, Piper." Teresa's tawny eyes radiated terror and anger as they bore into Tarian's.

"What the hell is going on?" he demanded.

"Soon you will know everything. For now, you just have to trust us," Piper exclaimed.

"No! You explain this to me right now, or I'm going to the High Council."

"No," Teresa yelped.

Her plea startled Tarian. He took a step back and looked at the three of them with confusion.

"Please, Tarian, just trust us," Piper said.

Teresa sighed, "He's right. He should know the truth."

Patrick and Piper both turned in surprise to look at her.

Teresa shrugged. "This is a family issue. Follow me, Tarian."

Teresa escorted her brother into the elevator along with Patrick and Piper. Patrick cradled his hurt arm, and Teresa held his other one. She reached to touch her brother, but he stepped away. Guilt, fear, and sadness cut through her like shards of ice.

Tarian stayed behind as they all stepped off the elevator

into the stone walled alley. Teresa held the door. She didn't speak to her brother, but she cast her kind eyes on him and waited for his breathing to steady. When he was ready, she led him to the end of the hall. She removed a small film from a pouch in her pocket, placed it on her finger, and touched a dark gray stone on the wall. The stone walls scraped and screeched as they parted to reveal a passageway. The four advanced inside.

Tarian's eyes grew wide at the sight of over a dozen bodies lying still and covered with white cloth. The crypt didn't smell of death. Instead, it smelled of cloves and cardamom. Teresa gingerly moved him farther into the room of bodies. He turned back to see Piper and Patrick had not followed. Piper rocked from her heels to her toes over and over again as Patrick stood alert like a cautious snake.

He looked at the two cages imprisoning two Wakers then back at his sister. Teresa nudged her brother toward the man sitting at a computer. The man concentrated on the screen with his back to them.

"Dad," Teresa said without panic.

"Hi, honey." Joe waved a hand in the air, still focused on the screen. "One minute, I'm just finishing up."

"Dad?"

Joe whirled around at the sound of his son's voice. He shot to his feet, his eyes wide and black as a starless midnight sky. Joe turned to his daughter then back to his son.

No one spoke.

Teresa finally broke the silence. "I had to tell him, Dad. You should've told him a long time ago. He almost killed Patrick. I'm furious at both of you right now."

"You've been alive this entire time?" Tarian's brows drew together, and his fingers curled into fists.

"No, Audrey woke me up six months ago."

"Audrey?" Tarian shook his head.

"Yes, but I insisted she keep my life a secret."

"Why?"

"Because of the High Council. I couldn't risk it. Harboring a Waker is punishable by death. I didn't want anyone to know."

"Why does Teresa know?"

"She already knew. Your sister's nosy."

"Dad." Teresa's face scrunched with annoyance.

"Well, you are. You followed Patrick and Audrey without their permission."

Joe took a step toward Tarian, but Tarian stiffened. He drew a ragged breath and swept the crypt with his eyes, then bolted out of the room.

"Tarian!" Teresa turned to run after him.

Patrick grabbed her arm. "Give him some time."

"You don't think he'd tell the High Council, do you?"

"Of course not," Patrick said.

"He's a rule follower. Loves order. I hope you're right." Teresa's shoulders slumped, and her eyes no longer wide with anger now glistened with tears. Everything she'd gone through in the past hour twisted her stomach and emptied her lungs of air. She gulped and doubled over in pain.

"Are you okay?" Patrick swooped her into his arms.

She buried her head into his neck and sobbed.

"I'll go watch over him." Piper vanished.

TWELVE

Audrey braced herself as she opened the door to Tarian's apartment. A fist-sized hole in the wall met her before she'd walked three steps into the living room. Teresa had warned her about Tarian's outburst after discovering their secret. The apartment looked like a crime scene. The couch lay on its side and pillows scattered around the room. Something must have hit the lamp because it lay on the floor in pieces. Several beer and orange soda bottles were piled high, empty or half drunk on the kitchen counter.

She tiptoed into the bedroom where she found Tarian fully dressed, two more orange soda bottles on the end table, and sound asleep. She stood in the doorway for several seconds. He looked peaceful. That wouldn't last. Thrilling anxiety traveled from her toes to her head, giving her nervous jitters. She swallowed but couldn't get enough air into her lungs. Finally, she spoke. "Tarian,

I'm home."

He didn't immediately awake like she thought he would. She expected him to bolt upright and yell at her, possibly throw a pillow at her face.

Unsteadily, he propped himself on one elbow. "Hi," he said, voice hoarse from sleep. He reached for the bottle and gulped down a mouthful of orange soda.

"I'm so sorry." Tears welled and stung.

"Me too."

"You have nothing to be sorry about."

"I must. You couldn't trust me."

"No, that's not it at all."

"Yes, you put your loyalty with my father, not me. I shouldn't be surprised."

"What's that supposed to mean?" Her heart beat faster and faster as anger over took her.

"I'm still the newcomer. The 'First Born.' You and Dad are centuries-old buddies." Tarian didn't smile. His eyes remained flat and emotionless. If they were black, he would've looked like a soulless Waker.

"Joe had a good point. You're the savior of our village, the 'Awakened Hunter' sweeping the streets of danger. I needed more time."

"Stop labeling me like I'm some pet." Tarian got out of bed and slammed the bathroom door.

Audrey dropped to the edge of the bed and waited.

He emerged clean and dressed.

"Where are you going?"

"To find another Waker."

"Who?" She asked without thinking. She wanted to take it back. She didn't want to know the names anymore.

"Judith Wright."

Audrey closed her eyes, remembering her friend Judy as she was before the monstrous change. "Don't you want to talk about your father?"

"No." He marched out of the bedroom.

She ran after him. "What about the Sleepers? I can save them. Isn't that worth it?"

He didn't say anything, but he stopped walking toward the door.

She continued, "We can awaken the Sleepers. They can have their lives back like your father and Patrick. I just need to bring a few Sleepers to the Technology District," she hesitated as he stared at her. "Actually, the Bar District within the Technology District ... I met with the Xias."

"Just tell me the truth Audrey! You're negotiating with strange creatures."

Was he asking or did he already know the truth? "Yes."

"From what I've read in the Guardian library, that's a very dangerous idea."

"It's the only way."

"You do what you have to do, and I'll do what I have to

do." He disdainfully glanced back at her before he stormed out of his apartment.

Audrey wandered around the mess picking up a few pillows. "G.O.D." she called. The personal robot with the Guardians of Dare emblem emblazoned on it hovered into the room and took over the cleanup. Audrey collapsed into a chair and cried.

THIRTEEN

BUSINESS MATTERS

Teresa knocked on the solid oak doors of the Chancellor's office.

Audrey opened the door ajar and whispered, "I'll only be a minute. Have a seat."

She motioned for Teresa to sit in the antechamber's chair that smelled of centuries old smoke and leather. Audrey didn't completely shut the oak doors and the voices traveled. Teresa resisted the urge to listen, but curiosity got the better of her.

"Mr. President, I'm sorry for the destruction of the building, but no one was hurt," Audrey said.

"Please, assure me that that will be the last time I have to explain to the people of the Entente why the Prevallers were able to break, once again, through our defenses."

"Yes, Mr. President, you have my word that will be the last time."

"Audrey, I'll hold you to that … Goodbye Chancellor," said the President.

"Goodbye, Henry."

Teresa heard the connection die and prepared to stand when another voice spoke.

"Audrey," Margaret said, "You can't make promises like that."

"Margaret don't second guess me. The Prevallers have failed. The Guardian spies and Entente Generals have assured me this was the last cell left inside the borders. They're done. They've scurried back to the Wastelands where they belong."

"It was also the largest cell we've ever encountered. It didn't match previous Prevallers' behavior," Margaret said, but it sounded more like a scolding to a child than an observation explained to a superior.

Teresa imagined Audrey's silver blue eyes turning to hard crystal as they bore into her Vice-Chancellor, and she was glad not to be in the room.

"And that's exactly, why we destroyed the entire building."

"You disintegrated it."

"They're no longer a threat, right? We are the hidden soldiers to the Entente and it's our job to keep this nation secure at all costs. I'm going there immediately to see to it personally that the people of the Technology District will have a new building, a better building."

"I should be the one to go," Margaret snapped.

"Why on earth would you go? Outside of this village, I'm Eleanor's successor, the Entente's Secretary of Border Affairs."

"Yes, but here, you are the Chancellor of the Guardians and head of this village. The villagers are scared, and they need you. Your absence does not help morale."

"That's why I have a Vice-Chancellor," Audrey said.

The escalating conversation had Teresa on the edge of her seat leaning in to hear more clearly.

"Tarian hasn't caught a Waker in over a week. He needs help, your help."

"He'll be fine."

Teresa scooted back as the doors opened completely and attempted to look innocent of her eavesdropping crime.

"Teresa." Audrey waved her into the office.

Margaret took a step into the antechamber.

"Hello, Vice-Chancellor," Teresa said as she walked past her.

"Hello, dear," Margaret said, but didn't exit the room.

"Thank you, Margaret." Audrey nodded. "That'll be all."

Margaret opened her mouth to speak, but Audrey cut her off, "You've done an excellent job briefing me on the state of affairs of the Guardians. Have a nice day Margaret."

Margaret traipsed out of the office with obvious misgivings.

Audrey waited in silence for Margaret to leave then shut her office door, shoving it with her arm for good measure. "Are we ready?"

"She's not buying your story," Teresa whispered.

Audrey eyes squinted.

"Sorry, I kind of heard your conversation."

"Eavesdropping can get you in a lot of trouble, but I guess it's my fault for not pulling the door shut. And just to clarify, I didn't plant a Prevallers' cell in the precise area I needed to travel."

Teresa slanted a suspicious glance her way.

"I didn't," Audrey protested.

Teresa laughed. "I'm just kidding, but the Vice-Chancellor seems upset."

"Don't worry about her."

"I think she wants your job," Teresa said.

"She can have it," Audrey sighed.

"And I'm pretty sure she thinks you're a control freak." Teresa smirked.

"Exactly why *I* should be the one to go to the Technology District to oversee the state of the building. It'd look suspicious if I didn't go. I personally need to ensure that it's properly rebuilt. And, conveniently, I will be able to look into that when we bring the Sleepers to the Bruja Blanca. Killing two birds with one stone."

"What?" Teresa asked.

"Just an old phrase, before your time."

Teresa shook her head. "Whatever. The sleepers, Daniel, Julia, and Jake have been prepped for the trip. Patrick is putting them on the plane right now."

"I hope this works." Audrey ran a hand through her hair then whipped it into a ponytail.

"Me too."

"Ready?" Teresa asked.

"Yes." Audrey grabbed her tablet. "Let's go."

Audrey and Teresa boarded the plane as Patrick closed the door to the private cabin in the back where he'd just secured the bodies of the Sleepers for the long flight.

"I still think I should go with you both," Patrick said.

"We'll be fine. Joe needs you here, and Margaret is already highly suspicious of my trip," Audrey said.

Teresa kissed him. "Love you. We'll be back soon."

"Love you too. Be careful. I don't trust these preta creatures. Roman told me all about Hu."

"Who's Hu?" Tarian asked.

His appearance surprised everyone. He stood blocking the passenger door.

"Roman's cousin," Audrey said flatly. The first two words she'd spoken to him in five days.

"Why can't she trust him, Patrick?" Tarian still stood in the doorway blocking Patrick from exiting and trapping him in the middle of an awkward situation.

"Nothing, Tarian, I was only joking. Let's go, they need to take off," Patrick said.

"I'm not going anywhere."

"What?" Audrey asked.

"I'm going with you."

"Fine." Audrey gritted her teeth and flashed a fake smile.

Teresa sighed. The tension between her brother and Audrey saturated her bones. She turned pleading eyes to Patrick.

"Good luck." Patrick winked at her then exited the plane.

Audrey spent the trip submerged in business negotiations for the Entente, occasionally glancing in Tarian's direction. His face was lowered into a book except for when he shot intermittent looks at her. Their eyes never met.

Teresa sat silently watching this stressful tug-of-war. She fidgeted, searching for conversation topics to break the invisible barrier between them. The silence became too much for her. She stood up to pace the aisle but before taking her first step was thrown to the ground by sudden turbulence.

Audrey threw out her arm with a pointed finger.

"Okay." Teresa understood the mimed instruction. "I'm okay, thanks for asking," she sarcastically mumbled under her breath as she hopped to her feet and bolted to the cabin. She lifted the lid of the boxes and saw Daniel, Julia, and Jake secure in their resting places. She turned to leave, and face planted into Tarian's broad chest.

"It's not that I'm not happy that Dad's alive." The words erupted from Tarian.

"I know, Tarian," she said softly.

"I just can't see him yet."

"You need to see him soon. We have a second chance with him. How many times did you pray for this opportunity? Come on, don't wimp out."

"I'm not," he said, drawing a ragged breath. "These last few days I haven't killed one Waker. I haven't come close to catching one. All I can think of is Dad and Patrick, and yet, because of my weakness, a thirteen-year-old girl is now fighting for her life in the infirmary, drained of blood with a broken back. That's my fault!"

"It's not your fault. So many people are alive because of you."

"And you," Tarian said looking down at her.

Teresa nodded. "Everyone agrees that the Wakers are too dangerous and can't be saved."

"Even Audrey?"

She looked up at him. "Yes, she agrees."

"Well, she hasn't told me."

"She's probably waiting until after the results of this trip." Teresa inspected her brother. Pain tempered his good looks lining his forehead and creasing his bloodshot eyes. She reached up and placed a calming hand on his shoulder. "Talk to her. She loves you."

He nodded but said nothing.

Another turbulent drop and Teresa grabbed hold of Tarian to sturdy herself. "We need to get into our seats."

Audrey glanced up to watch them reenter the main cabin, still on her business call. She offered a small smile. Tarian returned it with a slight upward curl of his lips before taking a window seat.

This is progress. Teresa's heart warmed, finally feeling some relief in the tight quarters of the plane. Unfortunately, the rough air brought twitchy butterflies into her stomach. She clutched the armrests of her seat and thought, *so much for a nice relaxing flight to Los Angeles.*

FOURTEEN

SALUD

The casket-sized boxes were brought into Qui's wine cellar whose temperature had been lowered a bit further to accommodate the Sleepers. The impressive room stretched deeply with rows of red wine bottles gleaming in the underground lighting system. Everyone dwelled on the obvious question, but no one dared ask if the bottles contained cabernet or blood.

"Well, I never expected to put bodies in my wine room," Qui said with a wry smile.

"Thank you again, for letting us use your home. I hope the colder temperature won't damage your, uh, wine." Audrey's nervous smile gave away her unease.

"No, it'll be fine. I have been gradually reducing the degrees since we last met as to protect the quality of the," Qui hesitated, "wine."

"Can we go upstairs now?" Tarian asked.

Once upstairs, Qui served her guests tea while they

arranged plans.

"It will take us forty-five minutes to get to the Bruja Blanca's home. We need to leave here at six o'clock. You have plenty of time to rest or freshen up. Your rooms are ready. Please excuse me, I will see everyone at six." Qui floated out of the room with a swan's grace.

"Ouch," Tarian said pulling his arm away from Audrey.

"Stop staring," Audrey whispered.

"Sorry, I've never seen a woman float before." Tarian rubbed his bicep where Audrey had pinched him.

"Oh my God, Tarian, aren't you used to strange phenomenon by now?" Teresa punched his other arm and laughed.

"I'm a little sick of you girls teaming up against me."

"Big baby." Teresa strolled toward her room. "I'm going to take a little nap to recover from that horrible plane ride."

Tarian and Audrey stood alone and uptight in the kitchen. They hadn't talked this much in days.

"Do all preta float?" Tarian asked

"No, I don't think she's actually floating. She just walks with extreme poise. Or her feet move so fast we can't see them."

"I want this to work," Tarian said.

Audrey's eyes squinted, confused. "Me too." She wasn't sure if he meant their relationship or this trip.

"I'm hoping you and Dad are right. I hope this witch has the solution to awaken the Sleepers properly."

"She created the two vials for Joe four years ago, and those worked well, so let's pray she can do it again. And Qui says the twins use her quite often to bring back mortals dropped into near death by intoxicated creatures."

"That's good. I mean for us. It's not good that creatures are nearly killing mortals." He shifted his feet and fumbled with his hands.

"Yeah." She smiled at his awkwardness. His youthful innocence surfaced every once in a while, endearing him more to her. Her tenacious Awakened Hunter boyfriend was still a young man of twenty. She wanted to reach out to him, hold him in her arms. Instead, she retreated to the bedroom to read.

The road wound precariously close to the cliff's edge. As the car reached dizzying heights, the view became breathtaking. The vast sapphire ocean outstretched to meet the powder blue of the sky. The waves rolled and crashed melodically against the rocky coast. At sea level, the border wall's oscillating electric and magnetic currents dulled the colors so they were almost imperceptible to the human eye, but far more apparent with Guardian vision. Whereas, the height unhindered the magnificent beauty.

The car abruptly turned into a steep driveway that veered up and away from the cliff's edge and into a canopy of overgrown foliage that hid a quaint cottage. Audrey had envisioned a haunted mansion at the end of such a journey but found a cute gingerbread house instead. Large trees with low-lying branches eerily caressed the fringes of the decorative, buttercream latticework around the perimeter. The house looked as if at any moment the forest would swallow it whole.

Qui and Audrey approached the front porch. A woman of about forty opened the door. She was neither beautiful nor homely. Her skin was the color of caramel, but her little face held features much too big to suit it.

"Good evening, Qui." The woman stood on tiptoes to kiss Qui on both cheeks.

"Hello, Ana-Clara. This is Audrey Gualtiero, Chancellor of the Guardians of Dare. May we enter with the others?" Qui asked.

"Yes, please do, but leave the Sleepers at rest for now. I must analyze her first." Ana-Clara turned her focus to Audrey.

Audrey gasped. The woman's eyes had turned lavender like Piper's, then with a blink returned to amber. Audrey regained her composure and stood eye to eye with Ana-Clara.

Ana-Clare took Audrey's hand and led her into the home. She didn't release her firm, warm grip until she had placed Audrey onto the lime-green, velvet-upholstered couch. She sat close to Audrey.

Qui, Teresa, and Tarian followed and sat in brightly colored chairs. The cheery interior of the home contrasted the spooky, winding drive.

Ana-Clara squeezed Audrey's hand. The witch didn't smile, and her eyes fixed on Audrey's silvery blue irises. "You are brave and powerful. You are true to this cause. I see it."

Audrey only nodded. Hope bloomed in her chest.

Silence seized everyone in the room as Ana-Clara remained quiet, closed her eyes, and continued to keep a hold of Audrey. "I will help you." Ana-Clara dropped her hand, got up from the couch, and grabbed Tarian's hand.

Tarian pulled away. She scowled, and he gave her his hand back.

"Ah, I see why you can't trust. A lot in your life hasn't been what it seems. Your doubt must go, or I can't allow you back into my home. This is a process of hope. It will take all of my positive energy. Your negativity will fight against me."

Audrey glared at Tarian.

"It's not his fault." Ana-Clara snapped her head toward Audrey. "He will come around." She smiled at him and gently stroked his face with her delicate hand. "See, he's already much calmer."

Teresa was the last to be touched by Ana-Clara, and she offered both hands without hesitation.

Ana-Clara took them then she pulled Teresa up to standing. She drew the girl's hands to her chest then moved them down to just above her stomach. A broad grin spread across her face. "I need you."

"Ok?" Teresa's expression slid into puzzlement.

"You'll help me," Ana-Clara said, still holding tight to Teresa.

"Sure." Teresa looked to Audrey for affirmation.

Audrey attempted a smile of encouragement but remembered Jun's warning that this woman trusted no one. Yet she seemed to be entrusting Teresa with an apprenticeship. This supposedly skeptical witch gazed at Teresa with the fondness of a grandmother, quite the opposite of what Audrey had expected.

"You're a gifted healer," Ana-Clara said joyfully. After a small pause, she released Teresa's hands and turned to face everyone in the room. "The process will take three days and three nights. Teresa will stay here."

"I don't like this." Tarian shot to his feet.

"I can take care of myself," Teresa barked.

"Your sister will be fine," Ana-Clara assured him.

Audrey sensed that this woman knew all their secrets. She knew Tarian and Teresa were siblings. What else could she see or feel? She saw Tarian's brow furrow with doubt. *Had he seen something in her touch with his gift of reading people? Could he read a Bruja Blanca?* She opened her mouth to ask him when he seemed to relax. His face flattened, and his eyes softened. Now wasn't the time.

"Okay bring in the Sleepers," Ana-Clara said in an energetic voice. She raised her hands high above her head, and her smile radiated happiness.

The bodies were carefully delivered into her home. She placed them in separate rooms and arranged in different positions. She laid Daniel on his back near a window. She placed Julia on her side away from the window. She put Jake on his stomach surrounded by a curtain. She stripped all three and painted them with ointments of different colors, red for Daniel, blue for Julia, and green for Jake.

Ana-Clara gathered everyone around a circular table. At its center was an intricately designed sundial made of many-colored gemstones. On the edge of the table sat a bottle of red wine and five glasses. She poured a splash of wine into each glass, lifted hers, and toasted, "Salud!"

After the glasses had been emptied Ana-Clara announced, "It is time for you to go. Rest, relax, have some fun, but do not leave Los Angeles nor return here for seventy-two hours. Hasta pronto!"

Gravel shifted beneath their feet as they left the strange home. Teresa and Ana-Clara waved goodbye from the porch. Tarian slipped his hand in Audrey's and squeezed, but he said nothing. Pride melted through her as the warmth of this palm in hers spread to her heart.

FIFTEEN

ROMANCE REKINDLED

Viscous tension simmered in Tarian and Audrey's bedroom as they stirred around the small space. She bumped into him when she attempted to scoot past as he shaved at the bathroom sink. She felt the brush of his anger as it seeped from his skin. Apologies rarely left her mouth, even when she was wrong, but she hated fighting with him, so she invited him to her meeting.

"I'm going to see the destroyed building and work some damage control on behalf of the Entente. I'd like it if you'd join me." Audrey smiled while offering her olive branch then braced for his rejection.

"Sure. I need something to take my mind off of my sister stuck in that rainbow-colored casa with that strange witch."

"Great." She clipped her word but kept her smile. It wasn't a reassuring answer, but she reminded herself that she'd lied to him, so any affirmation meant hope for forgiveness.

A Technology District transport vehicle pulled up to Qui's

house. They entered and rode in silence. Audrey reviewed the intelligence while Tarian checked the Realm training and kill status of the Awakened Hunters back home. Soon the vehicle's halt drew them back into the moment. Their eyes met without expression.

Glancing out her window, she saw the horrific consequences of her decision. One city block had been reduced to a terrible pile of mangled steel and ashy stone. She opened her door and stepped outside. Fine chalky particles too minuscule for the eye to see gushed into her lungs. She coughed to clear her throat but only inhaled more debris. Her hand flew to cover her mouth and nose.

"Put this on." The driver handed her a mask. "I apologize Madam Secretary. I should have prepared you better. You exited the vehicle too quickly." He pointed in the direction of the destroyed building. "Once we cross over the barrier line, we're inside the decontamination zone."

"It's alright. I'm fine. Where is everyone?" She could breathe freely again without the scratch of debris or sharp smell of burnt toxins.

"I apologize, we are thirty minutes early."

"No need to apologize. It gives me time to do some investigating on my own."

A group of unmasked picketers paraded in front of the destroyed building, their eyes swollen, the rims of their nostrils lined red, and their lips dried to the point of cracking from the unhealthy air.

"Get those people some masks," Audrey ordered.

The driver stood dumbfounded.

"Now!"

"But they're a nuisance. They delay our progress every day."

"Freedom of speech is what this nation stands for. It's what we fought for during the great Entente War."

"Yes, ma'am." The driver handed her two hard hats and retreated to find more masks for the protestors.

"Well, anyone inside that building is definitely dead." Tarian followed his harsh commentary with a cocked grin.

"We got all of the civilians out. The only people dead were supposed to be," Audrey replied.

"And incinerating an entire building was your best solution?"

"Yes. A long time ago, before you were born, our nation was polluted with terrorist cells. Let them alone and they multiply like cockroaches with devastating consequences. That will never be the case while I'm Chancellor or Secretary of Border Affairs."

"And you think that was the very last Prevallers' cell?"

"Absolutely, they're gone, Tarian. We wiped them out in less than a year. They first attacked you—well, Zachary had convinced us they were after you—in December, and here it is the twenty-fourth day of September, and their threat is over. I'm proud of that."

"Yeah, that's good work."

"We have your brother to thank, too. He led us to the underground recruiting system they created inside our most elite educational institutions."

"Now what?" Tarian asked.

"Now, we put on these hard hats and walk around. We need to scavenge the wreckage for weapons. The East is dead, yet the Prevallers have managed to secure advanced weaponry—"

"From Zachary," Tarian interrupted.

"Probably. Anything I can bring back to Headquarters to be studied will be valuable. All fibers of all materials can be scanned and identified."

"So Charlie was right?"

"Right about what?"

"There is life in the Wastelands."

"Of course, but it's unsophisticated. It was ruined a long time ago. But that doesn't mean someone won't try to rebuild it."

"Why isn't the Entente claiming it? Sending troops over to start new colonies?"

"We have started. So far, they've reported it's full of junkies and thieves."

"Don't you wonder how many junkies and thieves we might have in the Bar District? From what Roman has told me, his cousins run a pretty seedy establishment."

"Yes, but every nation has its Sin City."

"I guess."

She slanted a peek at him from over her shoulder. *How*

much had Roman told him about Hu?

They trudged through the rubble, gathering evidence for over an hour. The Governor had been held up on business, but once he arrived the meeting began, lasting less than twenty minutes. He applauded her tactics, and she offered financial support for the reconstruction.

Returning to Qui's house, they tracked gray muck all over the hand-woven rug in the foyer. Her disdainful scowl convinced them to strip on the outside porch and shake the dust from their garments.

"Give those to me," Qui said with a sigh and an eye roll, treating them like a couple of unruly children.

After a long shower and a quick nap, Audrey and Tarian were once again fussing inside their cramped quarters. Their idle minds filled with doubts and insecurities about the success of this mission. They needed a distraction.

"I'm hungry," Audrey said.

"Me too. Qui offered her Flux Geodesy to us," Tarian said, unable to suppress the eagerness in his voice even while his face remained calm.

"I know."

"Well, let's go."

"Okay but if we wreck her Geodesy, she'll kill us. Do you

know how expensive and rare that vehicle is?"

"Yes. Stop worrying. It's self-programmed. I can't wreck it."

"Fine. Let's go."

Tarian's wide smile reached his eyes as he slid into the Flux Geodesy driver's seat. He squeezed the soft, red leather and rubbed the shift knob.

"We're putting it on autopilot," Audrey said as her lips thinned and eyebrows cocked, but his excitement was contagious, and joy swelled her heart. He smiled like a child opening birthday presents.

"I know. A man can dream right?" Tarian started the hover engine. It roared to life but barely vibrated as it lifted from the ground. "Smooth as silk." He gave his coordinates to the car and sat back to enjoy the fluid ride; his grin still bright as ever.

The vehicle parked at a restaurant wedged into the cliff's side. Pacifica Steak House peered over the border walls and admired the glory of the ocean below.

The maître d' placed them at a table with an exquisite view. Audrey felt as if she were floating, a glass wall the only thing preventing her from falling to a mortal's death.

"I miss you," Audrey said.

"I miss us," Tarian replied.

"Can you forgive me for keeping your father's secret?"

"Yes." The crease running across his forehead disappeared as he reached across the linen tablecloth to squeeze her hand. "I'm going to talk with him as soon as we get back," he paused then added, "Mom has a right to know."

"Only if we're successful here."

"Why? Dad and Patrick are a behaving humanely. Isn't that enough?" The line returned to his forehead as the words bitterly dropped off his tongue.

The server arrived before she could answer. "Would you like to hear our specials?"

His presence startled Audrey. She fumbled for the touch screen to order, but there was none. The restaurant's intimate setting provided a personal touch to all aspects of dining. She'd forgotten how nice it was to be waited on.

"No, thank you. We'll take the Chateaubriand and a bottle of cabernet," Tarian ordered.

Audrey smiled at him. He came to her rescue. It may have been a small act, but she relished his gallantry.

The waiter trailed away and Audrey continued in a hushed voice, "I fear the judgment of the High Council. They could order Joe and Patrick to death."

"They wouldn't do that."

"I've seen them do far worse in the past."

"I won't let them."

Audrey looked at him, admiring his loyal courage but knowing full well that no one could change a High Council order. His broad, capable shoulders filled the chair. She wanted more than anything to leap over the table and wrap herself around him to not only enjoy his robust muscular body, but also to protect him from any future pain.

The delivery of the wine broke the spell of Audrey's thoughts. The server made an exaggerated presentation of uncorking the bottle and pouring the cabernet into their stemmed wine goblets. Sipping the smooth, bold liquid, Tarian once again reached for her hand. She took it without hesitation.

"You're beautiful," Tarian said without a smile but with a spark in his chocolate eyes.

The rough rumble of his tone caressed her ears. She melted as he gazed at her from across the table and longed to kiss his full lips, but instead she smiled softly and stroked the top of his hand with her thumb.

Tarian's glance fell, and he let out a long sigh.

"What is it?" she asked but he said nothing. "We have to communicate."

His chin shot up from his chest, he opened his mouth to sling a smart remark at her, but he stopped then calmly said, "I hate that you have centuries of secrets with my father, but I shouldn't because I love you both. Sometimes I feel like I'm just a shadow among the Guardians."

"You're not." Her words felt meaningless, but no words were adequate to express how much she loved and respected him.

"You can't even commit to me fully."

"What do you mean? Of course, I'm fully committed to us."

"Then why not share one apartment, instead of two?"

It was her silvery blue eyes that drifted downward this time. Again, she couldn't explain her fears. Her anxiety was unreasonable, and yet she stubbornly held on to her independence as if that would somehow shield her if he left her or died. It was stupid. She would've kept Joe's secret even if they'd lived together. She did have an unbreakable bond with his father, the kind that only existed when two people had shared centuries of heartache and happiness. That couldn't be changed, it could only be accepted.

The fragrant meat set on the table by the server thankfully drew their attention away from each other. They ate and soon found themselves laughing while watching the blazing sun sink under the horizon, leaving shimmering trails of orange, pink, and yellow.

"Delicious." Audrey sipped her wine and gazed at the now dark sky and endless horizon.

"Let's get out of here." Tarian's eyes sparkled with mischief. He quickly paid the bill, and they left Pacifica Steak House.

Tarian glided into the driver's seat then turned to look at her. "Let's program it to drop us off in front of Jun and Hu's Bar. What's it called again?"

"El Tunel." She entered the coordinates, and the onyx Flux Geodesy sped away. "Are you sure you want to go to a bar. It's very loud, and I'm so full."

"Don't act your age." He grinned. "I want to check it out.

I find it very intriguing that mortals come to these bars, and some end up dead because they're partying with creatures and don't even know it. How is this allowed by us?"

"We have a mutual understanding. There are hundreds of different species Tarian. We don't want to start a creature war."

Once at their destination, Tarian sprung from the vehicle and sent it to a secure location to park. He turned to face Audrey. A smirk plastered on his face. "I want this car!"

"We don't need cars in the village," she said.

He sighed and slouched.

Audrey hesitated to enter the establishment where she'd last danced with Hu. She knew Tarian would eventually have to check it out, but she'd hoped the two men wouldn't meet now. Not when she and Tarian were finally mending hurt feelings.

"Wait." Audrey placed a hand on his shoulder. She toyed with the idea of telling him what had transpired between her and Hu, immortal and preta, dancing in an illusionary forest. Her eyes flicked from side to side, but she merely said, "This place is, uh, loud."

"I've been in a bar before." He cocked his head and inspected her.

She nodded.

They took their place in line, flashed their passports, gave the man fifty credits, and strode into the arena of pounding music. Brilliantly colored lights flashed, bodies pumped, and arms flung to the beat.

"Let's get a drink," Audrey yelled.

"What?" The thump of the deep bass and high-pitched synthetic strings overwhelmed Tarian's acute hearing.

She grabbed his arm and led him through the crowd of people. She found a single chair at the bar and climbed into it. Tarian leaned up against her.

Audrey placed their order then turned to see Tarian watching a young girl at the end of the counter. He shifted his attention to the multitude of adolescents dancing ecstatically to the music and she took the drinks from the bartender.

"Here." Audrey handed him a purple soda. "House specialty." She shrugged and clinked her glass to his.

Tarian leaned in so she could hear. "Look at the girl at the end of the bar and tell me why she looks so familiar."

Audrey casually turned back toward the end of the counter, but no girl sat there. "She's gone?"

Tarian spun around to find an empty seat. "Maybe she's dancing." He scanned the dancing youth but didn't see her. "Hmm, she reminded me of someone. I just don't know who."

In the split-second Audrey had seen the girl she hadn't recognized anything unusual.

The atmosphere of El Tunel soon lifted them into another world, a place where all their cares vanished. The music lured them onto the dance floor, but unlike the illusion that transported her on her last visit, it remained a flat stage in an overcrowded club. Creatures intermingled. Pointed teeth brushed young, tender mortal skin. Strange vials of many colors parachuted down from the ceiling of infinite night. The mysterious liquid inside the vials eagerly consumed by the patrons. It all seemed highly illegal, or if legal, highly irresponsible, an environment hinged on disaster.

Audrey refused to see the dangers tonight. She tossed her head back, swayed her hips, and wrapped her arms around the neck of her gorgeous boyfriend. Her fingers played with the ends of his chestnut hair. She liked that he'd let it grow a little longer than his normal conservative cut.

They danced and laughed like never before. He was her life, her everything. He'd forgiven her. Soon she'd free her friends from their limitless slumber and restore order to the village. She delighted in her thoughts and in the arms of the man she loved. But when she kissed him, she heard a tiger's roar. With a jerk and a gasp, she tore her lips away. The sound disappeared. Her eyes saw only Tarian's warm chocolate orbs staring back at her.

"What's wrong?" he whispered against her ear.

"Nothing, I'm just feeling a little dizzy. It's probably that purple drink. I want to leave."

"Of course." He placed a solid, vigilant arm around her as he weaved a path through the crowd, sheltering her from clumsy dancers.

His snug, secure grip kept her safe, and she loved him for it. She didn't see Hu watching them from the railing above as the exit door shut behind them, but she sensed his presence.

SIXTEEN

HUNTER TRAINING

Margaret stood in her green suit in the middle of the circular all-white room, looking completely out of place next to the massive Commander General. She was an overly matronly and entirely non-athletic woman with chubby ankles and soft arms. He, on the other hand, had the sharp, defined muscles of a genuine war hero. Her hair stretched into a grandmotherly bun. His was shaved short. She was immortal, and he wasn't.

Eight Guardian Awakened Hunters and eight newly appointed Entente Elite lined the curved wall. They stood at attention to receive their weapons from the Commander General.

"You have all trained in the Realm before. Some of you were here only months ago for the game to assess Tarian's abilities as the First Born immortal. That landscape is not the one you will encounter today." Margaret's precise words and over-enunciation made her sound like a well-meaning, but annoying, schoolteacher. She swallowed and continued her speech in a much more forceful tone. "Now, we must succeed in the destruction of the Wakers that haunt the villagers' homes and hunt their children. With Tarian, our best Hunter out-of-town, it is up to you and so far, you've failed. Failure is not an option!"

In silence, Margaret circled the Commander General as he remained in the nucleus of the room like a giant mountain. She didn't like to yell so she calmed herself and reclaimed her saccharine, high-pitched voice. "You eight Elite Forces have impressive records and have been recruited to assist our Awakened Hunters in their mission. You are not immortal, and this is a potentially lethal task, but both the mission and this training are confidential. Should you die in performing these duties, your valiant efforts will be recognized only inside Headquarters. You do this mission for love of country and not for honors and awards. Now is the time to leave if you do not think yourself capable of following the rules I've laid out and are not willing to die for our cause." She paused. No one budged. "Wonderful! You are all very brave and have the respect and protection of the Guardians of Dare. Commander," she threw the conversation to him.

"Killing a Waker takes skill and finesse. You must either weaken them long enough to inject Death Serum or manage a sneak attack. The hunters are much more likely to be able to achieve this than the Elite Forces. You don't have the lightning speed of an immortal, but you are the best, and I have faith in you. We've been developing specific weapons to stun, trick, guide, and gather these mutant creatures, which you will use and test during the simulation. Take your positions," the Commander General ordered.

The sixteen men and women stepped into the cylinders. The doors closed. The compartments hummed and vibrated as they transported them into the Realm.

"Very well, let's get started." Margaret exited the room and led the Commander General into the control center.

Each bodysuit that the Awakened Hunters and Elite Forces wore transmitted their emotions during training. If they felt scared or confident, Margaret knew it. They each wore lenses and earpieces revealing exactly what they saw and heard. The Realm itself was monitored by thousands of advanced devices capturing not only audiovisual real time, but tactual, olfactory, and gustatory as well.

She watched as trainees entered the simulated village street in pairs, one Elite Force with one Awakened Hunter. The first test drill named *Bait and Stab* began. It was one of many plans Margaret had been developing for weeks. If it worked, Tarian would no longer be the only Hunter capable of killing these monsters.

The Awakened Hunter, Sasha Middleshire, exited her tubular pod and found herself face to face with her Elite Forces partner, Josh Farmington. The simulated street identically matched Rue de la

Magie, from the odor of bread and flowers to the shades of brown on the boards of all the windows to the uneven texture of each cobbled stone underfoot. The midnight noises of droning insects, chirping crickets, and whispering wind sounded just as they had when Sasha hunted last night. She grimaced as she remembered her failed attempt to catch the Waker.

Eager to get started, Sasha gave Josh a small disc. "Here, take this luring mechanism and place it on the bench over there. If it does its job, the frequency and pheromone scent will attract a Waker."

They hid and waited. The respite lasted longer than expected. Josh's body swayed and his feet fidgeted. Sasha glared, bidding him to be still. Finally, the Waker crept from the shadows in search of the sound and scents. Josh nudged Sasha. She silently gave a three count and then they attacked.

Sasha, with her immortal speed, ran around the building to charge the Waker from behind, hoping to get a clear shot at injecting the Death Serum needle. By the time she'd reached the bench, Josh was dead.

Josh lumbered to his feet brow drawn, lips pulled straight, and deep blue eyes tense. He sighed. Simulated blood gushed from his lacerated neck.

"Start over." Margaret's voice squeaked in their earpieces.

Sasha clawed at her ears but the hearing aid wouldn't budge. She stomped back to the bench and reset the scenario. Once back at the hiding spot she hit Josh square in the face with a direct, wicked stare of her maple brown eyes making it known he'd better not screw up again.

"I'm very fast. Why don't we switch directives?"

"Fine, let's try that." She ignored his eyes and stared at the bench. "Go!" she ordered once the Waker approached.

He shot out of hiding and she had to admit he was fast—she dared to hope he might live. She charged towards the beast, coming at it from the front. Using a black diamond corral stick she herded the beast into position, its back toward Josh. She'd done her part. All Josh had to do was thrust the Death Serum needle into the Waker's large posterior area. Fool proof, or so she thought.

Somehow Josh stumbled just as the needle came plunging down. "Shit!" screamed Josh, "Shit! I'm such an idiot! Shit!"

Josh held up his hand. The needle pierced straight through it. The event was pure simulation as the needle disappeared, but the horrendous pain lingered, as a reminder of how badly he'd screwed up.

"Begin again," Margaret said.

"Are you serious?" Sasha barked at Josh as they took position again. "Did you even go to the EMA? What was that? How was that even possible?" Her rapid questions went off like bombs and then she punched his arm.

"Ouch!"

She punched him again.

"Okay, I got it. This isn't helping our working

relationship." He rubbed the pain out of his arm.

She wanted to laugh, looking at his young, innocent face as he pleaded for forgiveness, but she wouldn't. The seriousness of their task bound her to be the leader, the cruel alpha dog. She told herself that if she managed to shape up his skills and complete their task, she'd reward him with a drink at the Tavern.

"How old are you?" she asked.

"Twenty-two, graduated last spring."

She shook her head, rolled her eyes, then backed away into the corner to lean against the wall. Thoughts of his precious mortality surged through her. Young blood sung to the Wakers tempting them in a way that old blood didn't. This young man had been chosen for his bravery but also for his tasty blood. He was green and had never encountered such a strange world of creatures before. He probably came from a nice mid-western family of corn producers. A sweet, mild mannered mom and hard-working dad, maybe a pretty little sister, or adorable baby brother he gallantly swore to protect. The EMA was his way of getting out of the doldrums of that life and into the exciting arena of the military. As she focused on her training partner and surmised his past, she wondered if he still thought his choice worthy.

Sasha had to endure five more failed attempts by Josh and two by her own incompetence, all ending with Margaret's annoying shrill call from the Realm's command center to "Do it again!"

"Listen, this is your last chance. You get this wrong and I'm flunking you out of this mission. I won't be the one to tell your darling cornhusking mama that you died killing the walking dead. Got it?" Sasha asked, but it was an order.

He looked at her completely confused. "Yes ma'am, but I'm from Seattle. My mom's a musician."

"Whatever! Just get it right. You're not dying on my watch." She threw up her hands and revised the image she'd made of him in her mind.

The device was once again set in place, moved to beneath the bench, which they had found to be a better distraction. Josh bolted out of the dark alley a lot faster than Sasha had seen him run before. Now, for her part, holding out the diamond rod she tricked and teased the Waker. Twice before the monster had managed to steal the new weapon away from her, but not this time. She was ready for the lunges and strikes.

She wielded the stick like a beloved sword releasing the electricity that traveled through it. With grace and precision, she flew through the air, the beast at her will as she prodded it into position. This time she received only one angry scratch, manageable.

Josh slid the Death Serum needle into the lateral muscle that ran along the beast's spine. He injected the fluid then gripped the monster in a headlock rendering it limp.

Sasha smiled wide and bright as she sheathed her weapon and strutted over to Josh's side to throw the beast over her shoulder. But he beat her to it and hoisted the large body over his shoulder. They walked side by side to the bonfire. Josh swung the

Waker into the flames Herculean style and Sasha laughed. She gave him a congratulatory pat on the back and let the blazing fire warm her cheeks.

Their few minutes of joy abruptly ruined by Margaret's squawking voice, "Moving on! Next simulation."

"Can we ignore her?" Josh asked.

"I wish," Sasha said with tired, dulled eyes. "What time is it, Margaret?"

"It's not quitting time," she responded.

"What time is it?" Sasha insisted.

"You have time for a few more drills."

"That wasn't my question."

"It's 1800, soldier. Now get in position for drill two," the Commander General's voice boomed into their earpieces.

Josh sprang to life and hurriedly reported to the next task.

Sasha moved at a much more leisurely pace. The General outranked her, but having fought for centuries, she'd earned the right to grumble.

SEVENTEEN

IDLE TIME

Following breakfast, Audrey and Qui left to attend a meeting with the Xia Council. Tarian shuffled around the house in a heather gray t-shirt and long plaid pajama pants, hot mug of tea in hand, snooping in rooms. The three doors he tugged on wouldn't open. He stepped back to inspect the third locked door.

I could bust it down. It'd be easy.

He abruptly turned around not wanting to be a spy and tromped into the kitchen. He was bored and torn between his need to stay to protect Audrey and his sister, and his desire to be home protecting the village from the Wakers. Thoughts of his father filled his head as he drank his tea and paced. His impatience grew. He wanted to have a civil conversation with his dad, renew their relationship, pick up where they left off, and yet, he was stuck in Los Angeles doing what?

Teresa has a purpose here. She's helping Ana-Clara. Audrey has Secretary of Border Affairs Entente business to tend to. Why am I here? I'm not needed.

Thunk! His mug slammed the counter and shattered into clunky chunks of ceramic. The hot liquid rolled out and over his fingers.

"Damn." He jerked his hand back. Advancing anger coiled up his neck, seething out of his eye sockets until he closed them. He inhaled a long, smooth breath and urged a sense of tranquility to travel through his lungs. "I wanted coffee anyway. Get yourself together, Tarian. Prying into Qui's things. Feeling sorry for myself. What's wrong with me?"

He mopped up the wet counter and floor, threw the mug in the trash, and put on running shoes.

Before leaving, he checked on the village. "Hi Margaret, what's the update on the Realm training?"

"Sasha and Josh made a kill last night." Margaret's voice sang with excitement.

"That's terrific. I guess partnering with Elite Forces was a good idea?"

"It's only one. The others were not successful, but no victims either, so yes, I would conclude this is a success." The confidence in Margaret's voice teetered with each thought.

"Eight more to go, but that's good news. Thanks, Margaret." Tarian allowed himself a teeny bit of celebration then he checked in with all his family members. Satisfied that everything and everyone back home was safe and secure, he headed out.

He ran with a destination in mind, the mysterious El Tunel

bar. He was suspicious of Hu, remembering Patrick's unease when Tarian busted in on their conversation about him on the plane. Something at Hu's bar had spooked Audrey the night before and put an end to their fun evening, and he had every intention to find out what or who it was.

His blood raced, his sinews throbbed, and his mind focused during the twelve-mile run to the Bar District. His boredom and fretfulness replaced with an energy that pulsed through him, invading every inch of his skin. He glistened with sweat in the mid-morning sun. Slowing to a walk, he took in the scene. The light now shone onto the alleys revealing a plethora of waste and debris that couldn't be seen in the night's darkness. A monotonous hum annoyed his hearing and grabbed his attention. Enormous black suction brushes attached to a moving vehicle whirled upon him within seconds, nearly knocking him off his feet. The machine swept through the streets digesting bottles, crumpled paper, clothing, plastic—anything that littered the pavement. This explained the lack of vagrants. The vehicular creature would suck them up too if they were lying around.

He attempted to open the doors to the bar, but all were locked, and no one came to greet him when he knocked. Continuing his quest, he found an underground path leading to a water canal. The stone steps appeared ancient, dark mold veining the surface and moss gained the grout. As he descended, the air thickened and the sunshine faded. However, there was light. The underground waterway glowed in a luminous shimmer, but Tarian saw neither torch nor electricity.

He was at least fifteen miles from the ocean and completely unaware of any existing water path. Before the trip out, he'd studied the area's geography, history, and current events. He wracked his memory, but he'd never seen an underground waterway on any of his documents.

"How did you get down here." A voice whispered into his ear.

Tarian spun but saw no one. An unsettling sensation spider walked down his spine. Then he saw her. The girl from the bar stood on the other side of the canal. "Do I know you?"

"No."

"Why are you following me?" he asked.

"It's you that's following me. How'd you get down here?" Her sweet melodic voice danced across the water.

"I just walked. I took the stairs. It's no mystery."

Without warning, she disappeared from the opposite bank and reappeared next to him. "That's impossible." She leaned in, studying him hard with her stare.

He jumped back from this strange wiry girl. She didn't seem threatening with her skinny limbs, tiny wrists and ankles, blunt hair, and short stature, and yet, she frightened him. Every fiber in his body pleaded for flight. She was definitely a predatory creature of some kind.

"What are you? A vamp? A witch?" She stepped closer.

Recognition drowned his words as he choked out, "You're

like Piper!" Her lavender eyes pierced into him. That's why she looked so familiar. "You can travel through space, and you have lavender eyes."

She turned away. "I don't know this Piper person."

"Well, she's a lot like you, and she's one of my closest friends."

"I knew it! You're not a mortal human!"

"No, I'm an immortal."

"Oh! That's why the stairway showed itself to you." Her posture relaxed until the roar of a boat engine echoed from down the water passage. She grabbed Tarian and transported him to a small nook in the wall as the watercraft sped past.

All Tarian saw was long flowing black hair, and then the boat faded into the distance.

"Where does this lead?" he asked.

"I can't tell you."

"Listen, like you said the stairs chose to reveal themselves to me, so you can trust me."

"Why are you here?" She stepped away and straightened her spine.

"I just told you."

"No, why are you in the Bar District?"

"I'm here on business."

"What kind of business?" she asked.

"How about you answer my question first?"

She paced, rubbing her hands on her thighs. "Rain's Gate

is a path for magical creatures to enter the Entente from the South."

Tarian was silent, but his mind raced. A breach in the border wall could be deadly if used by the Prevallers. "But mortal humans can't travel down here?" he asked.

"No. You said you know someone that looks like me?"

"Yes, the eyes." Tarian hesitated. The girl looked increasingly curious. Tarian withdrew. Could he trust her?

They silently scrutinized each other then Tarian heard footsteps and spun around. A man with similar features to Roman's strolled nearer. When he turned back to the girl, she was gone.

"Tarian?" the man asked.

"Yes, who are you?"

"I'm Hu, Roman's cousin. Where is your lovely girlfriend?"

"She's meeting the Xia Council with your mother today. How'd you find me?"

"A combination of scent and surveillance. The Bar District is large, but only a few of us control it. We have tracking technology throughout to prevent crime, but it helped me find you. I went to answer the door, and you were gone."

"I waited a long time."

"Come, let's get above ground. It's muggy down here."

Tarian followed Hu back up the old stairs. He'd read about Xia Preta lure, but he'd never expected it to be so enticing. A magnetic pull dragged him closer to Hu. A disconcerting, but pleasurable sensation slithered under his skin and took control of his limbs. It took Tarian several minutes and full concentration to block Hu's access to his emotions.

Hu halted and turned his gaze upon Tarian. "Interesting." Hu stepped back, relaxed his stare, loosened his lips then resumed walking.

A smirk slid across Tarian's face. Somehow, he'd blocked Hu's seductive powers, and by the look on Hu's face, this had never happened before. Pride swelled in Tarian's chest and lifted his height. He strode shoulder to shoulder with his new opponent.

"I suppose you don't trust us, but your curiosity had gotten the better of you. I mean, you have entrusted us with your sleeping immortals," Hu said.

"It's not a matter of trust."

"No, I suppose it isn't. It's a matter of last resort."

Tarian didn't know how to respond to the remark. He wouldn't show weakness during this standoff.

"Placing your dear friends' lives in the hands of hungry ghosts is a desperate move, is it not?"

"Actually, I've never met the Sleepers. They had died before I knew I was immortal."

"Fell asleep," Hu corrected.

"Fell asleep." Tarian nodded. "And my father has entrusted them to the Bruja Blanca. You and I really don't play a big role in this game."

"But your lovely Audrey does."

"Yes." Tarian's smile diminished as his protective instinct stiffened his spine. With every reference to Audrey as *lovely*, Tarian's stomach lurched. This man toyed with Tarian's emotions, throwing them around and bouncing them from attraction to pride to jealously to brotherhood. This internal circus cavorted just below the surface, and it took all of Tarian's will to keep it in check.

Hu smiled and opened the door to the club, defusing the bomb counting down inside Tarian.

"Come, I'll show you everything." Hu displayed the congeniality of a gracious host.

With a deep breath and purposeful stride, Tarian entered the door held open for him. He'd accept the terms of their unspoken fraternity but keep up his guard.

A drab dullness blanketed the giant room. Tarian recognized the massive dance floor, the stage for the DJ, the bar where he had a drink with Audrey, curtains, beds, VIP sections, all the usual attractive nightclub settings dusted in neutral, boring tones. No more magic. The night before, the bar had dripped with color and exploded with titillating excitement. People laughed and objects floated through the air. The beat of the music slipped inside the hearts of the bar patrons and created ecstatic moments of pleasure. And the ceiling had been an endless, romantic sky dotted with twinkling stars, a place of dreams. Today the ceiling was flat and white like a thick coat set on top of a magic hat to smother the magician's bunny.

"It's disappointing, isn't it?" A female voice from above drifted down.

Hu swept his arm from low to high gesturing a grand introduction. "Jun, meet Tarian."

"Nice to meet you."

"Likewise," Tarian said.

"We'll come up," Hu said to his sister.

"By all means," she answered with a wry smile.

Tarian followed Hu up a back staircase, and the three took seats at an office table.

"Did you and Audrey have fun last night?" Jun crossed her long, spider legs.

"Yes." Tarian hoped his outward smile disguised the squeeze in his throat.

"Sorry for being a voyeur. We keep tight security around here. You understand," she said.

Tarian nodded. He didn't entirely understand. He'd never been to a bar of this magnitude before. He'd been to sports bars where normal people ate food and watched games, but this establishment was a foreign beast.

"The mortals come here to have a good time, and we give it to them. They just don't know they're partying with preta, vamps, demons, witches - ya name it. All they're little brains know is they feel free to indulge in drink and lust. We entrance them with our spells. But if one of the esurients latches onto a mortal that person is helpless. Their free will gone, so it's up to Hu and me to make sure the creatures know the consequences of takin' advantage of the mortals. Have some fun, but that's all," Jun explained.

"But that's not all, is it?" Tarian's nerves fluttered as he remembered how easy it'd been to forget all his worries and live in a moment of bliss with Audrey. Had it been his true feelings or had he been spellbound?

Hu laughed, a hollow and disturbing sound that bellowed up from the depths of his bowels. "Fun is a slippery slope. We wouldn't need to employ the Bruja Blanca if people could control their limits of fun."

"What is the drug in the vials that float down from the sky ceiling?"

"It's whatever is needed," Hu said.

"Is it legal?"

"It helps heighten the experience. One night our bar looks like a forbidden forest and the next night it might be a circus tent. The vials are filled with potions that help to enhance the illusion we create with sets, lights, and costumes," Jun said in answer.

"And magic?" Tarian asked.

"Yeah, we have five magicians, three illusionists, and two witches on our payroll," Jun said.

"And you smuggle creatures across our border. You are breaking laws, both legal and moral here!" Tarian's brown eyes darkened as his lids narrowed.

"No, we do nothing immoral. Our guests want to escape.

They want to have a good time. What's wrong with that?" Hu asked.

"Nothing if it doesn't kill you because you're entertaining creatures that cross over illegally."

"Crossin' the border isn't legal by Entente law, I'll give ya that, but don't think your Guardian High Council doesn't know about it. As long as safety is our top priority, they ignore us. No harm done. It's in our best interest to keep people alive and safe, or else we go outta business," Jun spoke calmly as if she truly needed Tarian to understand the importance of their establishment.

"People need to relax. They need an outlet. Creatures too. And now because of us your immortals will live," Hu added.

"It's a win-win." Jun stood and patted Tarian on the back.

"So you expect me to believe that the High Council knows about you and all of this?"

"Yep." Jun nodded.

"I don't believe it. They would have suggested you to us instead of us sneaking behind their backs to come here."

"I'm not sayin' they know about our ability to bring the dead back to life without turning them into monsters, but they know about us." She strode around the room.

"You mean they know about the border penetration."

"Yeah." Jun tossed her hand into the air like brushing off floating steam.

"Do you go to the Southern continent?" Tarian's curiosity was piqued. Did the crossing go both ways?

"We have been, but we prefer to stay here." Hu puckered his lips and shook his head.

"Why? Is it as bad as the Entente wants us to think?"

"In South America no, in Eurasia yeah," Jun answered.

"So South America is a thriving country like us?" Tarian asked.

"I wouldn't say thriving but developed and mildly successful. Over there, people are happy and safe," Hu said.

"What about thievery and murders, destruction and rubble?" Tarian inched closer to the edge of his seat with every question.

"Not in the South. It's lush and green. Farming is abundant. They have plenty of everything they need. They're like the Entente only without a wall. The South American people don't travel outside the continent like us, but unlike us, they're not walled in. They're trapped by choice. The rest of the world is destroyed, and we're bordered up. No reason to go anywhere," Jun said.

"We are trapped by choice too. We built the wall for good reason," Tarian argued as he watched Jun stroll around the table. He felt as if she spun a web as she circled.

Hu leaned back in his chair looking satisfied with the load of information he had just dumped on Tarian.

Tarian pushed back into the seat of his chair. He didn't speak. He let this knowledge swirl inside his head. Again, he felt naive. Desire rustled in his stomach, a yearning to follow Rain's Gate to the other side. He always knew from looking at maps that the two continents were connected by land, but he'd never wondered why the two nations remained so separate.

Shouldn't we combine, work together, share? Then his mind drifted to Audrey. *Did she know about this? Had she kept this secret from me too?*

"How is AC doing with your friends?" Hu waltzed around Tarian's chair as he spoke. He brushed Tarian's arm with his fingertips.

Tarian flinched from the touch and pulled his arm away. The spot now tingled. "I don't know. She said we had to wait three days. Tomorrow we'll go back and see."

"Three days." Hu widened his eyes and cocked his brow. "That's not bad. We had one girl, seventeen, took AC ten days to bring her back. The entire city searched for her. It was a nightmare. But we took care of the vampire that took advantage of his powers."

"He can't come over the border anymore?" Tarian asked.

"He can't go anywhere anymore. He's dead." Hu flashed his sharp teeth.

"Oh."

"See? We keep our mortals safe."

"Gotta do, what ya gotta do," Jun interrupted. "Tell us about Roman."

"Not much to tell. He's a decent guy. Intelligent. Worked for Dad as an attorney."

"I remember your father. Joe, right?" Jun asked.

"Yes, my dad's name is Joe."

"Your dad's smart. He knew all about us in our little corner of the world. He had a plan too. Hired Roman for a reason. But I guess he died before he got the chance to do whatever it was he planned to do. He only came here once, then that vile man came."

"Handsome but evil. Wanted the power of the vampire, energy of a demon, casting ability of a witch. He wanted to rule all of us." Hu's upper lip curled.

"Zachary?" Tarian asked.

"Yes, is he still alive?" Hu leaned over to look Tarian in the eye.

"No." Tarian pushed back and pulled his face away from Hu's.

"But your dad's alive?" Jun asked.

"Yes, and I guess it's thanks to Ana-Clara."

"Probably. She's powerful," Jun said.

"It's been a pleasure, but I need to get back now." Tarian stood. "Audrey will be done with work soon."

"Audrey." Hu inched closer to Tarian invading his space once more as her name dripped like honey from his velvet tongue.

Tarian's insides gnarled into a knot. He balled his hands into fists but remained still.

Jun flashed her brother a narrow-eyed glare. With lightning speed, Jun appeared between Hu and Tarian. She nudged her brother back to give Tarian room to leave. "Nice talking with ya. Don't be a stranger." She grinned.

EIGHTEEN

BOYS

Audrey returned home with Qui just as the sun set in the tangerine September sky. Tarian's silhouette sat on a lawn chair in the backyard. She strolled over.

"Hi." She slid into an empty lawn chair.

"Hi." He lazily tilted his head in her direction.

"Beautiful sunset."

The blended orange hues melted and swirled as darkness stole the light. The air chilled and the high-pitched hum of insects droned in the distance like an army of miniature helicopters.

"How did it go today?" he asked.

"Well. We came to an agreement on the budget and squared up some deadlines." As she spoke about business, his face never turned to meet hers. He'd asked out of sheer politeness, but something else weighed on his mind. "What did you do today?"

He shifted to face her. "I met Qui's twins."

"Where?" She didn't like how his eyes interrogated.

"At the bar. I took a jog. I don't trust Hu."

"I agree." Unspoken words scraped at her throat like broken glass, but she wouldn't tell him any more. She could handle Hu.

"He seems hung up on you."

"He's a preta, Tarian. That's what they do. Intimidate their prey. Hu uses seduction. I know how you felt around him. I felt the same when I met him, too."

He took a deep breath. "Did you know about the underground waterway?"

She saw from the look in his eyes he thought she'd kept another secret from him. "No. What are you talking about?"

"Really?"

"Yes." Her heart sank. She'd impaled a dagger into his trust and feared it could never be removed. But she had no knowledge of an underground waterway.

"It leads to the Southern continent."

"What? How?"

"It's a passage that only creatures can pass through called Rain's Gate. Somehow it conceals itself from humans. It's a way for them to enter the Entente and party in the Bar District."

"That's dangerous."

"Apparently, it's been going on for a long time, and the High Council is aware of it."

"I see," she nodded.

He snapped his head in her direction. "Really? Because it

makes no sense to me!"

"Tarian, you have to understand that the High Council has been around since the beginning, before the immortals came to the New World and before we had established ourselves as the Guardians of Dare, protectors of North America. The council was formed to protect us, as we didn't know who we were back then. Other creatures were threatened by our existence, and we needed a governing body to liaison for us—"

"The Esurient Eternals."

"Yes. They are the council to the most deadly immortals that walk this earth. Creatures like vampires or the cursed. Creatures that have lived thousands to our hundreds of years. We were a bunch of frightened people, most of us commoners with no say, no power, no money back then. No idea why we weren't getting any older. Who knows what would've happened to us if it weren't for those four crafty, powerful immortals that were willing to go before the Esurient Eternal Council. And yes, sometimes they take it upon themselves to negotiate deals without informing me or the rest of us."

"That's what they've done. They've made an agreement with the local Xia Preta bar owners: keep the mortals alive, and the High Council looks the other way."

"I need to see this tunnel," she said.

"Let's go tomorrow."

Audrey nodded.

"I also ran into the girl from the bar, the one who

disappeared. The one I told you looked familiar."

"Yes, I remember."

"I spoke to her. She has lavender eyes. She reminds me of Piper."

"Really," she said drawing out the word.

"What?" The word saturated with skepticism.

There it was again, the tone of distrust. "Piper didn't come with us from England in 1857. We found her in Saint Augustine years after our arrival to the New World. She had come over from Spain. Banished by her mother on purpose. Something about her mixed blood. Her mother feared she'd be killed by her own kind. But I've never seen or heard of another Lavender Witch before."

"Aren't a lot of immortals mixed with witch's blood?"

"Yes, but not Lavender Witch's blood. They were legendary, kept to themselves. Pure bloods you could say. Very mysterious. They never let outsiders in so no one knows much about them. Then, like us, they disappeared. No one knew if they fled across the seas as we did. Or if they had been destroyed, as we had feared would be our destiny if we'd stayed in England."

"Could she be related to Piper?"

"Maybe. Strange. What did she say?"

"Not much. Hu showed up and scared her away."

"There's a lot more to this place. Hmmm," she growled low. She didn't like the idea of a tunnel for creatures. *Was it a mistake to reveal our one weakness to these creatures?* She took a deep jagged breath.

"What is it?" he asked.

"We hold power among the creatures even though the others have lived centuries longer. But we proved superior because we had almost no weakness."

"And now the Death Serum threatens us." He shifted again in his chair.

"Yes, and we've revealed our weakness to the preta."

"Because of Dad."

"But Joe would never have come here unless he truly trusted these people."

"Or he was desperate," he said.

They stared at one another. Clouds had eclipsed all but a sliver of the moon while they'd conversed.

"Let's go to bed." She stood and held out her hand to him. "I'll feel better in the morning after we go see Ana-Clara."

"I'll feel better after I get my sister back to the village."

Ten in the morning, Audrey and Tarian sat at the breakfast table waiting for Qui to return. She'd been summoned by Ana-Clara and informed them to remain at the house until she returned.

A rumbling hum of an engine caught Audrey's attention. "Someone's here." She ran to the window and peered outside.

Jun and Hu strutted up to the door.

"Hello, Lovely." Hu took Audrey into his arms and kissed

both her cheeks.

"Hi, Hu." She forcefully untangled herself from his embrace. The burn from Tarian's glare upon the back of her head annoyed her. Standing between the men made her feel like a prize to be won. She grit her teeth. "You've met Guardian Tarian Prescott."

Tarian stepped toward Hu.

Jun stepped in between them. "Apologies for my brother's stupidity." Jun twisted toward her brother.

Hu bowed. "It will not happen again."

Tarian glanced at Audrey. Her temperature flared. Jun's eyes widened in surprise, Hu flashed a wicked smile, and Tarian to leaped to her side.

"Why are you here?" Audrey asked.

"Mom sent us to bring you to AC's."

The four of them squeezed into Hu's sporty vehicle, and he gunned the engine to max speed. Audrey rolled her eyes and shook her head. None of them would die in a crash, but that wasn't the point. She liked speed as much as anyone, but she didn't have patience for showing off. On the other hand, Tarian's eyes gleamed from the thrill of the ride. She decided she'd buy Tarian a sports car for Christmas.

Why not? It'll be fun, she thought.

The sweet smell of ember flowers drifted out of Ana-Clara's front door as it opened. Inside, the warm, humid air sharply contrasted with the chilly chamber back home. Teresa appeared at the end of the hall supporting a limp, weak Julia. Julia's legs remained stiff and unsteady causing her to lean heavily from one side to the other.

Teresa greeted Audrey and her brother with a huge smile. The pride of her healing work danced in the twinkle of her caramel eyes. "Hi guys."

Julia looked up to see who'd come through the front door. It was a mistake. She lost her balance, teetered like a drunken sailor then collapsed, bringing Teresa down with her. The cottage floor creaked as the weight of their bodies thwacked it.

Audrey and Tarian rushed to lift the two girls up. Tarian swept Julia into his arms and placed her on the velvet couch.

"Hi, Audrey," Julia said in a rough voice. She cleared her throat with a cough.

Teresa hurried to grab a glass of water.

After gulping half the glass down, Julia said, "Thank you."

"How are Jake and Daniel?" Audrey asked Teresa.

"Still dipping in and out of consciousness, but they have strong vitals. Ana-Clara said she has seen people awaken four hours or four weeks after being injected with Awaken Serum."

"You look tired," Tarian said to his sister.

"I'm fine. I'll sleep later."

Ana-Clara trotted out from one of the bedrooms with gray clay covering her dress. "We are making great progress. Teresa is a huge help. I believe Daniel and Jake will be conscious by the end of the day and 48 hours after that it'll be safe to fly them home. They'll be weak of course, but they'll survive."

"Can I see the others?" Audrey asked.

"Sure." Ana-Clara's eyes spread even farther apart as if Audrey's request had surprised her. She turned to lead Audrey to the Sleepers, and Hu attempted to follow, but one glare from Audrey convinced him to return to the living room.

Audrey stopped short. Both Daniel and Jake were wrapped in a cocoon of colorful clay. No part of them was visible. "Daniel and Jake are inside these things?"

"Yes." Ana-Clara nodded. "Silly girl, don't worry. I haven't hurt your friends. Come here, look in this hole."

Audrey peered into a tiny hole. All she could see was someone's black eye staring back at her. It wasn't proof at all. She sighed audibly.

"Leave!" Ana-Clara demanded.

"What? Why?"

"Your doubt is diminishing the healing energy. Get out!" Ana-Clara barked.

Audrey darted from the room straight into Hu's chest. She tilted her head up to see his satisfied smirk. She shoved him with the strength of twenty, and he barely took a step backward.

He grabbed her wrists. "It's okay. Your friends are safe here. Stop worrying."

She stared at him, and he looked sincere. Her body relaxed, and he let go of her wrists. "I'm just concerned. I'm their Chancellor. I have to protect my people." She shuffled slowly back to the living room not wanting to get too far away from Hu and

Ana-Clara. She needed to know what they were up to. Ana-Clara took him into another room and closed the door. Audrey tiptoed back down the hall and listened.

"The girl will be fine. But make sure you get the creature that did this. This was a deliberate attack. You have an angry maldito among you." Ana-Clara's tone darkened. She spoke with urgency.

As Audrey turned to sneak away from the door she ran into Jun.

"The cursed maldito people were supposed to have been exterminated. The Queen of the Damned was assassinated a century ago," Audrey said.

Jun grinned lazily. "Do the cursed ever truly die?"

Audrey wanted to slap the arrogance off her face, but she calmed her temper. "You have more victims here?"

"Yeah, a young girl, and the club next to us has a twenty-five-year-old guy here to be treated."

"Treated? Is that what you call it?"

"I don't question you or your kind, so don't question mine," Jun said evenly without emotion.

Audrey's world slowed to a crawl as Jun towered over her. *Is she threatening me?* She felt hollowed out as Jun's yellow eyes searched her silver ones. "Fine." Audrey nodded. She remembered Ana-Clara's insistence on positive energy. She heard the creaking of the wooden planks coming from the other room. Ana-Clara headed toward them. She inhaled a deep calming breath, forced a smile, and willed her body to exude positivity.

"Nice try," Ana-Clara said with a knowing but kind smile. She hooked her arm around Audrey's and led her away from the twins back into the living room.

"Aren't the cocoons cool?" Teresa asked.

"Yes," Audrey replied.

"Amazing isn't it? Millions of tiny gemstones crushed into the clay. I thought I knew everything about healing, but Ana-Clara has enlightened me."

"Amazing? I'd call it intriguing," Audrey said.

Hu strode in behind Audrey and Ana-Clara. Tarian glared at her accusingly, as if she'd been conspiring with Hu. She had had enough. She couldn't deal with Tarian's jealousy, Hu's magnetism, and the mandate that she exude optimism at all times. Plus there were creepy, glittering mud cocoons that entrapped her fellow Guardians.

"Qui, will you take me back home now?" Audrey had no intention of getting back into a car with Hu and Jun.

"Yes, my work is done here." She stood. "Pleasure to meet you Julia."

"Likewise," Julia said.

Audrey noticed a patch of pink on Julia's cheeks. She was regaining color—evidence of healing that brought tears to Audrey's eyes. She didn't cry, but her voice quavered when she spoke, "We'll return tomorrow. Teresa, do you want to stay?"

"She must stay. Julia needs her. I will call when it's time

for you to come back. If all goes well, I will remove the cocoons at midnight," Ana-Clara said sternly. She softened her tone as she turned to Audrey. "Please, don't worry, hon."

Her eyes flickered lavender again. It was only for a second, but Audrey witnessed it.

"And you too, Tarian. Teresa will be fine."

"Yeah, I'm fine." Teresa grinned as she sat close to Julia, the two girls clutching one another. "Julia is making good progress, so I can't leave her now."

"It's wonderful to be back," Julia said.

Audrey had many questions to ask of Julia, but not with Hu nearby. The questions would have to wait, plus she figured Julia's experience as a Sleeper couldn't differ too much from Joe's, and she'd already asked him a million questions.

"We'll talk tomorrow. When there are less people here," Audrey said. She traded the brightly colored interior of the cottage for the overgrown canopy of trees. The morning dew still clung to the shaded leaves. Audrey dreaded another day on the west coast and wondered how she could make time go faster.

NINETEEN

BAD NEWS FROM HOME

Audrey entered the room. Tarian gazed out the window. He didn't turn to acknowledge her. His eyes remained focused on the vast city at the bottom of the cliff.

"What's wrong?" she asked.

"A lot. I should be home."

"Oh, you were just talking with Margaret, weren't you?"

"Yes. I thought the Realm training would help make it so I wasn't needed." Tarian paced the room.

"I know you're upset about the latest villager's death."

"Of course, I am. We have to get all the Wakers," he paused, "And honestly, I'm not sure I like this black magic voodoo science stuff. When people die, they should die."

"Well, they don't. News flash—we're not normal people." Audrey narrowed her icy eyes at him.

"That's not what I meant." He grit teeth forcing his anger to calm.

"Maybe you should fly home."

Tarian turned to look at her, but she looked neither upset nor happy. "You want me to leave?"

"I want you to be productive. I know sitting around here will only frustrate you. And yes, I'm a little upset that you think what we're doing is evil magic."

"In your five hundred plus years have you ever been a part of something like this?"

"No, but we're immortal. It makes sense that we would sleep, not die."

"Nothing makes sense." The words left his mouth as a bland comment but ricocheted back on him with a vicious punch, the tang of blood lining the inside of his cheeks. His shoulders sagged under the weight of his doubts: about Audrey and Hu, about the course of treatment for Sleepers, and about his own vendetta against the Wakers.

"I think you need to meet with Joe. You can't tell me that you're not happy he's alive."

"If I was happy, I would've already gone to see him." His heart sank at his words. He wasn't sure what he thought anymore. "It's strange."

"And living forever is normal. Sorry for your gift of life and that you have to live with us mutants!" Audrey stormed out of the room.

Tarian lunged down the hall after her. "Why are you pushing me away?"

"What?"

"You've been going solo for months now. I thought we were a team."

"I'm the Chancellor. I have more than just you to concern myself with."

Tarian jolted back, stunned that she thought so little of him. "I'm sure you'd love for me to leave."

"Don't act like a spoiled child."

Her words slapped across his face. He'd always feared she thought of him as a kid.

"Fine, I'll go." He straightened and strode back to the bedroom. "Now you and Hu can spend some time together." He regretted the childish remark immediately and glanced back to catch her reaction.

She threw up her arms and went outside to sit on the lawn chair.

TWENTY

EXPOSED

Tarian left for the airport without a goodbye, but could Audrey blame him? She hadn't attempted a goodbye either. The Awakened Hunter needed to hunt. What was her role? Should she stay here awakening Sleepers? As Chancellor, shouldn't she be doing more?

With each hour came a new layer of guilt. Guilt over lying to Tarian, the state of the village, the death of children, the elusive Wakers, the destruction of the building, lying to Tarian, the drone difficulties at the border wall, harboring Sleepers in the chamber, keeping Eleanor's sleeping body instead of burying her next to her daughter as requested, hiding Joe, holding Patrick's secret, lying to Tarian. She buried her toes in the lush backyard grass and tried to ground her thoughts. She felt so alone.

She ambled back inside the empty house in search of something to occupy her chaotic mind. She panned the bookshelves for an interesting book. She read for a little while, but none kept her attention. She investigated the pantry for ingredients to cook up a delicious meal for her and Qui, but still her thoughts turned to Tarian. Then her mind drifted to the lavender-eyed girl and the underground waterway. She and Tarian had planned to investigate it together.

In dark jeans, short boots, and a black top, she tucked away her Guardian weapons and set about on pursuit. Tangling with a creature was far more treacherous than combating a mortal human, but she felt confident and determined. It felt good to be doing something, to have a mission, even if her objective was blurry.

It didn't take her long to find the mysterious stairs. She easily spotted the aura of the magic that kept the stairs hidden from humans. She descended into the darkness. Rain's Gate bustled with creatures, so she fell in step with them and tried to fit in. The vampires regally strolled alone, while the demons travelled in large, boisterous packs, and the witches formed small covens of two or three.

"Ingenious," Audrey mumbled, admiring the clever waterway system, and the border crashers who passed through it. The creatures of the tunnel piqued her curiosity. They were apparently wealthy, based on their dress and jewels, but they were also at ease traveling this exotic pathway. They were regulars.

After the war, the Entente had erected its borders, and Eurasia had become a wasteland of war. Rumor had it that Eurasians had fled to South America to avoid North America's impenetrable wall, and the onslaught of refugees brought disease, hunger, and crime, crippling the South's booming economy. Based on the elegant creatures in the tunnel, they'd actually flourished and survived like the people of the Entente.

Her last two decades worth of assignments had kept her within the borders. What had she missed? An overwhelming urge to know the truth drew her forward deeper into the depths of the tunnel. She strolled for over an hour without coming upon a portal. Endless black water wound its way through infinite distance. Feeling stupid and lost, she stopped walking. A mission of this magnitude shouldn't be handled alone. She knew that. She was off her game. Arguing with Tarian and awakening the dead had tilted her head in a haze of misery.

She loitered too far away from the active hustle of the partygoers. The echoes of her boot heels reminded her that she walked alone, exposed to strange creatures or unfamiliar spells. The dampness soaked her bones to a brittle chill. She heated herself with her gift, but with her rising temperature, she began to glow. An effect she hadn't seen in a long time. She immediately cut off her powers. She'd have to remain cold. Glowing in the dark seemed like a bad idea.

Unease overtook her. She trusted her gut and ducked into a small nook in the stone wall. Blanketed by darkness she stilled and listened. Silence, then a familiar voice resonated from a boat drifting on the waterway. Hu and a woman stood in the boat arguing while a man piloted through Rain's Gate at idle speed.

"As I have already explained, these stories you're hearing

are mere rumors," Hu explained, his tone nonchalant but firm while his eyes focused straight ahead.

"You cannot support the insurgents," the tall woman said.

Hu turned to face the woman. "I can support whom I choose. The fact is I don't support anyone, not you or the insurgency. This is not my battle. If you want her sent back to Guiana, and you believe she frequents my club, then send someone to come and get her."

"I will and maybe while I'm in town I'll pay Ana-Clara a visit. I've heard the Guardians are hiding something." The woman's eyes leveled menacingly onto Hu's. He didn't flinch.

The gentleman in the boat perked up at the mention of the Guardians. Audrey gasped. She recognized him. The sound blended with the rumble of the boat engine, but fear found its way into her blood.

Hu stiffened and his eyes flicked in her direction.

Audrey's body tingled with the claim of a preta. The strength of the claim crashed down on her like a violent yet beautiful snowfall.

Hu released her as he gathered himself, but his guests in the boat were not fooled.

"What is it?" the man asked.

Audrey's astonishment returned with her senses. She knew this man's voice. It was Karl, a Guardian that had been banished by the High Council. She hadn't seen him in four hundred years.

"Nothing." Hu smiled. "Let's go Karl. Piritta hasn't much

time."

"Wait Karl! He's lying." Piritta turned her ferocious glare in Audrey's direction.

Arrested by Piritta's lavender eyes, Audrey froze. Was this the woman Tarian had mentioned? No, he'd said the girl was petite and this woman was very tall and bullish.

Audrey felt the rushing breeze as Hu and Piritta charged toward her. Hu's honey irises swirled like ravenous tornados; the red rim broke through in streaks of fire. He wanted to rescue her, and Piritta wanted to kill her. She prepared for both. In a split second, she balanced her stance, retrieved her weapons, and prepped her body for an attack. She saw Hu's outreached arms and steeled for his brutal embrace then he vanished.

Whipping her head around, weapons lowered, eyes wildly darting in all directions, she realized *he* hadn't disappeared, *she* had. She sat at a bar, but not *El Tunel*. Next to her sat a stranger, whose hand clamped down on her shoulder as she ordered both of them drinks. She smiled at Audrey then laughed and nodded her head as if Audrey had just told her a hilarious joke. Audrey tried to stand up but the girl's grip forced her to remain rooted in the seat.

The girl bent forward and whispered, "Smile. We need to appear friendly and put your weapons away." She leaned back, tossed her chin length brunette hair, and laughed.

Audrey laughed flatly, slipped her gun and blade back into her pockets, then tilted in to whisper, "Don't you think it's obvious we just appeared here?"

"This bar is full of creatures, and the humans are too inebriated to notice, or they think it's part of the bar's magnificent special effects."

"We need to talk." Audrey held her fake smile. The girl had lavender eyes, and Audrey knew who she was. "What's your name?"

She evaluated Audrey with an unblinking stare. "Vixy. Just be careful." She delivered her warning through clenched teeth then laughed again to fool onlookers.

Audrey asked, "Of what?"

"Of whom."

"Hu and Jun?"

"No, they're keeping the peace. Your presence is the disruption. You need to go back home."

"I will, but not until my mission is over."

"The more you're seen here the worse it is for Jun and Hu," she paused, "and me."

"Why?"

Vixy swigged her drink. "Many reasons. I don't have time to explain."

"Is it the border crossing? It's illegal, but we can work something out." Audrey swirled the colorful liquid around in the glass.

"You don't work things out with these people!"

"Only creatures can cross over, right? So as long as—"

"Yes, but they are taxed when they do so."

"Taxed?"

"Yes, the man you saw with Hu is the gatekeeper. His family of malditos makes a lot of money with the underground Rain's Gate. He knows your friend wandered down there yesterday, and now he wants him killed."

"Does he know who Tarian is?"

"No."

"Good," Audrey sighed. "What does he think?"

Vixy put her drink on the bar and slid it away. "From what I've heard, he thinks Tarian's mortal, and he's furious. He thinks there's a breach in the spell."

"That buys us time."

"There is no us." Vixy flung up her hand.

Audrey stared at her, wondering why she'd been deep in the tunnel in the first place.

"My fight doesn't concern you," Vixy answered Audrey's prying eyes.

"You're being hunted too. That woman in the boat mentioned she wants someone returned. It's you?" Audrey wanted to mention Piper, but her gut told her to keep silent. Audrey looked at this young, slight girl for a long time, but got no more answers.

"From what I can see you have enough to concern yourself with."

"What does that mean?"

"It means our battles are separate. But as you've seen in

the past, battles tend to get the innocent killed."

"Innocent?"

"People like Ana-Clara and the young girl that's helping her. Why do you think Hu attempted to save you from Karl and Piritta?"

Audrey drank her cocktail in silence. The liquid caught as the lump in her throat grew. She forced it down along with her fear.

"Hu and Jun are decent preta. Not all eternals are. Your High Council made a peace deal at one of the moon cycles with the Esurient Eternals a long time ago, but do you honestly believe any of the undying species would have accepted their inferior position if the Guardians had had any weakness at the time? Your kind has a weakness now. Pretas, vamps, malditos and the like need witches, fairies, and demons for their unique skills, but they don't need the Guardians. The Guardians occupy the North and impose laws onto their way of life in order to protect the mortals. What will happen once the word gets out that the all-powerful Guardians of Dare have created a Death Serum?" Vixy laughed again and tenderly placed her hand on Audrey's arm to maintain the illusion that they were a couple of girls out on the town.

Audrey played along but her blood raced with fire, and her breath chilled with angst.

"When Joe came here, when he hired Roman, he took a huge risk. But Hu and Jun truly want to help," Vixy whispered.

"And what about you and the other Lavender Witch.

What's your agenda?"

"I told you. It doesn't involve you."

"Then why did you help me?" Audrey narrowed her silvery eyes, no longer able to fake her happiness.

"Because someday, I may need your help!" Vixy smiled then vanished.

"Damn!" Audrey slammed down her drink and marched out of the bar.

TWENTY-ONE

FATHER

The stone of the chamber door scraped as it slid open. Tarian plodded inside. "Dad?"

Joe turned then stood up from his desk chair. "Hello, son."

Every cell in Tarian's body begged for his dad's hug, but he refused to give in to his emotions. He was a man now, an angry man. He'd been lied to and betrayed. His body remained unyielding as his dad took a step toward him.

Joe didn't take another step. "You want answers?"

"You're damn right I want answers," Tarian said. Then he shook his head and relaxed his stance. His emotions morphed from pigheaded fury to pliable calm. "I didn't come here to fight."

"I know. Have a seat." Joe sat back at his desk and offered Tarian another chair.

Tarian took it and peered into his father's bottomless black eyes. They were not vacant like the eyes of the Wakers he'd killed.

Life danced inside his darkness like stars in a midnight sky. Every sinewy muscle in Tarian's body melted with relief.

"Don't blame Audrey or Teresa or Patrick. I insisted they keep my secret from you."

"Why?"

"For several reasons, and I didn't think it was fair to ask you to lie to your mom."

"But it's okay if Teresa does?"

"Of course not, but Teresa has many gifts. It's not just curiosity or insight that led Teresa to discover the truth about Eleanor when she assisted her in the lab or to sneak down here and discover me. She's a seer, as well as a healer. I hear you have the power to steal people's secrets by touch."

"Yes."

"Your mom was adopted so when I married her, I didn't know anything of her true bloodline. After I discovered you were immortal, I began looking for answers. I found she is a descendant of the Crimsonfelts. A powerful coven of witches."

"I could've handled it. The secret. You think I'm weak," Tarian said.

"No, Tarian. You're not weak at all, and I didn't want to give you a weakness. Why do you think Audrey can't hunt the Wakers?"

"She thinks they're like you."

"Yes. She knows the truth. She knows she can't save them. But coming here and helping me every day seeing our success gives her doubt and doubt you can't afford because those creatures roaming the village and killing the innocent must be stopped. You must stop them, and I couldn't give you any reasons to fail."

He knew his father was telling the truth, but it still stung. "There're five left." Tarian closed his eyes in attempt to stifle his stubborn feelings of deception. He wanted to love and understand his father and rebuild their relationship.

"Then you know what you must do."

Tarian nodded. His tongue felt dry as sand. He swallowed hard.

"I'm sorry son, that this is your fate. Every life you take leaves a dagger in your soul."

"Why don't you trust the High Council?"

Joe grinned. "Their world is black and white. I've seen them send children into the hands of evil demons because it was Demon Law."

"Demon Law?"

"All creatures have laws. The High Council will often ignore the heart to follow the brain. They will allow millions to die to stand on their own principles."

"You're talking about the Entente War."

"The High Council is our ultimate authority. Whatever they rule we must follow, but if they make no rule then we have gray areas to work inside."

"So you keep them in the dark, and they can't make a ruling? Your secrecy gives you leeway."

"Yes. But it's a tricky leeway. Your job requires you to go in front of the Council on a weekly basis. I didn't want to put you in a position where you could be asked about me. Now if they ask, you must tell the truth. Lying to the council is punished by banishment. Eternity without your community is hell."

"What is the plan? Audrey will come back with three formerly dead immortals, and what will the Council do? You can't hide this any longer." He swept his arm around signifying the lab then pointed at the Wakers asleep in their cages.

"I know. I'll go before the Council with the three awakened Sleepers and plead my case that they are not Wakers."

"What about Patrick?" Tarian asked.

"He is to keep quiet until the Council delivers their verdict."

"You can't protect him Dad. He is what he is just like you are."

Joe smiled. "He said the same thing. But I can give him a little more time should he need it."

"Time!" Tarian laughed and rose from his chair. "We're cursed by time."

Joe stood and gingerly placed a hand on Tarian's shoulder. A moment passed while Tarian considered his father then he embraced him. He squeezed him hard and drunk in the sting of tears.

"I will kill the Wakers—all of them—before Audrey returns. We'll present a solid case, and we'll have our beloved village back." Again, Tarian glanced at the caged Wakers, but he decided not to ask any more questions.

As if Joe had read his mind he said, "Don't worry, I'll dispose of them humanely when the time comes. Good luck son."

Tarian smiled and strolled to the exit. The lumps of sleeping bodies surrounded him. He lifted one of the sheets, peeked at the frozen face then placed it back down. He turned to face his dad. "I hate that you are stuck down here."

"It's okay."

"You need to shape-shift and get outside."

"I know it seems creepy, but it's not. These are my friends. They're just sleeping."

Tarian nodded. In his twenty years, he'd never heard his dad complain.

TWENTY-TWO

GAINING STRENGTH

The young night hid Tarian in shadows as he hunched behind bushes. He'd been home for twenty hours. He'd seen his father and made his peace with him, but his heart remained heavy with jealousy. He'd paced the floor of the apartment while his mind wildly envisioned Hu cajoling his girlfriend. He needed the diversion of a hunt.

A Waker stepped out of the blackness and into the shimmer of the street lamp. Tarian pounced and thrust the needle, but he missed his target. The monster jolted to one side, leaving Tarian to stumble slightly. He regained his footing. The two circled each other like wild beasts, neither daring to make the first move.

The Waker's eyes flickered from side to side while Tarian's gaze remained locked on his prey. Wakers were too impulsive to withstand a long draw, but Tarian wasn't. He had the patience and self-control to wait for an opening move. As one of the few remaining Wakers, this one obviously had better survival skills. The world around them slowed to a crawl as the awareness of death to one of them became inevitable.

Tarian's fingers twitched eagerly. Was he off his game, or was this Waker more deadly than the rest? He'd been away from the hunt too long. He took a deep breath and banished his doubts.

The circle between monster and man tightened, and soon Tarian could smell the metallic stench of blood on the Waker's breath. It was now or never. Tarian lunged to the left as the Waker lurched forward. He managed to get under the monster's arms and tackled him. The two rolled over twice, the Waker ending on top pinning Tarian to the ground. Sharp, dirty teeth bit inches away from Tarian's face, but he managed to hold the beast's shoulders far enough away to avoid pierced flesh. With the full force of his immortal strength, he heaved the Waker off, and landed a kick to its gut, hurling the beast. Tarian heard the thwack of the monster's head on the pavement. He jumped to his feet, secured the needle in is hand, and jabbed it into the Waker's heart.

The beast didn't crumple like most. It fought death bitterly. It got to its feet and teetered, then to Tarian's surprise the beast ran. Tarian followed, keeping the Waker in his sights. No Waker had ever resisted the sting of the Death Serum. Eventually the Waker fell, convulsing on the ground and foaming at the mouth. Tarian waited and watched. He didn't dare hoist it over his shoulder until stillness settled on the beast. Tarian hesitantly approached the motionless body, fearing it'd spring to life once more. He grabbed its feet and dragged it to the bonfire leaving a crimson slimy trail in its wake.

The flame roared, and Tarian chewed on beef jerky. The hunt had exhausted him, and he needed food to reenergize. The fight played over and over inside his head. How had this Waker almost gotten the better of him? What had gone wrong? But as far as Tarian could tell, he'd done nothing wrong. This Waker was simply stronger and wiser. It had learned patience and gained strength. They were evolving. Four more remained.

A scream cut through the night air. Tarian took a last look into the bonfire. Satisfied that the monster had burned to ash, he turned and rushed toward the terrifying howl. He ran through an alley and out into the street to find Sasha, and her mortal partner Josh, being attacked by two Wakers.

They're lone hunters, not pack animals. More proof of their evolution.

Tarian pulled the dagger from his belt and hurled it. It lodged deeply in the skull of one Waker. It cried out in pain and dropped to its knees, giving Tarian time to drive a needle into its chest.

Before Tarian could stand back up, a body crashed down on top of him. Teeth like knives carved into the top of his head as claw-like fingernails gouged valleys into his arms. The monster rode Tarian, piggyback style. Tarian twisted in sharp jerks, but the Waker held on. He couldn't shake it, and he couldn't reach the Death Serum inside his pocket. Blood rolled into his eyes, blinding him. Rage boiled as the struggle persisted, but his knees weakened. His mind raced incapable of rational thought. Suddenly, he could stand erect again. The massive burden had fallen off his back. He turned to find a bloody lump folded on the street.

Sasha breathlessly said, "Are you okay?"

"I'll be alright," he said, but he felt dazed and uncertain. The cold fall air he sucked in hurt like slivers of broken ice chips. Until that night, hunting the Wakers had always been as uneventful as finding hidden deer. They'd been cunning and hard to catch, but retreated when confronted, and collapsed when injected. Until now.

"Thank God you came when you did. I thought we were done." Sasha bent over, her hands on her knees. Blood dripped from her nose and eyes. It oozed out of many slashes in her skin. "Welcome home Tarian, this is Josh Farmington, Elite Forces and life saver." She huffed out the words.

The right side of Josh's lips curled up into a smirk, and his hand made a sharp, short wave, but he had not the strength to say hello. His face and uniform were smeared with blood, but it didn't seem to be his. He held a long, black stick with red splattered all over it. His grip on the black diamond rod gave way and it bounced off the cobblestones, echoes rippling through the silence.

Tarian appraised them both, and his eyes fell on Sasha's many wounds. "Can you heal those?"

"I'm not sure. I don't have the energy to try," Sasha said.

"Try," Tarian demanded.

"Fine." She stood tall, exhaled deeply, and smashed her eyes together in concentration. Nothing happened. She opened her eyes to look at herself. Nothing. She slumped and lowered her head. "I don't think I can."

Tarian straightened his spine, regained his strength, and hoisted one body over his shoulder and dragged the other one by the ankles.

Josh inhaled deeply, took a swig of water from a thermos he had latched to his belt, reclaimed his rod, and seized the leg of the unconscious Waker in Tarian's grip.

Tarian gave the soldier a nod of gratitude. "Let's go." Pain seared through the gash in his head. His brain was on fire. He realized he wasn't healing either. "We'll drop these two into the bonfire, and then we need to get to the infirmary straight away."

"Okay." Sasha lumbered along next to them keeping a lookout for more evil beasts on the prowl.

Pain infused Tarian's body like a million microscopic pins puncturing his skin, but he ignored it as he threw one body into the fire. Josh took care of the other one. The blood orange flames reflected off of Tarian's eyes. He refused to leave the fire until no trace of the beasts remained.

Once certain the job of destroying those two hellions was complete, Tarian raised Sasha's arm and placed it around his shoulders. "Lean on me. You'll be okay."

Together they trudged back to Headquarters as Josh brought up the rear with his weapon in hand, alert and prepared to ward off any attacking Waker.

TWENTY-THREE

WE ALL CHANGE

Audrey yanked the curtain back and rushed into Tarian's space. He groggily shifted in the hospital bed. Her heart sank in both relief and agony. He was alive, but he looked badly beaten. Slashes ripped down the flesh of his arm and his skull could be seen through the scarlet gash in his tousled brown hair.

God, I love that hair. Even like this, it's beautiful.

She sat gently on the edge of his bed, stroking his chest and face with her fingers. She leaned down to kiss his cheek.

His lips curled up, but his eyes remained closed.

A smile spread across her face. All the anger she felt when he'd left her across the nation floated away. If she'd lost him, she shuddered to think of what would've become of her, what would she have done to get past the pain of losing him?

She watched him sleep for hours before she cuddled next to him on the twin-sized bed. She wasn't sure how much time had passed when he rolled over and nearly bumped her off the mattress.

He wrapped her in his arms, tucking her securely into him. "Hi." His voice gurgled as his mouth was full of sleep.

"Hi," she whispered.

"Have you been here all night?"

"I guess so," she said.

"They've gotten stronger." He swallowed hard trying to get the words to come out.

Audrey rose to her feet. "I'll get us some water." She zipped out of the cubby of a space and returned with two glasses and a pitcher of water. They both drank before speaking again.

"The Wakers are evolving. It's almost as if they are out to kill immortals. Last week, if one of them got close enough to scratch me, I would've healed in less than an hour, now look at me. I'm a mess." He studied the claw marks on his arm and fingered the wound in his head.

"Luckily, only two left."

"I need to hold a meeting with the hunters. We'll need to hunt in packs of more than two."

Her throat squeezed, and her stomach lurched at the idea of him going back to hunt.

Tarian stared at her, a smile in his chocolate eyes. A stray strand of her hair fell from her ponytail to lay across her cheek so he tucked it behind her ear. "Is everyone back here now? Teresa and the Sleepers?"

"Yes," Audrey paused. "Joe doesn't think we should

inform the High Council yet. What do you think?" She didn't wait for a response. "I think we have to. Margaret was waiting for me when the plane touched down and nearly jumped on board to inspect it. She was allegedly there to update me on all that had occurred in my absence, but she suspects something."

"They are all awake, right? It went well?"

"Yes."

"Then the High Council should be happy."

"I don't know. With this new development among the Wakers, they may fear the awakened Sleepers will change too."

"We all change. Look at Zachary. For five hundred years he was the ideal Guardian of Dare, and then I was born, and he turned into a power-hungry tyrant who wanted to make an immortal army and take over the mortals."

Audrey huffed a small laugh.

"That wasn't meant to be funny." His face flattened with seriousness.

"I know. I'm just at my wits end, stressed out. But your point is well taken."

Tarian swung his feet off the bed and sat upright. He gathered his strength and stood. He appeared a mangled mess, but his limbs were sturdy.

"What are you doing?" Audrey rushed to his side to help him walk, but he didn't need any assistance.

"I'm fine. I want to see Daniel, Julia, and Jake." He looked directly into her silvery blue eyes. "I'm glad they're alive. I'm glad

Dad is alive. Whatever voodoo magic Ana-Clara mixes up is good with me. I don't want any more of these Waker monsters. We need to get the High Council's blessing and awaken the Sleepers as soon as possible."

Audrey absorbed his words. Their positions had reversed during their time apart. He now agreed with all that she'd wanted him to, but she doubted the urgency of awakening the Sleepers. She worried that taking more Sleepers to Ana-Clara could be a mistake. If they fell into the hands of those wicked malditos Vixy had warned her about, the immortals would then have two weaknesses. *Maybe the immortal time has come to an end*, she wondered. God had given them hundreds of years, and now it was their time to die.

"What's going on in that brain of yours?" Tarian asked.

"Oh," she sighed, "Nothing, I was just thinking how right you are."

"I'm right? That's a first," he teased.

"Don't get used to it." She smiled to hide her unease. Having considered her options, she concluded she did need to awaken all the Sleepers and make the immortals strong again. Bring the Guardians of Dare back to their full power. Then she'd deal with the mysterious underworld. Something sinister brewed in the Bar District, but she wouldn't fight it until her immortals were fully healed and capable of winning a creature attack.

TWENTY-FOUR

WAGER

Audrey examined the four ghostly pale and unnaturally thin High Council members as they huddled around the evidence she'd placed before them. Hooded in their blackberry coats, they looked like a gathering of ancient witches stirring a pot. Murmurs, gasps, coughs, and sighs cut through the otherwise silent room. Councilors Harry and Elizabeth looked at Audrey then back at Joe, Julia, Jake, and Daniel. Audrey counted on Harry and Elizabeth to be the voice of reason since George was quick to favor banishment or death penalty, and Councilor William was unpredictable.

Joe, Teresa, Audrey, Tarian, Daniel, Julia, and Jake formed a defensive wall before the Council. Audrey had advised the newly awakened Sleepers to remain seated to conserve the little stamina they had. She couldn't expose their frailty to the Council members.

The four members stood as one, as if a purple lotus flower had just bloomed in the dank, dark High Council room. Four taut faces turned toward the awakened Sleepers.

From her position between Teresa and Tarian, Audrey squeezed a hand of each then she rose. This was her pack of pups, and she'd protect them as fiercely as any mother wolf.

Elizabeth ignored Audrey and walked directly to Julia. Her bony hand touched Julia's shoulder then she clutched her arm. She kneaded the muscle like a cat then she let go. Her fingers combed through Julia's long, wavy hair. Elizabeth separated and scanned the individual strands.

Julia remained still.

"Stand," Elizabeth ordered.

Julia stood, and to Audrey's relief her legs held without buckling.

"Can you speak?" Elizabeth asked her.

"Yes, hello Councilor Elizabeth. It's good to be home," Julia said with a wide smile.

Elizabeth smiled back, then her putty colored lips straightened into a flat, thin line. She steeled herself and turned to face Audrey. "She has the black eyes of the Wakers."

"Yes, as you can see Joe has been awakened for months now and his eyes remain black, but he shows no signs of violence. His neurotransmitters haven't been broken down in any way. No extra chromosome, no warrior gene, no change in serotonin transporter metabolism, no abnormalities found in the frontal or temporal brain regions, and when given Malevolence Serum to trigger aggressive behavior, Joe reacted as he has always reacted. No change from before he fell victim to the sleep of Death Serum.

I have concluded that the eye color is a simple pigment change, nothing more."

Audrey's heart pounded. Nauseating tremors rolled through her. Had she persuaded them? She was a warrior Guardian, not a scientist. Had she relayed Joe's and Patrick's findings accurately? Did she sound steadfast and convincing?

Councilor George approached. "I appreciate all of your testing and I've reviewed your results, but I will not be satisfied until I myself have conducted my own testing. I will take these four back with me. The High Council's ruling will depend on the findings of our independent tests."

"I understand." Audrey fidgeted trying to calm the storm brewing inside of her.

Tarian stood. "With all due respect, Councilor George, I don't think your private testing is any more valid than Audrey's private testing. Shouldn't we use Headquarters' main lab where the testing can be scrutinized by a full complement of experts? The transparency will lend greater credibility to the results."

Audrey swelled with pride at Tarian's astute observation and his politically savvy resolution. Why hadn't she thought of that? Why should they trust the word of the High Council? They were hiding their knowledge of the underground world in the Bar District, after all.

George's beady eyes narrowed, and Audrey braced for his rebuttal, but Harry spoke first.

"Agreed," Councilor Harry stated.

"Agreed," Councilor William stated.

"Agreed," Councilor Elizabeth stated.

The silence stretched to several seconds as everyone waited on George's answer.

"Agreed," Councilor George said calmly, as if he'd not just been circumvented.

"Terrific." Audrey's voice pitched high with excitement and relief.

"Other business," Councilor William said, "In your report you state that the two remaining Wakers wandering the village streets are more dangerous than the others. They have evolved to pose a more significant threat."

Audrey nodded.

"We are all in agreement then." William turned from Audrey and focused on Tarian. "You have proof that the Wakers have modified. They are capable of injuring immortals, possibly killing immortals. Is this correct?"

"Yes, Sasha and I suffered permanent damage from two Wakers, damage that had never happened before. And the Wakers have become more aggressive toward hunters. They no longer hide from us, they seek us out and fight."

"I see. Your top priority is to find and assassinate them," Councilor George ordered Tarian then turned his dark, beady eyes on Audrey. "Do you understand the repercussions if this information gets out?"

Audrey stared steadily back, but fear began to twist her

stomach in knots. His point was loud and clear: they both hoped her new Xia Preta colleagues could be trusted, and neither was confident that was the case.

George continued, "We are indestructible, and we must remain that way. Anyone or anything that threatens our durability will be eliminated!"

"I understand," Audrey said.

The Council had agreed to suspend judgment on the Awakened. Joe, Julia, Jake, and Daniel—not to mention Patrick, whose awakened status remained a secret. She doubted she'd ever reveal that Patrick had been awakened far before Joe. That he was the first Awakened. That he'd been the one to help Eleanor keep the Sleepers hidden and safe before all hell broke loose with Zachary. That he'd been there when she'd awoken Joe. Some secrets were just better left unsaid. If their existence in any way threatened the dominance of the Guardians of Dare, they'd be eliminated.

"Meeting adjourned." Councilor Elizabeth pounded her gavel.

TWENTY-FIVE

DAYS TO WEEKS

As the days melted into weeks, all lab workers labored diligently as a unified body. Even Margaret's hurt feelings at being kept out of the loop finally mended after repeated apologies, a basket of fresh cut flowers, and three boxes of chocolates. Finally, the weeks of testing ended, and the results confirmed the findings presented previously by Audrey: the Awakened were not a threat. The High Council ruled in favor of awakening all Sleepers except Eleanor in keeping with her own wishes.

Councilor Elizabeth stood at the rosewood table with her fellow High Council members as well as Audrey, Tarian, Joe, Margaret, Teresa, Patrick, and five other Guardian leaders, and read the final ruling. "The former Chancellor of the Guardians of Dare, Eleanor Dare, will be returned to Roanoke Virginia to be interred next to her husband and daughter, as per her directive." Councilor Elizabeth turned to Audrey and nodded sympathetically.

Audrey's heart dropped like lead in a lake. She'd feared this would be their decision. She knew they'd accept Eleanor's sealed note, the note left to Audrey stuck in the dirt of the grave. Months ago when Eleanor was believed to be dead, when Audrey knew nothing of Sleepers, Audrey had been tasked with the delivery of her body to its final resting place. Her grave was open and waiting for her, next to the family she had when she first traveled to the new world in 1587. Next to her only husband and daughter, the pair she'd lost so long ago.

Audrey almost hadn't given the note to them. She almost didn't pick it up off the ground after she'd crumpled it and tossed it aside in Roanoke, but her conscience got the better of her.

Now she sat in this dark room filled with regret, doubt, and confusion. She'd felt unworthy of the Chancellor title before, but now the permanence molded over her like scalding hot, melted gold.

Elizabeth continued, "Eleanor had prior knowledge of the effects of Death Serum. She knew her fate when she decided to take her life with a needle filled with the life-threatening serum. We all knew her as a strong woman of outstanding character, but nonetheless, a mother that never fully recovered from the loss of her daughter. It was her desire to remain asleep, and we must honor her last wishes no matter how we personally feel about her decision."

Audrey felt the warmth of Tarian's hand as it fell upon her shoulder then dropped to settle at her waist. She'd slump to the floor if not for his security. She'd not known a world without

Eleanor in a very, very long time. Even when Eleanor had been sleeping in the Chamber, Audrey could comb her hair and confide her deepest secrets and doubts.

Councilor William raised his brow. "The last order of business concerns the elusive Waker, Benjamin Stuthers. Have the hunters made any progress locating his whereabouts, Tarian?" The warning in his question hovered over the round table.

Audrey knew Tarian and the others had failed. She knew this fact tormented Tarian, and she hated watching him announce his failure out loud. She straightened and opened her mouth to speak on his behalf, but he nudged her with his fingers, and she kept quiet.

"No," a long pause followed, "But we haven't given up hope."

"We have," Councilor George said evenly. "Tonight, the Elite Forces will enter every household, vendor shop, and alley inside the village. They also have orders to search all residences and workspaces inside Headquarters."

"You can't do that!" Audrey said.

"We can, and we will," Councilor George said.

"You need probable cause to search private property," Audrey stammered. The villagers' right to security of themselves and their homes was sacred to her.

"We most certainly do not," Councilor George huffed.

Councilor Elizabeth spoke calmly. "We are taking extreme measures due to the extenuating circumstances of evolving Wakers.

Political correctness or politeness has no place in this war. Tarian and his hunters fought bravely against the two remaining Wakers but only managed to eliminate one. In that battle, Benjamin murdered two Elite Forces and one of our own Guardians. If he manages to escape the village, the outcome will be severe."

Audrey nodded acknowledging that a Waker capable of killing an immortal held dangers far beyond her wildest fears. She wanted every inch of the village searched. She just couldn't admit it to herself.

"Understood," Audrey said.

"As Chancellor your presence is required. The villagers and Guardians must witness your complete support of this operation. You will walk alongside our Elite Forces," Councilor Harry said.

"Of course," Audrey said.

Councilor Elizabeth handed Audrey an envelope.

Audrey pulled the card out and read, "Training Facility, Commander General Smith's office, 1900 hours."

"Enough long faces, we should be celebrating," Daniel said. "I appreciate all you've done for me. Tonight, I get to see my son and sleep in my bed. I'm a Guardian again!"

His kind words tugged at Audrey's soul. Then a broad smile fanned across her face, and she laughed. She gave them all warm hugs.

Joe let out a low guttural breath. "I need to go home."

Tarian glanced in his father's direction.

Audrey whispered in Tarian's ear, "Your dad's scared." She grinned.

"He should be." Tarian laughed.

"That's enough you two," Joe scolded. "You're not making this any easier."

"Mom's going to be pissed," Teresa said.

"Ugh!" Joe sighed.

TWENTY-SIX

Tarian stood with his mom in the hallway. He hadn't opened the door. He turned to face her then turned away, reached for the recognition panel then stopped.

"What's going on Tarian? Why aren't we going in your apartment?" Carolyn asked.

"Mom, when I open this door you'll see someone you thought you'd never see again."

Carolyn's caramel eyes narrowed with concern. She opened her mouth to speak, but nothing came out. The door swung open, and she gingerly stepped inside.

"You better sit down." Tarian gestured to the couch.

She sat, placed her hands on her knees and began to rub them.

Joe stepped into the living room alongside Teresa.

Carolyn's eyes widened as her breath caught. She shot to her feet. Then suddenly she collapsed back onto the couch, breathing like a startled animal.

"Mom!" Tarian and Teresa ran to sit next to her.

"Carolyn." Joe also rushed over but wouldn't get too close to her.

"I'm okay, I'm okay." She inhaled deeply then exhaled a slow, ragged sound. "Joe?" Tears overflowed from her eyes, and a nervous smile slid across her face.

Joe swooped in and embraced her wholeheartedly. They both sat arms wrapped around each other, hips and knees pressed together. Joe kissed his wife, and she kissed him back. She touched his face with her palm and let her fingers explore his skin up to his hair. She pushed them through his messy brown locks, and she stared silently into the infinite darkness of his irises.

Tarian bowed his head and strolled over to the kitchen counter with his sister. She took his hand and squeezed it.

"How?" Carolyn asked.

"It's a very long story. You already know that the immortals who are now Wakers were injected with Death Serum and then brought back to life."

"Yes."

Joe turned to look at his children.

"I've told her everything, just not about the Sleepers," Tarian said.

"Sleepers are the immortals shot with Death Serum that were never incinerated or awakened. There is a way to be brought back and not be a monster with the help of a witch, a Bruja Blanca.

She has an Awaken Serum, and if that's not enough, she uses her healing powers to bring the Sleepers back to life."

"Why didn't you tell me, Joe?" Carolyn's eyes crinkled with pain.

"I swore an oath."

Carolyn dropped her hands and turned away from her husband. "You swore an oath to me too!"

"I know. I didn't know how to tell you, and then everything spiraled out of control, and I didn't know who to trust."

"You trust your wife." She refused to turn back to him.

"What would I say? I'm immortal. There's a Death Serum. What's for dinner, honey?" Joe threw up his arms then clutched his scalp.

"Don't patronize me. I had to send the boys off to live with that jerk. I scraped pennies together to find out later you're a billionaire immortal. I thought I'd lost you forever!" She nearly screamed at him.

"Stop!" Tarian said. "Being angry doesn't solve anything. Believe me! The past is the past. Everyone is alive and well. We should be celebrating."

"And what about the children. Well, Charlie's not a child anymore, but Chloe and Junior. People don't come back to life, Joe."

"I've been dropping hints to Chloe, and I know she'd accept it. She already thinks the village is magical," Teresa said.

Carolyn huffed a small laugh. "Is this why you're never

home anymore?"

Teresa nodded and smiled.

Joe added, "She snuck into my chamber without permission and discovered me."

"Sounds like her. Too clever for her own good."

Tarian inched toward his parents. "Mom, her healing powers have tripled. The Bruja Blanca uses Teresa as a sort of amplifier."

"What?"

"Let's just say that without Teresa the awakening process would take twice, maybe three times, as long," Tarian said.

"Is this true, honey?" Carolyn asked.

"I guess," she answered.

"Are any of my other children going to have freaky powers that I should know about?" Carolyn's eyebrows raised, and a smile formed in the corners of her mouth. She began to find the humor in her bizarre situation.

Joe shrugged. "I don't know."

"You know Mom, this is partly your fault too," Tarian said.

"What are you saying?"

"Your family tree dates back to Alse Young, and in more recent records, to members of the Arianthe Coven. You and Dad are a wicked combination," Tarian said with a sideways grin.

"What do we do now?" Carolyn asked.

"Have a family dinner?" Tarian suggested.

Both Carolyn and Joe shot Tarian a surprised glance.

"Yeah, great idea," Teresa said.

"I'm glad the two of you can finally agree on something," Carolyn said, then shook her head. "I don't know. I just—"

"Why not? Dad's alive. Chloe and Joe Jr. will be delighted. They're young with vivid imaginations. They'll believe whatever we tell them. Like Teresa said they believe in magic. And Charlie is an adult who survived Zachary's world takeover. I think he'll understand. He might be angry at first, but he'll get over it." Tarian spoke like a kid trying to convince his parents to buy a puppy.

"Can I come home, Carolyn?" Joe's eyes pleaded.

Carolyn's frustration and anger fit her like armor. She struggled to shrug off the heavy feelings of deceit by her own family. She had the love of her life back, the father of her children home again, but she was vexed. She closed her eyes and took several deep breaths. As she opened them, she felt lighter, not entirely free of her anger, but free to be happy, at least for now. She took his hands in hers. "I need a little time, Joe."

He bowed his head but didn't pull away. "I understand. Take all the time you need."

"I love you." Her voice broke from the weight of her tears. Suddenly, the beseeching eyes of the three of them became too much for her to handle. She hurried out of the apartment.

Joe didn't try to stop her.

TWENTY-SEVEN

RAID

Audrey stood aside while the Lieutenant pounded on the door. It had been a long night, and she jumped each time his fist crashed down on wood. People opened the door in all different manners, some tentative and afraid while others aggressive and furious. Eventually, everyone cooperated knowing full well they had no choice. Most understood the necessity of such a raid, but none welcomed the men and women in uniform charging through their home.

She recognized the face of the woman who opened the door, Mrs. Appleton, the baker, Hope's mother.

"Yes, may I help you?" A white apron smeared with blue smudges wrapped around her robust waist. The scent of blueberry muffins drifted out the open doorway. Despite her rosy cheeks and matronly appearance, she wore a stern, unyielding expression as she crossed her arms. A wooden spoon coated with the batter stuck out from behind her elbow. She'd probably whack them all with it.

"Hello, Mrs. Appleton, the last Waker is still at large and has proven both deadly and beguiling. We're searching every home in the village tonight. Please step aside and allow the Elite Forces entrance," Audrey said with a forced expression of pleasantries. She attempted to brighten her icy silver eyes and soften the sharp angles of her face, but it was no use, her worry invaded every inch of her skin.

The Lieutenant's nonexistent patience allowed for approximately ten seconds before he shoved Hope's mother aside and barged into the home.

"Why?"

"You might be aware, that the Wakers are evolving. They're far more dangerous now." Audrey delivered the speech she'd already given fifty times that night. The words stuck in her throat. She felt like a traitor. How had it come to this?

"It's hard to imagine those savages getting any worse. Come in." She stepped aside for Audrey but remained rigid.

Mrs. Appleton no longer trusted the Guardians, many villagers didn't. Margaret's annoying voice rang in Audrey's head: *We need to work on our public relations. We must rebuild the faith of the people. The Sleepers can wait. You need to plan town meetings.* Mrs. Appleton's thin lips, defiant hazel eyes, and twitching ears proved Margaret was right.

Audrey decided to schedule more than a town meeting. She'd organize a grand celebration after the death of the last

Waker.

As the two women stood examining one another, a girl's scream ripped through the air.

"Hope!" Mrs. Appleton's large body charged forward, pushed past the Lieutenant, through the living room, and into the bedroom.

Hope shook and trembled with terror. Her wide eyes gushed tears.

"Get out!" Mrs. Appleton ordered the two Elite soldiers rambling through her home. "Why on earth would I harbor one of those monsters? You've seen my home and terrorized my daughter, now leave!"

"You heard her. Let's go!" Audrey yelled. Hope's fear was real, and Mrs. Appleton's hatred was more real, and now that Audrey had witnessed just how deep the distrust of Guardians went, she realized they had a long journey ahead of them. Audrey followed the soldiers out, but before her departure, she turned back. "I'm sorry."

Mrs. Appleton frowned. She held a tight grip on her daughter whose tears still fell.

Audrey bowed her head and stepped over the threshold.

Before the door shut, Hope asked, "What happens if you don't find the last one?"

Audrey turned to face the brave little girl. "We will. I promise."

"Daddy's at the bakery, will you check on him please?"

pleaded Hope.

"Yes." Audrey smiled.

Through Hope's fear and pain grew a giant smile. The resiliency of youth shined through the tear-drenched, red face, and the chance for unity flickered inside Audrey's chest.

She stepped back out onto the street. Black, gray, and gold uniforms marched like ants lining the road and filling the alleys. The raid was in full force and still the last Waker hadn't been found. Audrey rubbed her eyes as her gut twisted dreading Benjamin had escaped. She sensed he wouldn't be found. She'd failed. With all her effort placed on saving the immortal Sleepers, she'd forgotten the most precious life: mortal life. The blood he'd spill outside the village would be on her hands.

She opened the door to the bakery. "Mr. Appleton?"

"You've already looked in here," Mr. Appleton answered.

"I know. You should go home, sir."

"Why? What's happened? What have you done?" His voice trembled with anger.

"Nothing. Your wife and daughter are fine, just frightened. Lock up here and go home."

"Did you catch it?" He tore the apron from his rotund midsection.

"Not yet." She didn't offer any words of encouragement. Instead, she bowed her head and retreated, leaving the sweet smell of the bakery behind.

Audrey lumbered into the kitchen of Tarian's apartment. "Tarian!" No one answered. After grabbing a glass of water, she roamed until she found her boyfriend. "Hi, honey."

"Hi, beautiful," he spoke from behind the bathroom door.

"We didn't find him."

"Me either." His words barely audible, muffled from the door and the running water of the shower.

"You went hunting?" She shouted, then she heard the water turn off.

"Yes, we hunted outside the village borders. Not only did we not find him, but we also didn't find any evidence to suggest he'd escaped."

"What does that mean?"

"I don't know. He just vanished." Tarian stepped out of the bathroom wearing only a towel.

Audrey's heart skipped, her breath caught in the back of her throat. She melted as he walked toward her with a boyish grin.

"You could see my wet body every day, if I moved in with you." He threatened to drop the towel.

"That's a check on the pro list for sure."

He kissed her neck tenderly disarming every sinew, fiber, muscle, and bone inside her body. His gentle lips moved to hers. He lifted her into his arms and carried her to the bed.

As he lay her down on the pillowy comforter, she sank into the blood-thumping sensations of his touch and forgot everything. Her mind and body surrendered to the wonderful bliss of his embrace.

Early the next morning, Audrey jerked awake. She shoved Tarian's arm off of her waist and joggled his sleeping body.

"What is it? Are you okay?" Tarian's eyes slit as they fought against sleep.

"Piper vanishes."

"What? Yeah." His tongue struggled to find its voice. He cleared his throat.

"Benjamin. Somehow a Lavender Witch has stolen the last Waker!" Her chest heaved with panic.

Tarian propped himself up on the pillows. "Why?"

"I don't know, but remember when I told you about my encounter with Vixy?"

"Yeah."

"She's part of an insurgency and mentioned we need to keep our vulnerabilities a secret, that if the malditos got wind of our weakness, it could be drastic for us. They've done it. They've stolen our biggest weakness."

TWENTY-EIGHT

A STRAND OF HAIR

Audrey stormed into her office. "Good morning," she said to Margaret and Piper, who had been waiting for the last fifteen minutes. "I've called you here to discuss my future plans. As you both know, the last Waker hasn't been found. He's no longer inside the village. I've put him on the nation's most wanted list. So far he hasn't been seen anywhere throughout the Entente. I believe I know where he is, and I also believe the villagers are no longer in danger." Audrey motioned for them to follow her to the back wall where towering monitors showed feeds from critical places around the nation.

Piper zipped and Margaret shuffled. Audrey stopped at the image of the reconstruction of the destroyed building. The one she'd recently visited in the Technology District.

"Oh, it's coming along nicely, isn't it?" Margaret's jowls spread into a broad smile.

"Yes, it's ahead of schedule. The new drones are also

exceeding expectations patrolling the western border, and we've added them to all entrances of the Cavern System." Audrey picked up a control pad and zoomed in on an image. "This is the Bar District, a young adult playground of fun, for most. Drinking, dancing, and so forth, but there's an underground society of creatures rumored to be gathering information on us."

"Why?" Piper asked.

"Good question. Probably to destroy us."

"But the High Council has always maintained good relations with the Xia Preta and all the other creatures," Margaret said in protest.

"Yes, that's true. But when Tarian and I were there, we found an underground waterway. It's apparently legal by creature law. However, we met a young witch who hinted that some creatures used the waterway to gather intelligence on our predicament. I didn't take it seriously at the time, but now I believe her accusations are worthy of further investigation."

"What kind of witch?" Piper asked.

"I don't know," Audrey lied. There was only so much information she intended to tell Margaret. Eleanor had always trusted her, but Audrey preferred to keep some secrets.

"If it's covered under creature law then the High Council must be aware of it and monitoring those who travel through it," Margaret said.

"Yes." Audrey nodded.

"Then will you proceed as planned?" Margaret asked.

"I will. I'm taking three Sleepers to Ana-Clara as planned, but I'm also including a crew to go undercover in the area. If we're successful we'll come home with three Guardians and the ashes of a Waker and further intelligence on the activities of the foreign creatures mingling within our borders. Meanwhile, Margaret you're in charge. Contact all Guardians working on missions outside the village, and make sure they remain vigilant within their sectors."

"Christopher and Marcus too?" Margaret asked about the two Guardians currently on mission in the Wastelands.

Audrey hesitated, uncertain how far this conspiracy traveled or who it involved. "Yes. Tell them during their next check-in."

"That could be weeks." Margaret clucked her tongue.

Audrey ignored her fussing. "Do we have anyone in the Southern Hemisphere?"

Margaret shook her head.

"Very well. We need the village protection spells doubled and strengthened. Our perimeter must be impenetrable. I've enlisted the help of the Elite Forces. We need to use all of our resources—magic and man-made. They will be our first line of defense and positioned outside of the spell's range, therefore, out of sight from the villagers. It's our priority to reestablish the villagers' peace and their faith in us."

"By trapping them and lying to them." Margaret's polished guise couldn't contain her sarcasm.

"It's only temporary, Margaret. But as I said, their lives are no longer the target. It's the Guardians who will be attacked. While I'm gone you must keep the village secure and restore the villagers' trust."

"And how do you suppose I do that when their Chancellor is abandoning them?" Margaret crossed her arms pulling her green uniform taut.

"We're going to throw a party, a fall festival. Tarian and I will be there with the help of Piper."

"Me?" Piper flinched.

"Yes, you'll transport us just long enough to make an appearance. Like Margaret said, they must believe we're in the village and not know we've left them." Audrey strolled back to the other side of the grand room to her desk, formerly Eleanor's. She felt more at ease in the office of the Chancellor, but she still didn't feel at home. To her this space, this desk, the elaborate trimmings, would always be Eleanor's.

Margaret and Piper followed her and sat back in their chairs.

"What facts do you have suggesting Benjamin is anywhere near the Bar District?" Margaret asked.

"Margaret, I've explained your responsibilities. Please, leave us and get started," Audrey ordered dismissing her.

Margaret's eyes narrowed but she didn't speak out of line to her superior. Without a word she spun around and made a show of exiting the room.

Once the door closed completely, Audrey spoke, "Piper,

can you travel across the nation with passengers?"

"Distance is irrelevant to me. But honestly, I don't know. I haven't traveled like that in hundreds of years. I haven't left the village in centuries."

"But you used to, in the past?"

Piper nodded. She rocked from side to side. "Oh yes, when I first came over with the Spanish explorers, I traveled the entire nation without my colony even knowing I'd left my quarters."

"Great. What is necessary in order for you to locate us?"

"Nothing, only coordinates. But if I remember correctly, it does help to have a sample."

"A sample of what?"

"A strand of your hair, and Tarian's, would work."

"Really? That's interesting," Audrey's mind drifted back to the tunnel. *Is that what had happened? A strand of my hair had been left behind during the altercation between Hu, Vixy, and me. The woman did leap from the boat and come after me. With Karl's help and a strand of my hair, the village could've been exposed. Maybe.*

"What are you not telling me, Audrey?" Piper stopped rocking and focused on her friend.

"The witch I mentioned is a Lavender Witch. Her name is Vixy. She's part of an insurgency. I believe some sort of uprising is occurring among your kind. And she implied that the malditos and Lavender Witches would pounce at the chance to eliminate the immortals."

"But you're working with Roman's family, and they're preta."

"Not all creatures want this, only a certain group. The problem is I don't know how many. The secret waterway connects the Entente to the South. There may be thousands of malditos plotting against us for all I know."

"You must go to the High Council." Piper twitched and jerked trying to keep her feet planted in one spot.

"Not yet. I need more time and more facts."

Piper shook her head, but her feet had finally fixed in place.

TWENTY-NINE

WOLFGANG

An hour before sunset, Tarian arrived at Ana-Clara's home with Audrey and Teresa. They climbed the few steps and stood on the porch waiting to be welcomed inside. At their feet three fist-sized rocks covered the welcome mat. One red, one black, and one blue stone stood in line, on guard like snapping turtles.

Teresa leaned down to grab the blue rock at her feet.

"Stop!" Ana-Clara thrust the front porch door open.

Teresa pulled her hand away. "What are the rocks for?"

"Protection."

"From what?" Tarian asked.

Ana-Clara eyed him and after a long pause offered, "From Death." She spoke the word as if death was a person. She stepped over the rocks, parting Tarian and Audrey. "Get them inside quickly." She waved her hands gesturing for the Sleepers in the vehicles to be brought into her home. "Bring the gentlemen in through the garage and lay them on the beds in the back two bedrooms. The woman comes through the front. Lay her on the bed in the front right bedroom."

Tarian assisted the carriage of the two men. As the carts skidded down the gravel path to the garage, he saw more colored rocks hidden like Easter eggs among the flowerbeds and in the corners of the garage. Settling David's and Jonathan's sleeping bodies onto their assigned beds he noticed more stones inside. These rocks were tiny but just as noble. They hid like little toy soldiers behind the curtain on a windowsill, in a soap dish on the bathroom sink, or wedged in the crack of a door. Every nook and cranny contained a rock or a bay leaf.

The aroma he'd first inhaled entering the cottage now overtook him. Invisible clouds of fragrance filled the air, and he'd just passed through one. The strong odor closed his throat, and he gagged. "What's that smell?"

He turned the corner to find all the women gathered in the kitchen area around the colorful sundial table. Sour expressions on all their faces greeted him.

"What? It stinks." He spit out the vile taste that the scent had left on his tongue.

"It doesn't stink." Teresa rolled her eyes. "It's special herbs." She turned toward Ana-Clara for guidance but received only a fraction of a smile and a nod. "Lavender, Hyssop, and Patchouli?"

Ana-Clara's smile broadened from a slight curl at the edges to a gaping, teeth filled crescent that nearly filled her entire face.

"Good child." She sang the words.

"What's it for?" Audrey asked.

"Protection," Ana-Clara said.

"The rocks, the leaves, and the herbs are all for protection against death? Whose death?" Tarian pulled out a chair and joined them at the table.

Ana-Clara didn't answer him right away. Finally, she spoke in measured words. "It's just a precaution. You want your immortals woken up not pushed deeper into the sleep of death, correct?"

"Of course," Teresa said, "Ignore my brother, he doesn't get it."

"Don't be naive, Teresa. She's lying."

"Tarian!" Audrey squeezed his forearm.

Audrey was right. He should bite his tongue or risk removal from the property. He inched a forced smirk onto his lips.

"You're not fooling me," Ana-Clara said.

You're not fooling me either, lady, he thought but held his plastic smile in place.

"Can you give us a little more information Ana-Clara?" Audrey asked calmly.

"I just had a feeling, and I always trust my feelings," Ana-Clara said.

"A feeling? That's it?" Tarian asked.

"Yes." Ana-Clara nodded curtly.

"Well, my feeling is that I'm staying in this house with you two tonight." Tarian stood.

"No," Ana-Clara barked.

Tarian paced the room and glared at Audrey. "Do something!"

"Ana-Clara we will not interfere. We'll shut ourselves in a room until you tell us we can come out."

"No, this is extremely difficult work. Ask Teresa. Daniel nearly didn't make it last time."

"It's true. He had a relapse and almost died … for good." Teresa nodded obediently.

"I wasn't aware of any complications." Audrey looked from Ana-Clara to Teresa.

"I know. I didn't want to worry you. This work is hard. It drains my energy, but as you can see, I'm fine. After a few weeks at home, some rest, I feel good as new. But there are risks in healing, and if we fail by you staying, then all three might die. So, let's just do it the same way as before."

"Okay, we'll go to Qui's as we did before. You're right. You've been successful, but I'm posting guards outside," Audrey said.

"But if anything out of the ordinary happens you must tell us." Tarian stopped pacing and stared at Teresa and Ana-Clara.

"Yes," Ana-Clara said.

"Of course," Teresa agreed.

"Anything!" Tarian overemphasized each syllable.

"We have weapons." Teresa shook her head in annoyance

at her brother's overprotection.

"And we have Wolfgang," Ana-Clara added.

They all turned to see a giant growling dog. It had the coat of a German shepherd, dark face with black and gold fur blending down its back to the tip of its tail. Its head reached more than halfway up the doorway as its width brushed both sides of the frame, leaving not a millimeter. With ice blue glistening eyes and razor blade sharp fangs no one would dare pass. It was equal parts Herculean glory and gruesome mutant.

"Es seguro!" Ana-Clara ordered.

The dog barked in protest, frothy slobber spraying the air. It then lay down and rolled over as if it wanted someone to pet its stomach.

Tarian and Audrey stood still, but Teresa ran toward it without hesitation and rubbed its golden tummy. The dog licked her face and arms as a reward.

"Is it tough?" Tarian asked. "It doesn't look tough."

"It's a he, and he's obedient. If I had commanded him, he would've attacked you." Ana-Clara cocked her head.

"Where has he been?" Audrey asked.

"With my sister on the other side of Rain's Gate. I asked her to bring him over last week when I had a vision of a dark cloaked person walking in the mist."

"What does that mean?" Audrey asked.

"Could mean anything. Could mean I will get sick soon, or maybe I'll just stub my toe, or it could be Death."

Tarian sighed heavily and paced some more.

Wolfgang lifted his massive head and with his abdomen on the floor, forepaws outstretched, and hind leg toes driven into the wood, he studied Tarian's every step.

Tarian's eyes met Wolfgang's with a challenge. Tarian left the kitchen to track the entire house. Wolfgang trailed on his heels as he shut and locked all windows, drew all curtains tight, and opened all interior doors checking inside closets and bathrooms. Together, they secured all exterior doors while making sure not to disturb any bay leaves or colored rocks. Soon dog and master stood next to the front door. "Lock this door behind me and get started so we can all go home," Tarian said to his sister then patted Wolfgang's head. "I'm counting on you, mutt."

Wolfgang responded with a bellowing bark.

Tarian reached his hand out to turn the doorknob when Wolfgang's low rumble stopped him. The dog growled in his direction but not at him. He froze and listened. Several footsteps rustled on the other side of the front door.

Audrey froze too and drew her weapon. She waved Teresa and Ana-Clara back then tiptoed as far away from the front door as she could get but still have a clear shot.

A loud banging struck the door. Audrey glanced in Tarian's direction. He also had his weapon trained on the target and gave her the nod.

"Who is it?" Audrey beckoned.

"It's Elite Forces Jeff Statton, Madam Secretary, with two

unknowns," one of the guards Audrey had brought to protect Ana-Clara's cottage said through the closed door.

"It's Hu and Jun," yelled Jun in exasperation.

Tarian threw open the door, his weapon outstretched.

"Whoa, it's us." Jun nearly walked into the shiny steel of Tarian's gun.

Wolfgang barked, his hair on edge and feet twitching to pounce.

"It's okay Wolfgang," Hu said, and the dog stopped barking. Hu didn't spare a second glance at the dog as he charged inside.

Wolfgang never took his eyes off the preta.

Jun nodded toward the animal then flashed a glower at Ana-Clara. "You had a vision."

"Just a bad feeling." Ana-Clara frowned.

"Why are you here?" Tarian asked.

"Your missing Waker is gonna cross over Rain's Gate," Jun said.

"How do you know this?" Audrey asked.

Jun crossed her lanky arms across her chest. "A trusted source."

"Believe me, I want the bastard gone. Let South America have the beast. He's already murdered two of our clients," Hu said.

"How? Where?" Audrey asked.

"In the Crimson Rose Club, his handlers screwed up, didn't secure him. He seems like an average guy until he attacks.

He's scaring the crap out of our clientele," Jun said.

"An average guy, huh? He's adapting to his environment. Clever." Tarian glanced at Audrey.

She nodded then turned her attention to Jun. "How do you know this? Did you see him?"

"No, but the witness reports state that he's handsome and charming. Now his face is plastered all over the district on wanted devices. The District Police are on a major manhunt, scouring the bars and alleys. And I don't wan'em pokin' their noses in my business," Jun explained.

"Enough chit chat, let's go." Hu stepped toward the door. "We need to get the Waker before he crosses over."

"You got the Death Serum?" Jun asked. "To kill the SOB?"

"Yes, I have what is needed to kill a Waker," Tarian said.

Hu paced and glared at them. "We're wasting time!"

Audrey remained silent, ideas coursing through her veins. She looked at Teresa and ordered, "Call the Vice-Chancellor and give her all this information. Tell her to send reinforcements. Tell her I want this house and the Sleepers guarded 24/7. Tell her I'm contacting our local office for support once we've caught Benjamin. And tell her, if she doesn't hear from me within twenty-four—no—forty-eight hours to inform the High Council."

"Okay." Teresa nodded.

Tarian hugged and kissed his sister on the forehead. "Be careful, keep this door shut and locked. Keep your weapons on you at all times." He gave her a gentle smile, patted the small gun hitched to her hip that he'd trained her how to use, then rushed out the front door following Hu, Jun, and Audrey. He hesitated on the front porch until he heard the bolt of the lock and the pad of Wolfgang's heavy paws circling the room. A silent prayer crossed his lips, but he couldn't bring himself to turn away, to leave.

"Tarian," Audrey yelled from the vehicle.

He glanced at her from the front porch. Hu stood directly behind her, but unlike before, his predatory passion was not focused on her, in its place, a relentless drive for action centered on Tarian. Like a man with mud filled boots, he dragged on. He sank into the back seat of the car next to Audrey and leaned into her, letting the warmth of her body give him strength to leave his sister behind.

THIRTY

CAVE OF HANDS

Twenty minutes later Audrey and her crew entered the mouth of Rain's Gate. Nearing ten o'clock, the crossover hummed and sparkled with creatures dressed for a fun evening of revelry. Shimmers from glittery dresses and gleaming gemstones bounced off the black water, dotting the tunnel with tiny prisms of spectacular color. Stiletto heels clicked the pavement below, laughter flew from red lips, and none of them seemed fazed by the flashing wanted pictures of Benjamin.

Soon they reached the bowels of the tunnel. The dancing flecks of light exchanged for muted blackness, and the glassy water blended into the stone wall dark as coal. Every few feet miniscule lights shimmered cutting the shadows. The light glowed against the damp walls and rippled atop the water then faded away.

They finally reached a docked boat. Jun jumped in and started the engine, while Hu disengaged the ropes.

"Get in," Jun said.

Hu held out a hand for Audrey but Tarian grabbed her hand first and offered to assist her over the edge.

Disgusted by both of them, she snatched her hand back, shook her head, and hopped into the boat unaided.

The boat crawled into the onyx tunnel. The waterway curved ahead and out of sight, but they crept close behind the boat they believed held Benjamin and his handlers. Jun had an intricate tracking system at her helm.

"Are the smugglers using an illegal boat?" Audrey asked Hu for verification of what she saw on the boat's screen.

"Yes, only crafts equipped with both Bar District markings and maldito trackers are permitted to cross. Once the registered boat hits the borderline, credits are automatically withdrawn from the patron's bank account and deposited into the pockets of the South American Maldito Ministry, magic and technology working in harmony," Hu whispered.

Jun's boat purred like a kitten as she shifted it into low gear. Inching closer to their target, they heard the clanging of steel on steel. Three men had Benjamin chained and entrapped inside a barred cage. Benjamin thrashed around like a wild animal. The men threatened and hit the Waker to no avail. Benjamin wouldn't be silenced, and his restraints seemed to trigger his bestial instincts. When confined, the evolved, adapted, charming Waker reverted to the monster that he truly was.

Hu, Jun, Tarian, and Audrey drew closer and closer. The handlers became more and more frustrated with their captive.

Once in range, Audrey fired her weapon, taking out one of the three men. Tarian and Hu leaped into the smuggler's boat, thrusting daggers and wielding blades. They inflicted several knife wounds sending arcs of blood everywhere. Suddenly, the boat vanished, plunging Hu and Tarian underwater. Then the air filled with a loud echoing rumble.

"What's that?" Audrey panicked. "It sounds like a tidal wave."

"Brace yourself!" Jun yelled.

The wall of water crashed down dragging the boat deep under. Audrey tumbled over and over. She kicked her feet and swam but she was disoriented and couldn't find the surface. She clamped her lips tight refusing to let the rush of water pass her lips. Minutes later her breath dissolved, and the water forced its way inside her lungs. The pain of her body being filled with ravenous liquid got the better of her, and she let go of her weapon to clasp her waist and curl into a ball. She felt her consciousness slip away. She wouldn't die, but the burning, achy pressure rendered her mind numb. Her immortal survival kicked in and sent her into a state of protective hibernation. Then as quickly as the water had come, it left, pulling her body like a rag caught in a swirling drain and relinquished her on solid ground.

She drew herself on all fours, gagging until she vomited mouthfuls of water. She expected to see blood pooling from burst alveoli that stung like razor blades, but the discharge was clear as crystal. She heard a rough moan and turned to find Hu regurgitating transparent vomit. Hu's golden skin turned a grotesque, pale green as the water flowed out of him.

"Hu?" she gasped out.

He choked then rolled onto the mustard dirt ground and fell silent.

"Hu!" She got to her feet and ran straight for his limp body. She began resuscitating him. Thumping his chest then pressing her lips to his to breathe in lifesaving air until he smiled. She shoved him hard. "Idiot!"

He propped himself onto his elbow, grinning mischievously. "You were worried for my safety."

"Of course, I was. I, unlike you, am a decent person."

Hu jumped to his feet looking as if he hadn't just been spun through the rinse cycle, even his hair set in its perfect black spikes. "Come on."

"Why are you so calm? Where are Tarian and Jun?" She ran her fingers through her soaked, tangled hair.

"We've been flushed out, so the saying goes."

"What does that mean?" she asked.

"That means they've banished us."

"From the Entente?"

"Yes," he said.

"Are Tarian and Jun still inside the Entente?"

"Possibly, but more probable, they've been sent through another portal. There are five and this, my lovely, is by far the worst."

"Why?"

"Because we've been sent to the southern tip of the continent and stripped of everything but our clothes." He appraised her soaking wet body and sighed, "Pity."

She growled. She reached for her weapons but found none. No weapons and no mobile. Her blood boiled. As nervous sweat pierced her armpits and her shoulders trembled, her mind raced causing a scorching heat she hadn't produced in decades.

Hu stalked away from her. "Audrey, it's okay. Tarian's fine. I'm sure of it."

Closing her eyes and allowing breaths of earthy air to pass into her lungs, she calmed herself. She cautiously sat down, leaning against the cave walls. Taking in the dry, dim environment, she slowly regained her bearings and cooled her skin.

Hu held out a hand for her to take. "They've sent us through Cueva de las Manos."

"What's that?" She gripped his hand accepting his offer, too beaten up to be stubborn this time.

"The Cave of Hands, it's punishment. The cleansing they call it. It flushes people out of the Rain's Gate water passageway down to the bottom of South America. You either die or you're left stranded."

"But you assured me that Tarian is safe."

"Yes, since this is by far the worst of the five portals, I assume he's fine."

"Assume?"

"What do you think? Your boyfriend is the immortal Awakened Hunter. The best, so he says, so I'm deducing he's survived if we did." His clipped words and harsh tone cut through the air without any teasing or flirting.

"Sorry," she said and paused to assure her tone wasn't sharp, "I haven't had reason to venture into this part of the world for centuries."

"Welcome to my backyard," he sang like a sneaky pirate. "Follow me, I know of a man that can give us shelter. He'll help us find Tarian, Jun, and hopefully Benjamin."

The ground slanted slightly in the cave. Audrey tripped a couple of times until she got used to the incline. The air was hazy until the cave opened, and the light brightened, but the tinny smell worsened. Images of hands covered the walls. Thousands of hands in negative reliefs spread in lengthy ribbons of red, orange, black, and white. The ceiling rose and the path spread wider as more sunlight filtered in from the mouth of the cave, making the mural's sandstone colors more vivid and disturbing. The hands beckoned her onward. Audrey felt their pull and ran her fingertips along the rough cave walls until she found a hand to fit hers. She placed hers on top of it. Energy passed from the wall to her flesh, a vibration of some sort. The image of thousands of hands spooked but, at the same time, fascinated her.

"Whose hands are these?" she asked still exploring the cave walls with her fingers.

"They've been here for over ten thousand years. The

hands belonged to the indigenous people at the time, but they must've been creatures, not human, because this place holds a lot of magic. It makes for an easy portal."

"Easy." She huffed.

"Easy to spell bind it." He corrected. He stood next to Audrey placing his hand next to hers onto an image the same size as his. He turned his face toward hers and smirked. The two images of left hands matching the exact sizes of hers and his were painted side by side.

For a split second, Audrey kept her hand on the wall, her thumb gently touching Hu's pinky, then she withdrew it and whirled on her heels to exit. For an instant, she wondered if this was one of his tricks, an illusion, but her drenched hair and clothes were all too real.

The metallic iron smell of the cave gave way to the disturbing smell of rotting animals as Audrey stepped into the warm sun. An orange desert stretched before her. Breadcrumbs of bones, miles of rusty dirt, and a thin trail of bushes cut a path between the canyons. The sparse patches of green lined what was once a river.

Audrey's mouth salivated thinking about it. "There must be water. You can't have green plants without water."

"Well, it's gone now," he said.

"These plants are very, very green. The water couldn't have disappeared too long ago," Audrey said.

"Keep walking. We'll hit water by sunset and then it will

not be far from Ramiro's house." Hu prowled onward leading the way. As the tallest and largest, he walked in front, on guard for any animal, human, or creature designing to cross their trail.

The blazing sun mocked them as it lingered in the blue cloudless sky barely skimming the horizon. For what seemed like hours, it hovered in the same spot. Audrey tired of looking at Hu's back. His skin had tanned, and his shoulders glistened with sweat. She found herself unwillingly admiring his taut muscles. Finally, the sun broke the plane and at that instant, the ground below Audrey's step squished as mud oozed underfoot.

With a brief bolt of vigor, they hurtled forward to find the area where the stream ran deep enough to scoop out a handful of water. The coolness slid down Audrey's parched throat, soothing her dry mouth. Like oil to the Tin Man, the water loosened her tongue, and soon sounds of relief escaped as they smiled and laughed.

"So we are close now, right?" Audrey asked.

"I think. I have nothing to measure time or distance by, so I'm guessing we'll come across the house soon. It's been a long time since I've trekked this journey. If my memory serves me well, once we come upon the water the house appears soon after."

"And why were you banished before?"

"None of your business, my Timber Wolf." His flirtatious way reappeared as the water assuaged his tongue and cooled his reddened face. "It was long before the Entente War, before the border wall. But I have come here on my own accord since then."

"Did Rain's Gate exist before the continent disconnected itself from the rest of the world?" Tickles of uncertainty began to multiply along Audrey's spine. Time returned to her days as a young girl when she'd been scared and living in hiding in Elizabeth I's London, not knowing her true nature or the nature and laws of the other creatures inhabiting the world. But she'd fought hard and cleverly navigated through the rough streets to find answers. She'd been an officer inside the Guardians of Dare from its inception. She was the current Chancellor, and the High Council had the nerve to deem her unworthy of this information. *Had Eleanor known?*

"Yes, for as long as I can remember." Hu stood and stepped away from the stream. "Let's keep moving."

"Has it always been under the control of the malditos?" she asked.

"Yes," he answered. "They've grown rich over the centuries by smuggling whatever was needed at the time: people, drugs, medicine, weapons, anything to make money."

"Don't sound so pious, Hu. You've obviously gained from the malditos corruption."

"I have," he said, no shame in his tone.

He kept stride with her, and she felt his lure as his eyes danced upon her shoulders, but she looked straight ahead, realizing that her scornful words only tempted his lechery.

Unlike the stubborn sun that followed them all day long, the setting sun dove into the horizon thrusting them into blackness. With no flashlights and very few stars to guide them, their steps slowed. The temperature plummeted and chilled their bones. But Audrey's gift of micro-climate control wasn't needed for long. A light twinkled. A mere dot of straw yellow fixed against an onyx background beckoned.

"That's it," he said. After several more steps, the sharp square corners of the mud house materialized. "Yep, he knows we're here."

"How?" Audrey asked.

"We have a code. If the light in the window to the left of the door is on that means he's home and we can come in. If the right window had been lit then we'd be turned away."

"Yeah, right. I would've broken in," she muttered.

Hu knocked three times and waited. A white bearded man with skin as tawny and cracked as the dried mud of the house opened the door. He looked rough even dangerous without a smile on his withered lips, but his copper eyes warmly gleamed.

"Come in, I have food on the table. I've been waiting for you." Ramiro didn't hobble, instead he strode as he steered them into the kitchen area.

"How did you know we were coming here?" Audrey asked.

Hu answered, "Ramiro knows when someone breaks through the portal."

She glanced at Hu with one eyebrow raised demanding a clearer answer, but he offered nothing then the aroma of a homemade meal caught her attention. A set table with plates of steamed corn, boiled potatoes, roasted duck, and raw sparrow awaited their arrival.

Audrey devoured the food mumbling her appreciation amid bites while Hu barely touched his raw bird. He did drink an entire bottle of red wine though.

The old man refilled her glass of water. "So what do you have need of?"

"Weapons. And a mobile," Audrey said.

"Yes, yes, I know all that. I meant. What kind of creature will you be fighting?"

"We seek an immortal that's been captured and taken to your malditos headquarters," Audrey said.

"Headquarters?" asked Ramiro.

"Audrey means the malditos have taken this immortal man turned bloodeater to the castle," Hu explained.

Ramiro sighed, closed his eyes, and didn't speak for several long seconds, then walked into another room. "You are asking too much."

Large lavish furniture dwarfed the small den. A massive two door, ornately carved wooden cabinet stood against the back wall.

Audrey followed on his heels. "Why? What's in the castle?"

"Lautaro." Ramiro opened the cabinet. The interior of the door held several empty hooks and he sighed. One lone blade swung like a pendulum. Ramiro retrieved it then handed it to Audrey. "You will need blessed blades to fight inside the castle. He has Castle Guards, Maldito Ministry Soldiers, and the Apostólos. Only a sword or dagger blessed by a priest can kill Lautaro's Maldito Ministry Soldiers. It is rumored he has seventy malditos he calls his Apostólos that can only die if stabbed through the heart with a blessed dagger or decapitated with a blessed sword. Some say blessed bullets work too, but I'm not sure."

"Can you get more of these?" Audrey asked twirling the blade in awe.

"I know where I can buy two daggers," Ramiro said.

"That will do for now," Hu said with a reassuring nod at the old man who looked beyond worried.

"You'll be traveling thousands of miles. Okay. You'll need transportation?" Ramiro asked.

"Yes," Hu answered.

"Where's the castle?" Audrey asked.

"You go to where the waters meet. In the city, there's an opera house. Next to the house is a small white church with a golden cross. That's your destination."

Audrey nodded slowly. She opened her mouth to ask more questions when Hu took her hand and guided her to sit next to him on the sofa.

"The church is a portal to the castle. The castle within is hidden from the outside world." Hu inched closer to her. "Lautaro is not a maldito though he rules over them, even the Maldito

Queen answers to him. He is the present Grand Sorcerer. He's very old but not immortal. Nonetheless, he is all powerful at this moment, and all southern creatures, with few exceptions, answer to him."

Audrey scooted away. "So he controls the maldito underworld that run Rain's Gate."

"Yes," Hu said.

"If I can contact my Vice-Chancellor, I can enlist the help of the Guardians of Dare," Audrey said.

"Yes, help will be needed, but you must have a plan. Like the Entente, we too have a border. Anyone leaving the continent leaves a trace and a trail," Ramiro said.

"In other words, you might as well highlight your route home on a map in neon pink," Hu said.

"Okay, what about entering?" Audrey asked.

"Yes, entering or exiting, but there are ways around it. The cleansing we went through for example, or spells can be cast."

"Ana-Clara," she said.

"Yes." Hu's voice sounded far away and sad.

Audrey watched both men. Anxiety blanketed her in a shawl of shivers. She had so many questions.

Hu rose from the sofa, ran a hand through his black spikes, and stretched his long legs. "Tomorrow," he drawled out. He put a casual arm around Ramiro. "Come, let's get more wine, and then please show me to my bed chamber."

"Same place as before." The old man chuckled.

Audrey stayed behind stewing in the room. These men had a history together and secrets, but did it mean anything? Everyone had secrets and a past. Eventually, she walked back into the kitchen to join the men's toast.

Hu handed her a glass with exquisite golden rose buds engraved on it. The red wine's sweet aroma comforted her palette.

"Paz," Ramiro said as they all drank.

The next morning, Audrey stretched in search of Tarian's body to snuggle. She didn't find him next to her, her eyes flew open then her current predicament came flooding back.

"No," she groaned. "It's not a nightmare." Every muscle clenched as she forced them to extend long and far. With crackles and pops her neck and spine rattled back to life. She hopped to her feet and showered. Reaching for her towel, she found none. "Ugh." She stepped out, dripping steadily, and before long the tiny floor mat was soggy and useless.

The door creaked open just a sliver then an arm poked in holding a fluffy towel. "Need this?" the voice belonging to the arm asked.

"Give me that." She snatched the towel and slammed the door on Hu's arm.

"Not a morning person." He chuckled.

She said nothing as she got dressed and stormed into the kitchen following the scent of bananas. A plate of piping hot banana and cheese empanadas waited.

"These smell amazing." She reached for one of the oval shaped pastries.

Ramiro poured her a glass of fresh orange juice. "The coffee is percolating. It's almost ready."

He almost danced around the kitchen with a smile on his face. He had pulled back his long white hair and gathered his beard with ties to keep them out of his way for cooking. Audrey tried to guess his age, but she couldn't reconcile the white hair and wrinkled skin with the spry steps, so she gave up.

Hu strutted into the kitchen holding a list. "Good morning, Timber Wolf. Did you have a nice shower?"

She cringed once at the words then again when she saw the look in Ramiro's eyes. It wasn't surprise or suspicion or even disdain. It was understanding, as if he'd pieced together a puzzle.

Hu placed the list next to Audrey's plate.

"What's this?"

"My list of requirements. Feel free to add anything you desire," Hu said in a purr.

He leaned over her as she read through the items. He had all the necessities: communication, transportation, and weaponry. There was nothing she needed to add. She handed it back to him without comment.

"Nothing?" he asked with velvet smoothness.

She didn't respond and continued to eat, but her irritation at his advancements made it hard to swallow.

"Well then." He handed the note over to Ramiro. "What

do you think? How long?"

Ramiro appraised the items. "Untraceable communication devices will take the longest. And I'm not sure there's a vehicle in town. Everything else I should have by late afternoon."

"We can't leave without a form of communication," Audrey said.

"I know. I will do my best, but I'm afraid the devices will have to be made not purchased. If parts are in stock, then twenty-four hours, if not, seventy-two."

"That's too long." Audrey threw down her napkin.

"If I rush the job more than that, it will raise suspicion."

"You do your best Ramiro," Hu said without urgency and patted the old man on the back.

Ramiro turned off the stove and hurried out of the house with the list.

Audrey's head fell into her hands. She dug her fingernails into her scalp drawing blood.

"Coffee?" Hu asked.

She lifted her head just enough to glare at him.

He ignored her and poured the thick, black coffee into her cup.

"Why are you so calm? You were frantic when you came to Ana-Clara's house to get us," she asked, her words bitter on her lips.

"Yes, I didn't want that monster in my territory."

She huffed and nodded.

"What?" he asked.

"You were just protecting your turf." An unpleasant sigh snorted from her nostrils. She would've been embarrassed if she weren't so enraged.

"You make me sound like a dog." His arrogance never wavered, but his yellow eyes sank at the comparison.

"Give me one good reason to think of you as anything other than a mutt," she said, deliberately suppressing any empathy she might have shown this preta.

"You can sit here and stew in your loathing of me, or you can make the most of a terrible situation, which, by the way, you brought upon yourself. You're the one who brought this nightmare to me and my family."

Her mouth opened but she couldn't respond. He was right. She could hate him, but why? Because he flirted, because his preta nature compelled him to be attracted to her? No, she knew it was more than that. She also knew she needed him, and she hated needing someone she didn't fully trust. At least, he was intelligent and skilled, and she hated to admit it—charming.

THIRTY-ONE

ANGEL FALLS

Tarian's swollen eyes burned as the remnants of water oozed from under his eyelids. It took great effort to prop his head up, and once he had, the landscape in his vision spun. He laid his head back down. Carefully rolling onto his side, he attempted another look at the world. This time the items within sight remained in one spot. He took several deep, steady breaths before pushing up onto one elbow.

"Audrey." Tarian's weak, ragged voice called out. No answer. He raised himself to a seated position but remained still until the nausea in his stomach calmed. Lush greenness surrounded him. Trees and plants covered the land, obscuring Tarian's view of anything beyond his immediate vicinity. He rose on shaky limbs, gathered all his energy then screamed, "Audrey!" He heard a swooshing sound as leaves parted and someone approached. He reached for his weapon, but he had none.

"She's not here." Jun's long, black leather covered legs

stretched and stepped through the thick jungle. She carried a small bucket of water.

"Where is she?"

"Don't know," she shrugged, "There are five flush outs, and it looks like they split us up. I'm guessin' my brother's with her, and I got stuck with you, but then again, maybe they got sent individually someplace else." She drank out of the bucket and then handed it to him. "Here, this is water you can actually drink."

He took it and sipped it slowly. He heard and saw water all around them. He threw her a curious glance.

"You don't remember?" One of her black spikes of hair lilted over into a curl.

"Remember what?"

"You were delirious with thirst after the flush out."

"That makes no sense. The last thing I remember is drowning." He patted his hair and clothes feeling the dampness. He ran his fingers through his tousled brown locks creating a wave of chestnut that swept up and away from his forehead.

"It's a trick, poisoned water all around." She waved her hand in a circle. "Even though you almost drown you enter on this side thirsty as hell. You go to drink and vomit yourself into a coma. You're welcome, by the way."

"For what?" he asked.

"For havin' to deal with your disgusting puke, when you didn't listen to me. I told you not to drink from the stream, and what did you do?" She smirked. "You drank from the stream.

Now, from here on out, you listen to me."

He squinted and clenched his mouth shut. He said nothing. Her gritty endurance overpowered his feelings of pathetic nausea, so he decided to accept her demands—for now.

"You may be the best damn Awakened Hunter, but I've been here before. I know what to look out for, and I know how in the hell we're gonna get down from the top of this three-thousand-foot waterfall. Got it?"

"Sure." He took another sip. The purified drinking water dashed through his veins at lightning speed, giving him energy and strength.

"Eat this." She handed him an odd plant leaf that he'd never seen before. It looked like an aloe stalk, but it was candy apple red. The gel inside resembled aloe but tasted sugary sweet.

"What does this do?"

"Coat your intestines, and believe me, they're shredded from that poison. I don't envy your first crap," she snickered.

His face contorted into a scowl. He did feel the need to use the bathroom. His arm wrapped around his midsection in terror.

Jun laughed even harder vibrating her spiky hair.

Tarian nodded his head, but looking very disagreeable said, "Let's get going. We need to find Audrey and kill Benjamin." He started patting at his clothes. "The Death Serum is gone."

"Yep! That's all part of the flush out. Don't worry, I know a guy."

"No one has Death Serum except the Guardians!"

"I know, but he has weapons and communications. We can contact them."

"I don't know." Tarian eyes locked in a gaze of concern.

"What don't ya know?"

"I don't know if I want to contact anyone else. I don't want anyone else's life in danger."

"Well, I sure as hell am not fighting the Ministry Maldito Soldiers with no help. If ya want to get your Waker, you're gonna need help, and a lot of it."

"Just get me to your guy. I'll think about a plan." His words sounded like rough, gravel rocks rubbing together as they spilled from his mouth.

They didn't walk far, but it took them almost an hour to get to the exit hole. The tangled web of branches made the path nearly impossible to navigate. They climbed over large stumps and under thorny vines. They pushed apart hundreds of flowery leaves that curtained the trail. Strangely, there were no animals, only remarkable birds of every size and color.

Finally, Tarian could see the blue sky above. Below, Mandevilla vines spread and wove like a rug, covering the ground making a giant circle with a small opening in the middle. The plant vines spilled into it and disappeared like a fragrant and colorful black hole. White, pink, yellow, and red blooms sucked into the abyss.

"Now, we jump." Without hesitation Jun hopped up,

suspended for seconds above the opening, straightened her legs and pointed her toes, squeezed her arms into her sides and fell stiff as a pencil into the pit.

"Uh," Tarian grunted, then he swore. Before she disappeared, she gave him a sarcastic smirk, then he watched her descend downward. He paced the jungle floor. She hadn't given him any directions. How long was he to wait before following her down the tunnel? He paced a little while longer then repeated her pencil jump into the unknown darkness.

The drop exhilarated and terrified him like a steep and lengthy slide. It spit him out at full speed onto an unforgiving grassy field. He tumbled so far that he nearly dropped off the edge of another cliff.

"Took ya long enough." Jun rolled her eyes causing the scar above her eyebrow to wave.

He sighed but didn't bother to argue with her. "I see we're not at the bottom."

"Of course not. These falls took me and Hu two days to rappel down the first time we ended up here."

"How many times have you been here?"

"Let's just say before my brother and I ran a respectable bar business we did a lot of crazy shit. Two more chutes."

"How old are you?" Tarian asked.

"One hundred and seventy-two. Born in 1940."

"Oh, that's a lot younger than I thought."

"Yeah, well, it's a long story."

"Hmph." He didn't press her, although he wanted to know all about her, and how she became a preta. He'd ask her another time.

Once at the bottom of the falls, he turned and tilted his head as far back as it could stretch and still couldn't see the top.

"Amazing, isn't it?" she asked.

"Yes, it's inspiring. Is it natural or magic?"

"Oh no, it's real. Made by the one true magician."

Tarian cast a puzzled expression at her.

"God!"

"Oh, yes. I see."

"The mortals call it Angel Falls. It holds a significant amount of magic—that's why it's used as a portal. Like I said, the God that made this." She thrust her arm in a semicircle fanning the spectacular land that surrounded them. "She's the ultimate magical creature."

Tarian continued to look around at the tremendous beauty that sprawled out before him.

"What is it Tarian?" she asked as he stood still and quiet.

"I've never been outside of the Entente. I've never seen anything like this before. I mean our coast is rocky but nothing like these massive boulders. And the flowers are colors I've never seen, and these leaves are larger than animals. I don't know," he shook his head and paused, "I guess, I always pictured the outside world as destroyed and ugly."

"A lot of it is, but not South America. Granted, it isn't all as lavish as these falls."

She scavenged for rocks in the stream that flowed at the base of the falls.

"What do you need? I can help."

"We need a stone with three bright white stripes and the rock itself will be shades of three different browns. Plus, it will have a black dot on each end."

"What does it do?"

"We give it to the man running the boats. He takes it, and it releases a spell, so he'll recognize us even though we've never seen him before. He'll take us to Felipe's dock."

"Felipe is the man that will help us?" he asked.

"I hope so." She threw two stones away and picked up another.

THIRTY-TWO

The raft-boat that the young boy piloted through the narrow river hit Felipe's boathouse with a thud. Tarian stumbled into Jun. He uncomfortably pressed against her to rebalance himself. She growled.

"Sí," the young, eager boy said nodding his head rapidly.

"Sí," Jun answered and handed him coins.

The boy smiled wide, revealing stained, crooked teeth. "Gracias, gracias."

Stepping onto the dock, Tarian asked, "What did you give him?"

"Old money, silver dollars, not worth anything inside the Entente anymore."

"I read about the old money in school. A silver dollar is only worth a third of a credit," Tarian said.

"It's worth ten times that here," Jun said.

"Where'd you get it?"

"Like I said, this isn't my first flush out."

Suspicion brewed in Tarian's gut. Had he lost everything in the flush out or had she taken his weapons? He didn't have time to stew as a lanky, tanned man with medium length jet-black hair and deep-set eyes strolled out from the boathouse's screened backdoor and onto the connected dock.

"Jun." He drawled out the syllable.

"Hi, Felipe. This is Tarian." She flicked her wrist in Tarian's direction.

Felipe charged in, took Tarian's hand in a tight handshake and slapped him hard on the back. "Hola, young man." Felipe turned his thick accent to Jun. "What is he?"

"He's a Guardian," Jun said.

Still keeping a firm hold on Tarian, he spoke again, "Ah, I've never met a Guardian before. But my father told me stories. What brings you across the border?"

"He's lost his beast, and while we were attempting to kill it, the malditos flushed us out," Jun said.

"I didn't lose anyone, I …" Tarian tried to explain.

"Don't bother. I prefer to know as little as possible. You've come to me for weapons and communications."

"Yes," Tarian said.

Felipe released Tarian's hand and pushed him down the floating dock and through the creaking screen door. The floating house was spacious inside with tastefully decorated tables, chairs, and an inviting linen sofa. A refreshing river breeze from the many open windows swept across the living room and tunneled into the kitchen. Loose papers on the desk and the wildflowers arranged in a glass vase fluttered.

The humid tropical environment seemed entirely foreign and awesomely strange to a Northeasterner. His dampness from the flush out had evaporated during his sail down the river under the bright sun, but now, trapped inside a room with no air conditioning his skin glistened, his clothes clung, and his hair wilted. This southern paradise quickly morphed into an uncomfortable mess.

"You are in luck, my friends. The powers that be are with you. I won my poker game last night," Felipe said with a buccaneer's smile.

"Good for you. What does that have to do with us?" Jun asked.

Felipe's face deflated. "Jun, you take the fun out of everything."

"Thank you." Tarian gave Felipe a look of understanding and a genuine smile.

Felipe's grin and enthusiasm reborn, he continued, "I won the pot. My gambling mates are five fellow black marketers, and one of my prizes is a blessed sword."

"No way!" Jun gasped.

Felipe's glee turned sinister as he leveled his thinned eyes on her. "It's going to cost you."

"When has it ever *not* cost me?" Jun huffed.

"Touché!"

"Ya want tickets to the big game, and a free pass through Rain's Gate?" Jun asked.

"Yes." Felipe's eyes lit up with delight. "For two."

"Two?" Jun's glance skipped to the flower-filled vase. "That explains why this place is so clean and nice."

Felipe's smile reached his eyes. "Her name is Claire. She will join us for dinner tonight."

"Dinner? We've got to get to Audrey," Tarian said.

Jun turned toward him, her face blank and unyielding. "Your precious Audrey is fine. We will head out in the mornin'."

"Fine, first thing in the morning!"

"First thing," she said evenly.

Tarian loosed a ragged impatient breath and paced, not knowing what else to do in this alien room with no communication device. "Can we contact Margaret now?" he asked Jun.

Jun glanced at Felipe who answered. "Yes, I'll bring in the phone and the weapons and the rest of my winnings." He strode out of the room. His footfalls on the stairs leading to the second story echoed loudly as if he carried the weight of a man three times his size. Then the shack shook with each step down the stairs. Felipe dragged a large chest. Crash, thump, crash, thump.

Tarian inhaled to calm his nerves and assured himself that the shack would not sink.

Jun found a comfortable chair and lounged like a teenager with no cares in the world. Her easy appearance infuriated Tarian.

He increased his pacing changing his direction and placing his path directly in front of her. She remained stoic, and he added a grunt to his steps.

"Why don't you go help him? It sounds like he could use it," Jun said with lazy words.

This was a good idea, but he refused to give her any credit. He reprimanded himself for not thinking of it first then dashed out of the room to find Felipe. He snatched the opposite handle and lifted it without any effort while Felipe struggled. Tarian eventually took the whole chest and followed Felipe back into the living room where he gestured to Tarian to set the chest down next to the coffee table.

Felipe keyed the lock and popped open the hood to reveal many items. He took them out one by one and placed them on the table. Daggers, phones, communicator bracelets, rings with poisoned gems, and more. Many items were old and useless, then he withdrew the sheathed sword and handed it to Tarian. "This sword kills the Ministry Maldito Soldiers of the castle, even the most powerful Apostólos closest to Lautaro. I don't know your plan. I don't want to know it. If you merely have dealings with a local creature, you won't even need this sword even though one scratch would be lethal. But if you go inside the castle, you will not survive without this."

Tarian didn't know anything about the Southern Hemisphere. He grew anxious. Was Audrey safe? He stared at Jun for more information.

"Before you panic, let me call Mom." She made a show of untangling her legs from their cozy seat. She huddled over the many goodies and grabbed the most modern communication device she could find. "Untraceable, I assume?" she asked Felipe.

"Of course." He nodded.

After she spoke with Qui and Tarian spoke with Margaret, they still had no better idea of the whereabouts of Audrey and Hu. What they did have were orders from Guardian Headquarters that they would set into action at dawn after a fitful night's sleep.

THIRTY-THREE

A DIFFERENT HEMISPHERE

Audrey wrapped her arms around herself as the air chilled with the setting sun. As she stood silhouetted against the tangerine and marigold sky, she felt Hu's eyes on her back. She refused to turn away from the beauty to look at him. She needed to see the colors change from gold to fire to spice. The clean indigo lines blended and faded to a deep midnight blue. One by one the sky popped with pinpricks of starlight, and the cold reached her bones.

"Nothing like watching the sun set in a different hemisphere," Hu said.

She nodded. He hadn't spoken to her in two days since she'd insulted him. He'd spent his days with Ramiro. She'd spent the time alone and miserable thinking only of Tarian and her family of Guardians.

"We finally found and purchased a vehicle," he said. "It's old, so it will not have hover capabilities or autonomous features. If we're lucky it will have air conditioning."

"That's fine. I'm thankful to have it," Audrey said.

Two days trapped in the rust and jade countryside, away from and unable to communicate with the modern world of the Entente, had humbled her. After Ramiro had shooed her away from his workbench, she'd done nothing but sleep.

"Me too. We'll leave after midnight and contact the Guardians once we are hundreds of miles from here."

"The mobiles are untraceable right?" she asked.

"Yes, they are supposed to be, but I won't take that chance. Ramiro is a good, kind man, and I won't risk him being connected to us."

"I understand."

"Come inside. It will be very cold soon, and Ramiro has made you dinner."

She let him gain a few feet ahead before she followed him into the mud house.

Strewn across the table among the plates of food were communicators, water and food containers, and a variety of weapons. She recognized them all. At some point in her long life she'd used every one. She fondled them to check their authenticity.

She picked up the old luger and squeezed the wood checkered grip. She'd used a gun just like this one in World War I as she attempted to sneak a friend out of Germany. Its clumsy weight surprised her. She'd become accustomed to the sleek, feather light weapons of the Guardians.

"These old firearms and blades can't compete with

modern technologies or enchanted weapons," she said.

"I know, but these weapons have no tracers and have been blessed. All advanced weaponry factories are run by the malditos, and very little can be smuggled in due to the border trackers."

"You said spells could be cast to hide imports," Audrey said.

"It's possible with more time. But any magic powerful enough to mask that of the grand sorcerer's is rare and most witches will not risk it."

"Why?" Audrey asked.

"Because if they are caught, they and all in their bloodline will be killed. Witches will not risk that for anyone, especially not for a Northern creature."

Audrey placed the luger back on the table then ran a finger along one of the four long, thin triangular blades. "I've seen this stake before. It's not old."

"No." Ramiro's eyes surveyed her before darting to Hu's.

"Vixy had two of these." Audrey tapped the triangular weapon.

"She knows a Lavender Witch?" Ramiro asked Hu.

"Not really," Hu said.

Ramiro turned wide eyes on her.

"She saved my life in Rain's Gate. I met her briefly." Audrey held her tongue about Piper. She didn't like his stare.

"This Vixy must be an insurgent," Ramiro said.

"Yes, why?"

"Because any other Lavender Witch would not have given you the time of day."

"Did this weapon come from the insurgency?" she asked.

"Not directly, I don't involve myself with them, but my dealer has a few connections."

"Why don't you help the insurgents?"

"They don't need my help, and like the malditos, the Lavender Witches wouldn't hesitate to slice my throat."

Audrey paused. The image of a severed neck put it all in perspective. "Thank you for helping us."

"He owes me," Hu said with a wry smile.

Audrey picked up the stake, and the awareness of its power swept over her. "These are the true blessed blades. Aren't they?"

"They are all blessed," Ramiro said.

"Not like this. The power inside this metal is far stronger." Audrey twirled the blade in her hands. The power seemed too strong for such a lightly weighted metal.

"Yes, the Lavender Witches' weapons are the purest and said to have originated from a congregation of religious sisters inside the Papal States centuries ago. It is said that one nick from these blades in any part of the body will instantly kill a Maldito Ministry Soldier or Apóstol." Ramiro shrugged his bony shoulders.

"You don't believe this tale?" Audrey asked.

"Too many stories, old and new, and yet my countrymen still suffer at the hands of this brute Lautaro."

"It would've been nice to have a sword as well," Hu said.

Ramiro nodded. "I know. If I had more time …"

"There's no more time," Audrey said then turned from Hu to Ramiro, "You've done well. Thank you. I'm sure Tarian and Jun will also gather some blessed blades. We'll be fine." She rambled on, not knowing if she was trying to convince Ramiro or herself. The flimsiness of the stakes made his hopeful stories seem implausible.

"Eat," Ramiro implored. "Enough sober talk. You must leave soon. Get a good start before the break of dawn."

After dinner, Hu walked Audrey outside to load the car. She took one look at the vehicle and laughed. "You weren't kidding when you said old. That looks like a vintage police car."

"It was. It's a 1970 Plymouth Belvedere Pursuit."

"Wow." She slipped into the driver's seat. The steering wheel seemed huge. She wrapped her fingers around the worn leather. Memories of long drives along the coast and through the mountains rushed her. "Do you remember how to drive?"

"I grew up in the 1950s. I remember."

She smiled. Her foot found the gas pedal then the other smaller pedal on the left. "Oh my God, it has a gear shift. I haven't seen one of those in … I don't know how long." She shook her head, losing her mind in nostalgia.

"I know." He grinned down at her.

She looked up at him. "When did you change?"

He hesitated. "1965."

Unsure if he wanted to talk about it and feeling the urgency of this mission, she slid out of the driver's seat and continued stocking the car.

"We have a long drive ahead. We can exchange life stories then." He smirked.

After two hours of driving along the Atlantic coast Hu whipped out the mobile and called his mother. She didn't answer. He called twice more, never leaving any message. That was the code. Three contacts, no message from a strange number meant return contact. In less than one minute, Qui was talking with her son.

As soon as the call ended, Audrey asked, "Has she heard from Tarian?"

"Yes, my sister has already spoken with her. She's with Tarian, and he has arranged things with the Guardians."

"Okay what's the plan?"

"We are to meet in Manaus as expected. No contact is to be made until we see them in person. Apparently, our faces are plastered all over the city."

Audrey jerked in the passenger seat. "This is bad. We'll be recognized."

"Not necessarily. Yes, the city is as modern as any inside the Entente, but the majority of the continent isn't. The country invested in agriculture rather than electronics, so people are fed but without the technological advancements of the Entente. Just as the Guardians have maintained law and order in the Entente via the government, Lautaro's Maldito Ministry Soldiers have done the same, only more viciously and with widespread corruption. Most of the rural South American people simply stay away from the few thriving cities that are left," Hu said.

"So, we'll be fine until we get to Manaus?"

"Definitely. No one around here will pay attention to us. The people of the countryside live simple, hard working lives, never complaining even when droughts or disease cause loss of life and suffering. Those that speak out either disappear or show up at their family's doorstep as a brutalized body puzzle," Hu explained.

"But once in Manaus, if surveillance is anything like the Entente's we'll be caught." Audrey's shoulders slumped as she turned away from him and gazed at the Atlantic Ocean whizzing by her passenger side window.

"Don't worry, Timber Wolf." He continued to speak to the back of her head. "Remember I have the power of illusion."

She whipped around. "The forest!"

His smile broadened, and a soft laugh left his lips. "You remember."

"Of course, I do. You bit me."

"Let's not focus on the negative. It was fun."

Fun? It was scary and seductive, but not fun. "Just tell me how it's going to save our lives?"

"Basically, I can glamour us until we're deep inside the

castle. All illusions die in Lautaro's presence."

"Will Jun glamour Tarian?"

"No, she has no such abilities, but I'm sure they'll find another way to disguise themselves."

"What about your existing as a tiger? Is that an illusion or real?" She needed to know all the rules of this deadly game.

"No, that is a part of me. I'm the tiger and the man," he purred.

Forty-four hours of continuous driving and they were finally half way to the city. The eight-hour shifts had them ahead of schedule, but the monotony set in. Audrey awoke to find Hu pulling the Plymouth into an old-fashioned diner.

"Where are we?" she said in a groggy rumble, eyes still heavy with sleep.

"Fred's."

"Fred's?"

"Yes, it's an old favorite of mine. The original owner, Fred, was from Las Vegas. Remember Vegas?" There was a longing in his voice as his eyes softened.

"Of course." She was actually becoming comfortable around him. He'd been respectable and decent during the long journey. They shared a fondness for the eighties and joked about big hair and rubber bracelets. They argued about past politicians and legalizing drugs. She felt guilty for enjoying the company of a man who had lived more than twenty years, but it was nice.

"Well, Fred ran into trouble with taxes back in the eighties and came here, opened this diner, and it's been handed down generation to generation." He held the rickety screen door for her to walk through. The smell of greasy fries and hamburgers filled the air.

She followed him to a small booth in the back by a window.

He waited for her to sit first.

She halted mid-step, ran her eyes up and down him searching for his ulterior motive but found none, plus she was far too exhausted and hungry to put up a fight. The sound of sizzling beef patties and the smell of buttered buns lightened her mood.

"Hungry?" He swatted at the flies buzzing around the table.

"Famished. This smells like heaven. I'm sick of bananas and nacho chips."

"Amen." He laughed.

She smiled back. "You can't possibly find this food enticing?"

"Do you like chocolate?" he asked.

"Yes."

"Well, food is like candy or, in the case of healthy food, like a supplemental vitamin. I don't necessarily need it, but I enjoy it. I especially enjoy the aroma," he paused to sniff the air, "more than the taste. Smell is a powerful aphrodisiac."

And there it is. The predatory grin and growling purr reminding her of the tiger that lay beneath his honey skin and high cheekbones.

Thankfully, the waitress came by before the awkward silence lengthened. The black-haired woman was a veteran, and took their order the old fashioned way. Pulling a pencil from her thick hair bun, she wrote two sodas, one cheeseburger with bacon, and one hamburger with veggies, both with fries. She scurried away to return shortly with fizzing caramel colored pop.

"You look familiar, meu lindo," the waitress said.

Audrey stiffened, but Hu remained relaxed. "I'm sure I do. I stop in here about twice a year."

"Maybe. We don't get many Asians around here. You from the city?"

"Yes." He nodded.

"Only thing that keeps us in business is the city goers travelin' back and forth. Jesus knows the folks round here can't afford nothin'." The waitress hurried away to tend to another customer. She spoke both English and Portuguese but neither one properly.

"You said our faces wouldn't reach the countryside," Audrey whispered.

"Calm down, I think she's mistaken me for someone else, but she may have also recognized me from the past. She's been a waitress here for many years."

"Okay." She leaned back in the booth and tried to relax. She felt Hu's eyes on her, and she knew he meant no harm. He was simply concerned for her. She'd been jumpy and agitated from the beginning of their drive. She struck up a conversation to stop the awkwardness and his uneasy staring. "How did you get turned in 1965?"

"Ah, so you want to know about me." One side of his mouth curled up mischievously.

She rolled her eyes and he laughed.

The ink-haired waitress flung their two plates of food onto the table. A few fries zipped to the corner and the flies swarmed.

"My mom was not a typical Chinese lady. She was born and raised in an extremely traditional Chinese family in San Diego, but she was a free spirit. She married an Australian archeologist, my father, who was fascinated by the mythology surrounding the ancient Chinese dynasties. In 1965 my sister and I were twenty-five years old, and we were on an expedition with them. We discovered several bronze implements and a tomb. It was evidence that proved the Xia dynasty was real and not myth. And that's when it all happened." He paused long enough to eat the last two bites of his cheeseburger and smash the fly that threatened to land on his food.

"What happened?" Audrey asked, not letting him swallow his last bite.

"It was a feeling I can't explain, but me, my sister, and my mom all felt it. Not my dad, he didn't have Xia blood in his veins. When we touched the pieces that dated back to our ancestors something awoke inside of us."

"A curse?"

"Yes. Three months later my dad drove our car off a cliff. He'd lost his mind like he wanted to kill us all. He was the only one that died, the rest of us walked away without a scratch. Of course, that was when we knew we were cursed. We put two and two together, and it led us to the dig. Months of research and visits to Chinese Wu, spirit mediums, the shaman," he said, gesturing with his hands.

"I understand." Audrey assured him so he'd stop moving his hands in circles.

"When we touched the ancient relics of our past ancestors, we were punished for forgetting about them. The Xia people are legend, mythological, and forgotten. When we didn't die in that crash, we went into hiding. My mother was sick with worry. She didn't know what was going on, but her gut told her it wasn't good. She never went back home. To her family we'd died in that fiery crash. An unsolved mystery since the only dental remains were of my father. We lived with a Wu for five years trying to understand what had happened to us, learning the legends of the preta, finding out that our survival meant feeding off of others' energy through blood or worse. Sis and I rebelled. We ran off and went crazy for a while. Sowed our wild oats I guess you could say. Got caught up in running drugs in Miami in the eighties, which led us to the Los Angeles drug market where we soon discovered there were more creatures like us. We stayed in LA, and over time the Xia community grew to what it is today."

Audrey hadn't realized that she hadn't taken her eyes off of his. His story had entranced her.

"That's it," Hu said. "That's the story of me."

Realizing she still stared, she shifted her eyes to the waitress.

"You've seen other creatures, right?" he asked.

"Yes, of course." She shook her head trying to remove the sense of awe he'd evoked. Feeling the need to explain her strange behavior she added, "I love to hear the stories of the creatures." Her eyes fell to the table as her hands fiddled with the last French fry on her plate.

"What?" he asked.

"Nothing."

"No, you are thinking about something."

"It's nothing really."

"Please, tell me." His yellow eyes opened wide with sincerity.

He'd shared his past with her. She owed him. "Okay. I've always wanted to collect all the creature stories. I know each species has their own chronicle, but this would have them all in one place, in one catalog."

"That's a great idea."

She smiled feeling both silly and appreciated.

"It'd be a very big book."

She laughed. "But I'd bet we all have a lot in common,

more than we'd like to admit."

"Do you think a preta and a Guardian have ever had sex?" Hu said with a devilish sparkle in his eyes.

All the happiness she'd managed to muster flew out of her like a popped balloon. She scooted out of the booth. "Let's go!"

"What? I was only curious is all." His grin stretched from ear to ear.

THIRTY-FOUR

Teresa jolted awake sucking in the night air. She hadn't wanted to fall asleep, too much was at stake. But her body's need for rest had won, and she'd slept for three hours straight. Wolfgang sprawled across her lap. His large head jerked up and tilted, pink tongue flopping. Teresa laughed at his incredible ugly-cuteness.

"Get off," she said, but she scratched behind his ears. He wasn't going anywhere. Wiggling her legs free from his dead weight, she rose to her feet, and walked to the window. "Still there." She sighed. The armed Entente Military guards lined the perimeter of Ana-Clara's little house. Their presence calmed and unsettled her.

She went immediately to check on the Sleepers. She gingerly opened the door to the woman's room. Lauren remained snugly tucked into her bed. Relieved, Teresa shut the door. David had not awoken yet so she didn't bother checking on him, but Jonathan had woken up earlier that day. She found him crumpled over his walker.

"Jonathan! I told you not to get out of bed." Teresa rushed to his side. As she wormed her small body under his large arms Wolfgang held the walker in place. She smiled and winked at her furry helper.

"I know, but I called for you, and you didn't answer," he said.

"I'm sorry. I fell asleep. Where's Ana-Clara?"

"I don't know. Neither of you came to help me."

Teresa furrowed her brow as worrying tingles spread through her stomach, but she swallowed her feelings. "It's okay. What do you need?"

He smiled. "I have to use the bathroom."

She smiled back. The littlest things delighted the Sleepers once they awoke. "Then we better hurry." Teresa guided Jonathan to the bathroom, then back to his bed where he fell with a hard wallop onto the pillow. "Don't worry, it gets easier."

"If you say so." He looked as if he'd just run the Boston marathon.

"You've been asleep for a long time," she said, but Jonathan's eyes had already fluttered shut. She stuck the intravenous line into his port and added two more units of recovery medication. Soon he'd be strong enough to help her with the others. It was a plus when a Sleeper healed quickly and could provide an extra set of hands.

She left his room, put her hands on her hips, and looked at

Wolfgang. "Where's Ana-Clara?"

Wolfgang barked then sat looking at her, dumbfounded.

"Well, a lot of help you are."

She inspected the narrow halls of the small cottage but never found Ana-Clara. Knowing it was a bad idea, but doing it anyway, she shut off the alarm and opened the back door. She crept around the backyard sneaking behind bushes but saw nothing except the patrolling guards. She tiptoed around the grounds hugging the edge of the exterior walls, casting her glances deep into the treed forest but still found no Ana-Clara.

"Hey, you!" a guard called out, weapon drawn in her direction.

"It's me, Teresa. Sorry, just looking for some herbs." Her shaky voice gave her fear away.

"Is everything alright inside? Do you want me to come in?" the guard offered in a softer tone lowering his weapon.

"No, thank you." She scampered on the balls of her bare feet up the front porch, but the door was locked. She smiled a guilty grin. "Oh, yeah, I left from the back door."

"I'll walk you." He stood at attention waiting for her to descend the front porch stairs.

She didn't move quickly enough for him. He cleared his throat and scowled at her with eyes as fierce as an eagle's. She soon found her footing and pranced around to the back and slipped into the house. Like a frightened child, she returned to the couch she'd been sleeping on, beckoned for Wolfgang to join her then drew a throw blanket over their heads. Her head felt heavy as sleep seeped back under her eyelids then she heard the clink of a teacup on a porcelain saucer. She whipped off the throw and turned to face the brightly colored, sundial kitchen table.

"Hello, dear," Ana-Clara said sipping tea with Piper.

"Piper!" Teresa gasped, she leapt from the sofa and skipped over to Piper throwing her arms around her. Then she turned a sour face toward Ana-Clara. "You had me scared to death!"

"I'm sorry, sweetie. Piper brought you a surprise." Ana-Clara's eyes bloomed like lilacs.

Seeing the twinkle of lavender, Teresa took a double take at her mentor until she heard footsteps come around the corner.

"Patrick!" Teresa's heart sank to the bottom of her gut then jumped high into her throat in a dizzying jumble of emotions. She ran to him, jumped into his embrace, and planted her lips onto his without hesitation or reserve.

Ana-Clara cleared her throat after several seconds, but the kissing continued. She gave up. "Ah, young love."

Patrick placed Teresa back on her feet, and she gathered herself together. "What's going on? How's my brother and Audrey?"

"They're in Manaus, South America," Patrick said.

"What? How?" Teresa asked, shaking her head in disbelief. "They went through that waterway thing, didn't they?"

"Yes, but not by choice. Tarian and Jun are hiding in

Manaus awaiting Audrey and Hu's arrival. For the past five days, Margaret and the High Council have made several attempts to get inside Manaus to meet with a man named Lautaro who is holding Benjamin. He's a grand sorcerer with a vast maldito army. The mortals think he's some sort of religious king. It's been unsuccessful," Patrick said then sighed heavily.

"What are they going to do?" Teresa's heart that just beat with glee stilled with worry for her brother's safety.

Piper twitched in her seat, tapped her toes, and blurted, "Me, it's up to me. I'm going to travel into Manaus with a syringe of Death Serum." Her lavender eyes flew open wide as her face stretched out with anxiety. "But I'm not sure I can do it without detection, and if I fail, I can get everyone killed. It took me three tries to get here, and Manaus is a lot farther away." Piper rocked in her chair; face horror struck as she held a jittering teacup in her unstable hand.

Watching the brown liquid flirt dangerously with the edge of the cup, Teresa sighed and sank into Patrick.

"I arrived here successfully for the first time two days ago," said Piper.

"What? I didn't see you." Teresa felt tricked.

"I know. You were tending to the Sleepers. I scared Ana-Clara half to death. She almost knocked me out with an iron pan. Then yesterday, for the first time in many years, I took someone with me, your dad." Piper's rocking paused for Teresa's reaction.

"Where's my dad?" Teresa demanded.

"Home now."

Piper's response left Teresa's questions unanswered. For clarity, she turned to Patrick.

"Joe visited the Cavern System," he said.

Teresa's shoulders sagged. All he'd done was create more questions. "Why would he go there in a time like this?"

Patrick didn't speak at first. Instead he looked deep into her eyes. She felt as if he was seeing her as a woman for the first time and not just as a silly teenager. She turned seventeen today, but with everything going on only her mother had wished her a happy birthday hours ago.

"I don't know. It was a High Council direct order," Patrick finally said.

"Okay." She didn't have much knowledge about the vast Cavern System that had gouged into the Earth after the great meteor showers. Things down there were top secret. She remembered months ago when the Prevallers first attacked, the Guardians top priority had been the protection of the tunnel of caves.

A unique tremor ran up Vixy's spine as she sat perched in her makeshift tree nest above Ana-Clara's cottage. She smiled and knew what it meant—a Lavender Witch had broken the plane. She'd started to doubt herself, but she knew the immortal kid knew another Lavender Witch, and she also knew the Guardian Chancellor woman was hiding something, and both of them had disappeared without a trace.

Vixy stood and stretched her tight legs. "It's time for us to meet."

Two Entente military guards below heard the leaves rustle. They aimed their weapons upwards at the tree but saw nothing but twigs, mud, and leaves bunched together between the branches.

"Go check that out," one guard ordered to another.

Without a sound, Vixy appeared behind the wall that separated the kitchen from the hall leading to the multiple bedrooms.

Piper's perpetual movement stilled, and her eyes darted to Ana-Clara in question.

Patrick turned to look at Teresa who looked at Piper. The fine hairs on Piper's arm stood up.

Wolfgang growled.

Ana-Clara said, her voice calm and sweet, "Show yourself, witch!"

Vixy strolled around the corner, her boot heels clunking on the wooden floor. She stood with her feet wide apart, hands on hips like a cowboy in an old western. But her blue ripped leggings, short thin figure, and chin length, angled, black hair were not menacing. Even so, everyone knew she could be deadly.

Piper slid her chair away from the table and rose to her feet, her eyes beaming a straight line at Vixy's matching lavender irises. "Why are you here?"

"Gee, I don't know, maybe because your friends came snooping around and now they've gone missing along with my Bar District contacts. My group no longer has a safe haven. We have nowhere to meet!" Vixy stomped her foot at Wolfgang who kept growling at her. "You better shut him up before I lose my temper."

"It's okay Wolfgang. Place," Teresa said, and Wolfgang reluctantly lay down on his bed, never taking his gaze off of the intruding witch.

"Are you here to help?" Patrick asked.

"That depends. I need to know what's going on."

"I need to deliver a very valuable weapon to Manaus without detection," Piper said.

"Ha!"

Teresa couldn't tell if the girl was impressed or peeved by Piper's suggestion.

"I know about your insurgency. We can work together," Piper said.

"Why would I risk that?"

"Do you want a bloodthirsty immortal running around your country?"

"Plenty of horrible creatures run around my country already. Hell, a horrible creature runs my country, and your High Council has never seemed to care."

"I'm sorry about that, but maybe we can now work together. The quicker Piper gets to Manaus the sooner Hu and Jun return to their bar," Patrick said.

Vixy said nothing.

"Then it's possible to pass through the border undetected? The way we travel that is?" Piper asked.

Vixy remained silent. She lifted her nose into the air, closed her eyes, and frowned. After a long pause, she dropped her head back down. "It just may work."

Piper's jitters returned and she tapped her toes again. "Really!"

For as twitchy and light as Piper was, Vixy was equally as calm and dark.

"You're half immortal, right?" Vixy asked.

"Yes," Piper said.

"You know if they catch you they'll kill you. They'll find a way and it will be gruesome."

"Who?" Piper asked.

"The Lavender Witches. All mixed bloods are hunted." Vixy shifted her hips.

"Are you mixed? Is that why you fight against them?" Piper asked.

"No, I'm pure but I fight for my friend who isn't … wasn't. They killed her so viciously I was sick for days. Then I ran away and joined the insurgency. We have a powerful group, and we were making great progress but something is stirring. Something big. The Ministry Malditos and Lavender Witches have been seen negotiating on several occasions, which is extremely unusual, and now they have your mutant Guardian."

"Exactly. We have the only thing that can kill him, and I need to get it to Manaus. Can you take me there?" Piper asked.

"Yes, but we'll have to travel separately. I'm traceable via vading but you won't be because no one knows you exist."

"Vading?" Piper asked.

"Yeah, disappearing and reappearing someplace else. That's what it's called," Vixy said.

"Oh." Piper smiled. "I like that, vading. Vaaa-dinng." She spoke the word slowly, rolling it around on her tongue.

Vixy narrowed her eyes at Piper's strangeness then reached into her pocket and pulled out a worn, dirty square of fabric. "Here." Her hand shot out to Piper. "Carry this! I have a feeling you might get lost without it."

"Thank you." Piper took the fabric. She rubbed it between her fingers and on her pale pink cheek. It was thick and lush.

"Give me until," she looked at the clock that just struck midnight, "noon LA time, then vade where that fabric leads you. I'll take Rain's Gate and meet you."

"What if I get there and you're not there?"

"People are already there."

"Okay." Piper's feet still tapped, and her torso jerked side to side. She managed to stop her feet, but her fingers started to wiggle. Her brows squeezed together, and she looked entirely petrified.

Vixy smiled at her and shook her head. "Hey, you need to toughen up. You're a powerful Lavender Witch. Start acting like it."

Teresa blinked, and Vixy was gone.

Piper stopped moving. Her face stuck with concern.

Teresa's stomach twisted with angst. She drew Patrick closer to her and buried her face in his chest.

He kissed the top of her head and whispered, "Happy birthday, sweetie!"

She didn't look up. She couldn't because the tears would ruin his perfect words. Having his chest to protect her entirety and his touch to warm her heart was just the birthday present she'd wished for.

THIRTY-FIVE

MANAUS

The old Plymouth Belvedere Pursuit's engine puttered, hissed, and clunked from the long journey and blazing sun. The steering wheel bumped and jerked in Audrey's hands. She glanced at the watch strapped around her wrist to measure the amount of the time she had left in this vehicle. The watch, like the car, was manufactured from old technology, and she longed for the Egg. She laughed at the memories of that modern-day miracle. So many times she'd thrown it across the room, furious at its inabilities, and now she drove a car with foot pedals that ran on gasoline, using a paper map, and telling time by a hand watch. *Oh my goodness!*

"What's so funny?" Hu roused from a five-hour nap.

"Nothing, I've just lost my wits having to deal with all this old equipment, and I think this car is going to die soon."

"Nonsense, it's been running for as long as I have," Hu said not bothering to raise the passenger seat from its recline. He looked as if he was lounging on a beach-chair in the Caribbean without a care in the world.

"That's my point. I'm glad you're up, sort of." She glanced at his relaxed position and smirked. "We're getting close to the trackers you warned about. That is, if we can trust the map and watch."

"You can trust them better than any mobile. I guarantee it."

"You sound like Joe."

"I knew he was a smart guy." Hu winked.

"I think I turn here," she half said and half asked.

He lifted his head just enough to see over the dashboard. "Yes, and the gas pedal is the one on the right by the way."

"Funny." She mouthed a fake obnoxious laugh. "I've been driving top speed while you've been snoring away."

"Uh huh," he mumbled. "I don't snore."

Her right hand shot out from the wheel and struck him hard in the chest.

"Ouch!"

"I'm hot, filthy, and pissed off. Get up and navigate."

"I love it when you're angry." A Cheshire grin slid across his angular face as he cranked the passenger seat to its upright position.

Her skin shined with angry heat causing Hu's smile to widen even farther.

They drove another hour and pulled into a deep cave where they left the car after wiping its entire interior and exterior with a malodorous liquid. They changed into caped costumes perfect for hiding the weapon-filled vest underneath. Audrey donned an abstract mask depicting sunken eyes with crimson tears and sharp cheekbones. Hu's mask was shaped and formed in the mold of a predatory animal with red eyes and silver white fangs. The city's El Día de los Muertos celebration was underway. Cloaked and disguised as the dead, they walked through the gilded gates of Manaus.

Audrey had never traveled to this city, but she suspected the lavish towering gate with its leaves of gold was a recent addition. A domineering symbol meant to imprint the ultimate power of Lautaro upon all that passed below its iron greatness. To the mortals he was a Holy Man descended from the Monarchs of Portugal, and the tentacles of his ministry sprawled from coast to coast, twisting through the Amazon and over the deserts touching all parts of the continent. He was also the President of the Federative Republic of Brazil. In the creature world of the Amazonas, he was the Supreme Sorcerer. Either way, his influence and wrath were legendary to the southern people.

They crossed over from beat-up gravel roads to smooth black paved boulevards. As they walked deeper into the city, its wealth became more obvious with the appearance of lofty skyscrapers and pedestrians dressed in silk and ruby-encrusted costumes. Bright yellow sporty vehicles whizzed by fluttering Audrey's long, hooded satin cape. For those whose workday hadn't finished, they hustled across the street from building to building in polished shoes and designer suits. Tattered beggars could be found shuffling or squatting among the festive costumes and fancy people.

A beggar woman partaking in the Día de los Muertos reverie had painted her face, or at least Audrey hoped it was paint, because the woman had no face at all. Audrey jumped at the unsettling effect, side-stepped the woman's grasp and sped up. But she couldn't shake the haunting sensation.

"Are we close yet?"

"Yes, four blocks," Hu said.

The street inhabited half vagabond and half high-class. The clinking sound of coins dropping into cans rang through the air. The generosity of the wealthier struck Audrey, but so did the nonchalance on both sides, as if asking for handouts wasn't frowned upon. Blank faces dropping unwanted coins. As she took it all in, her steps slowed and soon she barely moved. People had to tread around her.

A pinch of her hip gave her a start.

"You're causing a scene and drawing attention to us. Walk faster." Hu put his arm around her waist and nudged her forward. "Remember, surveillance is everywhere."

She picked up her pace but remained focused on her environment, scanning and absorbing this new world that threatened her Guardians. She soon fell into unison step with Hu as he kept an uncomfortable hold on her. As much as she ached to move away from him, she noticed other couples in costume arm in arm. She glanced up at Hu, and he smiled down at her, his eyes communicating a silent warning.

Narrow one-way roads fingered out from the main street, and as she walked past, she looked down each one. She saw residences, little shops, general stores, and lots of cafes and restaurants. In most aspects, it was a city like any other.

Hu turned down one of the side streets. "It's this one, look for number fourteen forty."

Audrey slid out from his arm's reach.

He feigned a sad face, but arrogance glinted red in his butterscotch eyes.

She turned away, a sliver of guilt for her abruptness crept into her conscience. It didn't seem necessary to keep up appearances any longer. The last thing she needed was for Tarian to see them arm in arm. She had enough to deal with without an eager preta battling a jealous Awakened Hunter.

She searched for fourteen forty, anxious to get on with the mission. She finally spotted the numbers above four little stone steps and a plain wooden door. She knocked twice, waited, then knocked five times then waited, and finally rang the doorbell.

This was the code Hu had used last time he'd been there. He had warned Audrey that it had been a very long time ago and to be prepared to be shot at in case the code had changed. Hu put the old, intricately designed, bronze key in the lock and turned. They withdrew their masks and entered slowly. The people in the house hesitated to show themselves until finally Tarian burst from his hiding spot to lift Audrey into his arms. He kissed her lips then her neck and inhaled the fragrance of her skin and hair.

Jun came out to greet her brother in an unceremonious fist pump. "So, where'd it dump you guys?"

"Cave of Hands." Hu grunted.

"Jeez, long drive. No wonder it took ya so long."

"Yeah." He nodded. "I'm thirsty."

"You're in luck." Jun walked her brother up the stairs and into the kitchen. She opened the fridge and pulled out two bottles of garnet liquid. "Hooked us up good." She removed the seals of the bottles swigged one and handed the other to Hu. "Tastes like a fresh sacrifice."

Hu took the bottle, portentously poured it into a glass and drank like he attended a social cocktail hour.

"What did Ramiro feed ya?" Jun asked.

"All he had was raw Sparrow." Hu crinkled his face in disagreement.

Jun made gagging sounds.

"But I did stop at Fred's."

"Bro, I'll never understand your love for the human's hamburgers."

"You can take the human out of the preta, but you can't take the preta out of the hamburger." Hu laughed.

"You're an idiot," Jun said laughing along.

Audrey peered into the refrigerator and saw rows and rows of red bottles. "Anything in here for me to drink?"

"Not in this fridge," Jun said with a wicked grin.

Tarian escorted her to the other side of the long granite island countertop. He opened another refrigerator door. "This is ours."

She saw fresh squeezed orange juice, cola cans, breads, meats, cheeses. She smiled wide. She hadn't had a good meal since the hamburger joint two days ago.

"Sit, I'll make you something," Tarian said.

She plopped down on a stool, pulled up to the bar counter, and watched as Tarian prepared her a nice plate of cheeses and charcuterie. He poured her a glass of soda. He placed it in front of her and glided onto the stool next to her.

"Thanks." She stuffed her face and felt joy return to her hollow stomach.

"I get it. Jun and I were starving too."

"Where were you guys, and how long have you been here? And have you contacted Margaret?" Audrey's questions jumped from her lips.

"We got flushed to some place called Angel Falls. It would've taken us a lot longer to get down its massive cliff-side except Jun had already been there and knew the short cut. We went to Jun's liaison, Felipe. He fed us, gave us one blessed sword, and some antiquated technologies. When we contacted home, the only orders we got were to find a safe house in Manaus and wait for further instructions. Jun's friend sent us here. He said we'd get our instructions once we were inside this house. So far nothing and we've been here two days."

"Just waiting?"

"Yep! Bored out of my mind. We were told by the house not to use any devices, not to try to contact anyone and to just wait," Tarian said.

"The *house* told you this," Audrey said.

"Yep, I haven't seen one person since I got here. But every day there's new fresh food and drinks and notes on the board. I have no idea how they appear on that, over there." He pointed to the four-by-six-foot white board with blue lettering that said, *Your friends will be here today. They will knock twice, wait, knock five times, wait, ring the doorbell, then use their key to enter. No code, shoot on site!*

Audrey strolled over to the board to get a closer look.

"Don't touch it. The blue writing smears and goes away with only the slightest touch." Tarian's eyes widened with this mysterious information.

Audrey giggled, "It's a dry erase board."

"What's that?"

Jun snickered from the other side of the kitchen.

Audrey glanced at her then back at Tarian.

Tarian glared at Jun. "So, you were messing with me!"

Jun burst into a full laugh, side bend and all. "He was so damn fascinated by it, I had to." She couldn't stop her outbursts. "Idiot!"

"I'd never seen such a thing. Everything back home is on screens. You talk and words appear, you swipe and things happen."

"He was talking to it," Jun spurt out the words as she doubled over in glee.

Tarian scowled.

Audrey nearly gagged trying to contain her guffaws. "It's okay. It's just that there isn't anything special about the board itself. It's just really old and spell bound."

"Everything is old around here." Tarian crossed his arms.

"Except you," Hu said laughing along with his sister.

"Have your laughs. Ha ha ha. Being old isn't something to brag about." Tarian walked away to sit on the couch.

"The city isn't old. I saw plenty of modern vehicles and people walking with the latest mobiles. I even saw a kid with a Hoverboard Max800." Audrey plunked down next to him.

"It's been years since I've done business here, but it's a mix of the old and new worlds," Hu said.

"Pre- and Post-Entente War," Jun added.

"Their advancements were stolen from us, weren't they?" Tarian asked.

"Not really, South America wasn't as damaged by the war as the rest of the world. They've always had universities, but yes, the maldito's sent spies through Rain's Gate. It's just all the knowledge and control remains with the government, hence with the maldito. Free enterprise died with the war. When businesses couldn't trade with North America and the Wastelands across the oceans were all but destroyed, they looked to the government to fill the gap in their wages, and it did. But now the people are beholden to their corrupt governments, and since Lautaro's control snakes everywhere, the people are ruled by him," Hu explained.

"All the nations of the South are in bed with Lautaro," Jun added.

"And the person who writes the notes?" Audrey asked.

Jun shrugged her shoulders.

"Is this how it always happens?" Audrey turned to Hu for answers.

Hu strolled over. "I've used this house four times, and every time has been a different experience." Hu placed his hand gently on Audrey's shoulder.

Tarian glared at him and the amicable atmosphere evaporated.

"So we just wait?" Audrey placed Hu's hand on Tarian's shoulder and smirked at the two men.

"Mom is in touch with your Guardians and will contact us soon with instructions," Jun said.

"You've been here two days and haven't heard from her?" Hu asked.

Jun's eyes fell to the floor, and she shook her head.

Another knock on the door silenced the foursome, but the pattern was different. Tarian ran to the board. It read: *Three knocks pause, followed by four knocks, then answer the door.*

Jun answered the door while the others stood with weapons drawn.

Vixy waltzed through the entrance. "Hello guys," she said

with a flick of her head.

"What are you doing here?" Audrey asked.

"Meeting Piper," she said.

"What?" Audrey asked.

"No!" Tarian said.

"Thank you, I believe, are the words you're looking for. I shouldn't be helping you guys at all. Some appreciation would be nice." She wagged her finger in Audrey and Tarian's face. "You sure as hell haven't helped our cause, but these two, I happen to need." She nodded at Hu and Jun.

"So why are ya here?" Jun rolled her eyes at the little woman in ripped, stockings.

"I started keeping an eye on Ana-Clara's house to see what you all were up to, and Tarian made me curious about his friend he said had eyes like me. I know all the Lavender Witches and I'd never heard about this Piper before."

"If Piper comes here she'll be tracked and killed," Tarian said.

"No, she won't. The maldito think they've tagged all of us. Piper can vade here and no one will be the wiser."

"Vade?" Tarian asked.

"Travel through space and time," Vixy said annoyed.

"She can't," Audrey said. "She's out of practice. We tried back home, and she failed. She told me she needs some sort of artifact from the place in order to get to it."

"Which is why I gave her my cloth." Vixy strutted over to

the floor length curtain and lifted it up to reveal a square cut out of the hem.

"How'd you know we'd be here?" Audrey asked.

Hu glanced at Vixy.

She recoiled looking embarrassed as she shifted her gaze from person to person. At last, she confessed, "This house is my safe house. I told Hu and Jun about it a long time ago, when I needed help getting rid of someone. I knew it was perfect for this mission."

"Your house or the insurgency's house?" Audrey asked.

"Mine. The insurgency doesn't know about this place."

"Have you been the one writing on the board?" Tarian asked.

"It's a seeing spell," Vixy answered.

"What about the food?" Tarian asked.

She didn't answer. In fact, she looked puzzled.

Audrey waltzed over to Vixy, eyeing her sideways. "Why do you have this house so close to Lautaro?"

"My boyfriend. He's a human Castle Guard. He doesn't want to be a part of Lautaro's Maldito Ministry, but if he leaves, he knows they'll kill his family. He's kind, and he's probably the one who's been bringing the food. We planned to fake his death when the insurgency defeated the Lavender Witches, but then Lautaro and the malditos helped them and set us back." She snorted and grinned but the false smirk faded and revealed her true sadness. "Years of planning, gone!"

"Can this guard … your boyfriend … help us?" Audrey hated to ask this of her, but she had to think of her own family and nation.

"No!"

Audrey and Vixy glowered at one another, and Audrey felt the force of her will. Audrey finally said, "Fine! When will Piper be here?"

Vixy pointed to the whiteboard. *Fifteen minutes.*

When Piper appeared, her hair tangled in a chaotic mess of purple smudges and her legs wobbled. She didn't look anything like she did in the Guardian Village library where she flip-flopped in and out of sight without a strand of purple golden hair out of place. She grabbed her stomach, reached for the nearest chair, and collapsed.

"Are you okay?" Audrey rushed over to her.

"Yeah! A little dizzy. Can I have some water?"

"Of course." Hu brought her a glass of water.

She sipped it a few times then smiled. "I did it. I did it!" She pulled the needle filled with Death Serum out of her shoulder bag. "Look! I did it."

"You're a genius." Tarian took the needle and placed it in a secure holder inside his belt.

"Has Margaret given you instructions?" Audrey asked Piper.

"She and the High Council have been working on negotiations of some sort. I told Margaret I could get the Death

Serum to you. She told me no. Told me it was too dangerous. But then she and High Councilor Elizabeth met with me and said they had no way to get into the city. Lautaro won't meet with them, and they fear he's planning something horrible with Benjamin. Then they gave me permission to come here." Piper got to her feet steadily. Faded pink patches emerged on her pale skin as her energy returned.

"Now, we have to get into the castle undetected," Audrey said.

"I can glam us," Hu said.

"All of us?" Audrey asked.

"Yes, as long as we stay close together, and until we reach Lautaro."

"It will have to do," Tarian said.

The turn of a lock in the door echoed up the stairs and startled all of them. The white board went blank. Five weapons whipped out and Piper stood up ready to cast her power. But a young girl carrying a sack twice her size ventured up the staircase.

"Put down your weapons," Vixy yelled. "Lola, what are you doing here?"

"Dante sent me. He gave me these." Lola opened the bag and dumped its contents on the dining table: olive guard uniforms, half a dozen Sedation Serum filled syringes, modern communicators, one sheathed blessed blade sword, and one pearl white gun.

Tarian picked up the sword and unsheathed it then looked

at Jun with a smile. "Now we have two."

Jun nodded.

"We brought stakes," Hu added, then he gently picked up the gorgeous gun. "A blessed gun." Hu stroked the weapon as if it was a beautiful woman. "Where'd you get this?" he asked Lola in an unfriendly tone.

"I … I … didn't. I swear. Dante handed me the bag, and I ran straight here," Lola stuttered in fear.

Hu caressed the pearl finish one last time, flipped it then handed it grip side to Audrey.

"Okay," Tarian said, his voice flat with impatience. He picked up one of the communicators and asked the young girl, who behaved far older than she appeared, "Are these traceable?"

"No."

Audrey surveyed the goods. "Did all of this stuff come from inside the castle?"

"I think so." Lola walked over to the fridge and pulled out a rare ribeye steak. She smiled devilishly and bit into it.

"You stocked the fridge?" Vixy's question sounded more like a revelation.

"On Dante's orders," she defended.

Vixy paced.

"So you told your boyfriend about us. Who else have you told?" Audrey asked.

"I told him only because I wanted him to know someone would be in this house so he wouldn't kill you."

Hu strolled over and placed a brotherly arm around Vixy without flirtation. Audrey noted that he'd been making occasional sincere gestures like this for the last few days. It was getting more difficult to despise him.

"Dante is smart, and he knows you too well for you to lie to him. I will make sure he's safe," Hu said.

"You can't protect him in there. Lautaro is too powerful." Vixy's confident voice shook with nerves.

"He's only given us supplies, nothing more," Jun added.

"He gave me this, too, and he said to burn it after you read it." Lola pulled a wadded-up piece of paper out of her pocket and handed it to Vixy.

The note said: *The immortal beast is being held in cell thirteen underground. It is the most difficult cell to reach, as there is only one way in or out. Expect several guards.*

Audrey turned quickly in Hu's direction. "Can you make an illusion to hide Tarian from the guards?"

"Of course," Hu said.

"Your communicator should have a map of the castle on it." Vixy grabbed it and searched its functions.

"I've looked, and I can't find one," Tarian said.

"Yeah, these are several models old. Probably the only way he could get ones that couldn't be traced. But I have a map." Vixy left the kitchen then returned with a paper map. She laid it on the table. "We'll have to do this the old fashioned way. This is the underground cell." She pointed on the map. "And this is where we enter." She pointed to a door several yards away and two floors higher than the cells.

"That's a long way to walk undetected," Tarian said gritting his teeth.

"The guards always travel in threes, so you, Tarian, and Hu will go to kill Benjamin, while Jun, Piper, and I keep watch at the door. When the target is eliminated, use the communicator to contact Jun and get the hell out of there," Vixy said.

Audrey gauged Vixy's leadership skills, surveying the map for a better plan but found none. "Can you get us fast transport out of the city? We're going to be hunted like rabbits."

"I won't involve any of my people. This is not their fight."

Audrey shut her eyes to think.

"I know of a vehicle." Lola's face had a layer of dirt and dust on it, and her clothes were tattered at the knees and elbows like the beggars on the street. "I can drive, too." She stood tall but looked young.

"No!" Vixy barked. "No." Her voice cracked.

"If she gets me the vehicle starter I can use it to vade straight to it," Piper said.

"Great, problem solved," Jun said.

"Except, I've never driven before," Piper added.

"Are you shitting me?" Vixy threw her arms up and paced. "Fine. Lola, you bring her the key. Once you and Piper are at the car, you drive." Vixy turned menacingly toward Piper. "You had better protect this girl with your life or so help me Goddess!"

Piper nodded rapidly.

"Let's do this!" Hu said.

Audrey glanced out the window. "Once the sun sets."

THIRTY-SIX

ARE YOU TWELVE

Darkness fell over Manaus, and everyone but Lola and Piper had left the safe house. Lola helped herself to a giant bowl of raw tuna ceviche. While she ate, Piper plucked a single strand of her straight honey brown hair and shoved it into her pocket alongside the five other strands of hair she'd secretly retrieved earlier. She'd have to keep Lola's separate from Audrey's since they were similar in color, texture, and length.

Lola's hand flung up to the back of her head. She scratched at the place that was now missing a single strand. She swung her body around to face Piper. "Why'd you do that?"

Piper jumped back. Lola was the first to feel the tiny tug.

"Why'd you do that?" Lola asked again, louder.

"So, I can find you if I need to."

"Oh." Lola scrunched her brows and puckered her lips.

"It's a trick." Piper smiled.

"How old are you?" Lola asked.

"How old are you?" Piper reversed the question.

Lola hesitated. "Twelve-ish, but I asked you first." Lola planted her feet directly in front of Piper's. They were eye to eye. Lola placed her hand on top of Piper's head then drew an imaginary line across to her own head. "Are you twelve?"

"No," Piper laughed. "You're just tall and I'm short."

"Like Vixy."

"Yes."

"Vixy may be small, but she's really strong. Are you strong?"

Piper thought, then slowly nodded her head. She hadn't had to use her true powers at their fullest capacity for hundreds of years. She'd been the Guardians' Librarian nearly all of her life.

"Bye, I'll be back in forty-five minutes. There's more ceviche if you want some." Lola bolted out the front door.

Piper peeked into the fridge, took a look at the fleshy, red fish and cringed. "I'm not that hungry."

THIRTY-SEVEN

MARE OF DIOMEDES

Audrey, Tarian, Jun, and Hu trooped under Hu's protective glamour until they reached the plain white church with the golden cross that sat behind the grand Opera House. They ascended the five steps and entered the unassuming wooden doors as if they attended service regularly. To mortals it was a small chapel with loyal parishioners. The diminutive interior held only a few pews. Colorful mists of light floated in from two stained glass windows and four ancient wooden chandeliers above them. A statue loomed over them at the end of the rows elevated on top of a platform.

The statue was made from smooth white stone that almost glowed in the shadows. A humble man dressed in robes carried a cross twice his size over one shoulder and offered his other hand to a woman kneeling beside him. The man resembled Lautaro. Audrey was certain this was intentional to confuse potential attackers. The woman's indistinct face emanated all the beauty and strength of a saint.

Their footsteps echoed in the empty room, and Audrey hustled to her destination. She stopped in front of a door. "This is it, right?"

"Yes, don't open it yet." Hu turned to his sister. "Be careful."

In a hushed voice with sober eyes Jun said, "You too."

"I don't like leaving you here alone. Maybe Audrey should stay with you," Hu said.

"I'm fine. We have communicators. I'll use it if I'm in danger."

"Give me your word."

Jun squared her jaw at her brother, both irritated and thankful for his tenacity, and recited the oath, "I swear by the bones of my ancestors and to the King of the Gods."

"Thank you." Hu kissed his sister gently.

With a powerful sigh and a serious face, Hu turned away, opened the door, and stepped into the sorcerer's world. The fight began. Three guards quickly proved worthy opponents. They were trained maldito soldiers, but Hu had a secret weapon. In the blink of an eye, the tunnel leading from the false church into the castle became a hall of foreboding trees in a deep, dark forest.

The three soldiers took pause. Their heads darted back and forth, and their eyes narrowed with fear. That split second of uncertainty proved deadly for the two. Hu came down with his monstrous tiger paws and struck them both in one clawed blow. As they lay unconscious, Tarian ran the blessed stakes through their hearts. The last soldier disappeared among the trees. Audrey stalked the forest, looking and listening. Nothing. Suddenly an arm wrapped around her throat, squeezing the air from her lungs. She kicked at him, but his inhuman strength wouldn't budge. Blackness glided over her eyes. On the brink of passing out, she found the resilience to flip him. He landed with a hard thud on his back at Tarian's feet. Tarian sliced off the maldito's head with the blessed sword.

Audrey stumbled backwards and fell. She sat gasping for breath and holding her throat.

Tarian ran to her side. "Are you okay?"

She nodded and swallowed away the pain.

The forest around them disappeared, Hu returned to his human form and motioned for them to catch up.

"We have to go." Tarian slid his arm under Audrey's and hoisted her to her feet.

"Follow me! Audrey you must keep up," Hu ordered, and she nodded. "If we act like Maldito Ministry, they'll think we are Maldito Ministry. I have glamoured our faces, and we have the uniforms. No more bloodshed should be necessary until we've reached Benjamin. Can you walk alone Audrey?"

She stepped away from Tarian's grasp and steadied her footing. "Yes, I'm fine." The room spun slightly, but she said nothing. She was the Chancellor. She had no time for weakness.

The medieval corridor opened to a giant octagonal cathedral with eight hallways running away from the center, like spokes on a wheel. A majestic circle of stained glass dominated the middle of the twenty-story high ceiling. Complex scenes like Lautaro carrying a cross with the gentle woman at his feet were depicted in this magnificent glass centerpiece.

As Audrey marched on through this glorious house of horror, her stomach lurched and twisted violently. She drew in a long, calming breath. It sickened her that this devil mocked the house of the Lord or worse, considered himself a god. The thought that such overwhelming beauty belonged to someone like Lautaro brought fire to her belly and rendered her motionless. She took one last look at the beautiful house, drew in another deep breath, and ordered her feet to move. In her heart, she wanted to run and leap at every maldito. Kill them all. Protect her Guardians. But she remained tormented and hidden behind Hu's glamour as a dutiful guard marching in formation, as if all was right with the world.

The carved white stone zigzagged like a maze through the castle. Thousands of alcoves held pedestals topped with ornate statues of devilish-looking winged angels, nurturing plump women with arms open, or regal gentlemen browsing books or wielding swords.

The three of them descended staircase after staircase, meandered through unending serpentine halls with sloping floors. Audrey thought Headquarters was a shifting puzzle, but this labyrinth was far grander. She appreciated Hu's leadership on the mission as he led them confidently through the deceptive corridors. Her admiration grew and the heat of pride flushed her cheeks as she looked at him. To her surprise, she thought of him as a friend. She actually liked him. After a few seconds, she snapped out of it and jerked her eyes upon Tarian. Relief surged once certain he hadn't seen her admiring Hu.

Her heart pounded for Tarian. She regarded his youthful, princely face with chiseled cheekbones and pronounced jawline. He was handsome, courageous, and loyal, and she loved him. He strode with confidence. *His broad shoulders can hold mountains.*

He and Hu seemed so sure of their surroundings while self-doubt plagued her. She needed to pull herself together, end the turmoil inside. She followed their example of predatory focus and banished the brilliant walls, sculptures, and ceilings from her thoughts.

The hallway merged with another, and Hu ran into another guard. The guard didn't look surprised to see them, he merely marched ahead. Before Audrey knew what was happening, Hu had silently knocked him out. He stripped the guard of his jacket and replaced his own.

"His rank is far superior to mine." Hu pointed to the four stars on his olive uniform. "Tarian, hit him."

Tarian injected the guard with the Sedation Serum to extend sleep and erase memories. Then they shoved him into the shadows and walked on. They had finally reached the underground cells. All thirteen were monitored. Hu and Audrey entered the glass room while Tarian hid outside.

One of the two guards turned to face Hu. Four stars

decorated his uniform. He was handsome with tanned skin and full cheeks, his upper lip slightly fuller than his bottom with a natural, youthful pink color. He handed two thin square devices, one large and one small, over to Hu. "Here's the chart and key. He's in thirteen. Lautaro is expecting him in the parlor in fifteen."

Hu's face made a barely visible twitch as he accepted the unexpected items.

The other guard in the room paid zero attention to her superior's conversation. She had two-stars and sat in her chair diligently flipping buttons and swiping screens.

As Hu pivoted to leave the room, Audrey read the four-star guard's label. *Dante,* Vixy's boyfriend. Audrey wanted to smile and acknowledge his act of treasonous bravery, but she maintained her cover as she turned on her heels. This man had cleared their path to Benjamin, at least for now.

Audrey feared stepping into a cell with a powerful and clever monster. It would take the strength and skill of all three of them to take him down. Fresh notches and bloody marks scattered all four walls and ceiling. Benjamin had obviously tried in vain to break through.

"My new Chancellor," Benjamin drawled out Audrey's title as he stood leaning against the corner. His lips curled and one eyebrow cocked.

Audrey braced herself for an attack. In her peripheral vision she saw Hu and Tarian reach for their weapons, ready to pounce.

Benjamin didn't move. "I'm not going to fight. I don't want to be what I've become."

Audrey's heart sank, loaded with the many memories she shared with this man, her friend, her fellow Guardian. "I'm sorry Benjamin."

Hu and Tarian wasted no time. Hu dropped Benjamin to the floor and Tarian slipped the needle under his skin. Just as he said, he didn't fight them. He simply drifted off to sleep.

"Let's get out of here." Hu bolted for the door leaving Benjamin's slumped body.

"We have to burn him," Audrey said.

"What?" Hu questioned.

"Death Serum alone won't work. His body must turn to ash," Tarian said.

Hu paused, drew in a long, growling breath, then sank his shoulders with an exaggerated exhale. "That information would've been helpful."

"What do you mean? I explained it all to you in the car, on the way up here." Audrey threw up her arms in exasperation.

"Whatever! It doesn't matter. I'll carry him on my shoulder," Tarian said.

"Okay, I'll glamour him."

"So what will he look like?" Tarian asked.

"A backpack," Hu smirked.

They left the underground and zigzagged through the halls and staircases again. To Tarian's and Audrey's surprise no one noticed the full-grown man draped over Tarian's shoulder.

Just before they reached the exit door the room transformed into a forest.

"What are you doing?" Audrey asked.

"That's not me." Hu gritted his teeth.

Just then Audrey realized Hu existed in man form.

"For Christ's sake, turn into a tiger," she ordered.

Hu obeyed, his lethal tale whipped back and forth.

A horse galloped down the hall of trees. As the massive white furred animal drew closer, Audrey saw it was no ordinary horse. The unnatural bulge of its muscles and the fierce snarl of its lips revealed an animal worthy to be the Mare of Diomedes. By the fix in its cunning eyes, it too had a hunger for raw human flesh. Without warning, fire flew from its mouth nearly lapping the tiger.

Lautaro sat atop the Herculean horse with a gun. Bullets soared through the air in all directions.

Tarian dove out of the path of the four ferocious hooves taking Benjamin's body with him.

"Tarian! Benjamin is visible again. Get him out of here!" she yelled, but there was nowhere to go. They hid. She drew her blessed gun and stake. He gripped Benjamin's body.

Lautaro's human form melted as he became the horse-beast and lunged for the tiger. While tiger and horse-beast fought, Audrey fired upon the oncoming row of Maldito Ministry Soldiers. They charged by the hundreds.

Audrey turned to Tarian. "Run!"

THIRTY-EIGHT

HARD AND FROZEN

Tarian started to run then stopped. He turned toward the tiger and caught Hu's savage yellow eyes. A silent agreement passed between them. Tarian hurled Benjamin's lifeless body into the air. The tiger caught him in his fanged jaws then tossed him high just as scorching flames burst out from the throat of the fire-breathing horse-beast. Flames grabbed hold of Benjamin and spread quickly across his skin, devouring his flesh. The body blazed orange and red tendrils that stretched down the lane of trees and climbed up the trunks along the branches and plagued the leaves. Lautaro's army backed away and his imagery vanished. The trees disappeared and the castle returned to stone, but the fire remained. The Mare of Diomedes vanished. Lautaro stood as a man.

He didn't look like a holy man or a king or even a sorcerer. High Councilor Harry looked more a wizard than this formidable man resembling an ancient conquistador warrior. Hu remained in tiger form, and Tarian didn't blame him. Large paws and claws seemed a better match to this brutish man, but Lautaro wasn't running to attack Hu. His eyes fixed on Benjamin's burning body.

"No!" Lautaro ran to the Waker encased in fire. He smothered the flames with his body, seemingly immune to pain. The witch fire clung to Benjamin's body as if it knew its purpose. The body charred to ash within seconds. Lautaro seized a handful of ashy bone and shoved it away in a pocket. Then he turned wild eyes upon Audrey and Tarian. With his outstretched hand he cast a powerful force toward them. They flew through the air crashing down several feet away.

Lautaro turned his focus to the tiger that charged in his direction. With a swipe of his arm through the air the tiger fell over writhing in pain.

"Stop!" Audrey bolted to her feet and ran to kneel by the tiger. She stoked his fur, blood coating her hands.

Tarian saw her eyes fill with rage and screamed, "No, Audrey!" But it was too late. She barreled toward Lautaro.

She got within inches of his face, her stake thrust out, when he used his wicked magic to hurl her over the railing and send her tumbling down three flights of marble stairs.

Tarian had managed to get close to Lautaro while he focused his energy on Audrey. With the strength of the immortal Awakened Hunter, he thrust Lautaro onto the concrete floor. His heavy fists met Lautaro's face, bones cracked, and teeth dislodged. Lautaro pointed at the wall of fire and Tarian saw it drop. Lautaro's men charged. Tarian took one last punch and leaped over the railing to Audrey. Her unmoving body ripped his heart in two. He raced toward her. For nineteen years he'd lived as a mortal, with mortal ideas about death, but he pushed those thoughts out of his mind and convinced himself she wasn't dead. She's an immortal. But Lautaro was no mere mortal man, not a common wizard either. He wielded the magic of a supreme sorcerer. *Maybe he could kill her?*

As gently but as quickly as he could, he gathered her limp body into his arms. Her head flopped backwards, and he tried to cradle it in his chest, but he had to run. He had to get away. The soldiers closed in on him. Every hall he sprinted down had soldiers entering. He turned back to try a different direction, but it was no use. Soldiers came at him from all sides. Fighting all of them would've been difficult, but with an unconscious Audrey in his arms it was impossible.

The soldiers led Tarian back up the stairs to Lautaro who stood holding a spear aimed at Hu. Hu crouched down with one leg extended out and kneeling on the other. He tried to stand but fell over, catching himself with his left hand until that gave way as well. He crashed down on his elbow and lowered his head. Blood dripped from his nose and mouth. He lifted his head to speak but said nothing.

"What do you have to say to me, Lautaro the Grand Sorcerer?"

"Fuck you," Hu gargled.

Lautaro jabbed his spear at Hu's crimson streaked face but

did not strike him. Hu flinched and Lautaro laughed a cruel, guttural sound. "I will not kill you quickly, you lousy hungry ghost. I know your weakness, and you will starve for weeks before you are dead." He turned his attention to Tarian then motioned to his soldiers. "Lock them all in the cells."

The soldiers roughly hoisted Hu to standing, but he could barely walk. They dragged him and forced Tarian at gunpoint to follow the bloody trail. He still held Audrey. When they reached the cells, Hu was thrown into one and Tarian walked into his. He turned expecting them to shut the gates but instead two soldiers followed him.

"What?" Tarian asked.

"Give me the Chancellor," one soldier said.

Tarian backed away. "No, she stays with me."

"Give me the Chancellor," he said again.

Tarian squeezed Audrey more tightly.

"If I force her out of your hands, I will hurt her more. If you hand her over, she will remain the same. Either way, the Chancellor comes with me."

Tarian's eyes darted from soldier to soldier. A Castle Guard stood outside the cell.

Dante!

Dante nodded so Tarian passed Audrey's collapsed body over to the arms of the Maldito Ministry Soldier. His torn heart sank to the valley of his bowels. He paced the cell until his racing mind exhausted itself. He fell to the stone bed that protruded from the wall. Everything around him was hard and frozen, including his heart.

THIRTY-NINE

Audrey's eyelids fluttered open. A wicked pounding walloped around inside her skull when she attempted to lift her head. She gently placed it back down and drew in a deep breath. After several seconds her patience grew thin, but her ache remained. Rolling over and pushing up onto her side, against the protest of her muscles as they screamed in pain, she turned to peer out of the large window draped with layers of both solid and sheer silver silk.

The light from the setting sun highlighted the division line where the two rivers met. On one side a deep indigo blue, and on the other side a syrupy brown, neither yielding. She let the phenomenal beauty soak in before falling back on to the fluffy pillow. Soon reality crashed down upon her, and the memories of how she came to lay in this luscious bed flooded her mind.

Someone knocked on the door.

"Chancellor?" the female voice on the other side asked.

"Come in." Audrey sat up, willing her head to stop

throbbing and forcing her tortured body to prepare to stand.

An awkwardly tall, young servant girl walked into the room carrying a tray of food and a garment bag.

"How long have I been healing?" Audrey asked.

"Three days." The young girl smiled timidly.

"Where are my friends?"

"I don't know." Her eyes swept the floor.

"They're in the prison, aren't they?"

"I'm afraid I truly don't know."

Audrey decided not to scold this young woman.

"I've brought you dinner. You must be famished. The Grand Sorcerer has requested your presence after dinner for dessert." She opened the garment bag and hung a sleek pale blue dress in the closet.

Audrey noticed many dresses hanging in the closet. She swung her feet to the floor and walked to the petite table where her tray of food awaited. She sat and offered the other chair to the girl with grasshopper limbs.

It took several attempts before the girl realized she meant her.

"No ... No. Thank you ... I have work to do."

"Please, I have some questions before I meet Lautaro," Audrey said.

The girl sat on the edge of the chair as if a bomb were strapped beneath it, ready to explode at any given moment.

"In the Entente ... you know where that is correct?"

The girl nodded.

"Okay, good. In my nation, the creatures stay hidden from the mortals, well to most mortals. We disguise ourselves. You are a mortal correct?"

"Yes," she said.

"Human?"

"Yes."

"And yet you know what Lautaro is. So, am I to assume that you know him as a sorcerer because you work in the castle, or does this nation not hide their creatures?" Audrey asked.

"No, the creatures try to remain in disguise. The humans that work inside the castle are sworn to secrecy. But I would never tell, I've seen what happens to those who talk too much," she said with wide mocha eyes.

"How has this nation been doing after the Entente War?"

She smiled and shook her head. "I don't know Chancellor. I'm just a servant. I spend my days trapped in this castle."

Audrey didn't speak. She didn't accept this weak answer and pierced the girl with her stare.

"We do fine," she said through shaky breaths. "The Ministry sees to it that our bellies are full, and our technologies are advancing. There are talks of continental travel once again."

"What?"

"I really don't understand, but that's what I've overheard. All I know of the outside world is what my great-grandmother told me about her mother's life. She is the only one left from the old world. When I was young, she told me stories. She told me her mother was a businesswoman that traveled all over the world until it was unsafe to do so, and then the war. She told me of places covered with snow and others with desert. People who spoke with funny accents, and in different languages that she couldn't understand. Unlike today, she had no technology to understand a foreign tongue, but she said that made it more interesting, more challenging. She always said she hoped I'd be able to travel outside the tracking barrier one day. She schooled me every day on proper English, Portuguese, and Spanish in the hopes that maybe someday I could be a businesswoman." The girl lowered her eyes and sighed. "But I'm afraid my destiny is here."

Audrey put her fork down having eaten half her steak and rice and feeling the drum inside her head lessen to a tolerable pitter-patter. "Yes, I think it's time I do some traveling beyond the walls too. See the people. Maybe I could talk to your great-grandmother?"

"She no longer talks or listens. Unfortunately, she is ready for death. For the last three years she hasn't had her wits, only her strong beating heart." Her lips turned down and she swallowed.

"I'm sorry she suffers. Sometimes death is very bitter."

The young girl nodded.

Audrey ate the remainder of her meal, and the girl sat politely. "Are you going to escort me to Lautaro?"

"No, a Castle Guard will come and get you soon."

"Okay, thank you. You don't have to keep me company

any longer," Audrey said, realizing the girl awaited her dismissal.

She stood from her chair with lowered head and humbled face. She scooted the chair back in place but hesitated to walk away.

"Don't worry, I won't tell anyone about your great-grandmother's secret stories."

"Thank you," she said in a whisper.

"On one condition."

The girl snapped around with fly eyes.

"You continue to study and learn about the past, and if in your lifetime the continents reopen to one another, you travel and see the world."

The grasshopper girl smiled. She nodded in agreement, but the smirk on her mouth and the softening of her eyes suggested this idea was ludicrous. "Maybe my children will be lucky to see this world, God willing. Good evening, Chancellor."

"Good evening."

Audrey pulled on the dress and brushed her hair before another knock pounded the door. Her eyes danced around the room in search of a weapon. She found nothing except the steak knife. She wiped it clean and plunged it between her breasts. She wiggled, but it was no use. She'd be uncomfortable all night.

Another knock came, this time louder and harder.

"Come in," Audrey said.

"I'm here to escort you," the guard in an olive uniform said.

Audrey had hoped to see Dante's familiar face, but this man was much older. His hair had already turned white.

"Good evening, Chancellor."

"Good evening."

"You look lovely."

"Thank you."

"Shall we go?"

"Yes." She followed him down many long, shiny hallways and up two grand staircases into a private room. Below her feet were vibrantly colored antique woven rugs. The intricately designed rugs led to tall double doors that were swung open. Wispy rings of smoke floated in from the balcony, and Audrey strolled toward it. She found Lautaro puffing on a pipe as he leaned against the railing and admired the starlit sky.

She withheld the urge to push him over.

"Beautiful night, Chancellor," he said to her without turning his gaze from the sky.

"Yes, it is from this lavish balcony. Probably not so much from the prison cells or the huts your people outside the city live in."

He turned to show his calm expression not the least bit affected by her jab. He wore makeup over a severe bruise on the left side of his face courtesy of Tarian. "Your nation brought on the Great War, and then shut its resources off to the entire world. South America is alive and thriving thanks to me and my Maldito Ministry. My people are happy—poor or rich. They live a full life without judgment," he stated, without anger or regret on his tanned weathered face, puffing contentedly on his pipe one elbow propped up on the railing.

"The Great War was not started by the Americas, North or South," Audrey clarified.

"Yes, but you did what you had to do to save the North as I did the same for the South."

"Democracy still lives inside the Entente."

"Two sides of the same coin." He puffed a ring of smoke into the crisp air.

Audrey sniffed. She hardly agreed that dictatorship guised under religion equaled a democratic republic, but she said nothing. "Aren't you going to offer me a drink?"

"My apologies." He clapped his hand, and a man dressed in a white linen suit came onto the balcony. Then he turned to Audrey. "What would you like?"

"A local red, please."

The gentleman bowed his head and left to retrieve her wine.

"Despite what you might think, I never wanted to destroy the Guardians. Benjamin was a bargaining tool. I have more valuable things that can be used in a bargain. Your High Council can be quite intransigent at times."

Audrey smiled, but she didn't believe him, not for a minute, until he picked up an object from the table next to him. He ceremoniously removed the velvet sleeve revealing a transparent box with a vial of golden liquid inside. Her heart pounded boiling blood through her veins, she felt beads of sweat dot her hairline, and it took all her strength to trap the heat inside her skin as to appear unresponsive to his revelation. She knew exactly what that liquid was.

"Chancellor, we need to work as one," he said, but was interrupted when the gentleman returned holding Audrey's blood red wine.

"Thank you," Audrey said.

"You're welcome, Chancellor. Enjoy." The gentleman quietly exited the room.

"Lautaro." Audrey watched him cringe at the informal address. She smiled and took a sip of her wine. "Hmmm, very nice. Your vineyards must be extraordinary."

"They are. Maybe one day you can visit them."

"Maybe, but as I was saying, Lautaro, there will be no joining forces if Hu or Tarian have been injured or tortured in any way while I've been healing from your cursed magic."

His mouth twitched, and his eyes shot up. "They're still alive."

"That's not what I said."

"Come see for yourself." He set his pipe down, kept a firm hold on the transparent case, and waltzed into the room. He waved his hand in front of a screen on the wall. Tarian appeared.

Audrey's heart skipped at the sight of her love. He looked unharmed as he paced the floor of his cell, but she saw the anguish in his face at being trapped and helpless. "And Hu?"

He switched the screen to display Hu's cell to find Hu in a heap on the concrete floor, gorily battered. He didn't move. "He's alive," Lautaro reassured her.

She wanted to scream and fight but remained calm. She was the leader of the Guardians and had to act like it. "I want to see that man receive water and food right this instant."

"Very well." Lautaro swiped a pad on his desk and within seconds a man appeared on the screen helping Hu sit up and sip from a bottle of blood. A tray of raw meats was also sent in, but Hu never touched it.

Audrey watched the screen, continuing to suppress the heat inside her that so desperately clawed to break out. She wanted to escape, to walk back out to the balcony where the lights of the city skyline danced on the river, and the sky shimmered with starlight. However, she remained where she stood and kept her stoic expression.

"I believe it is time to rebuild across the oceans. There is half a world out there we aren't claiming. By now the radiation has gone, the poisons have faded, and the spells have weakened. This is a task I can do myself, but I'm offering the Guardians a chance for global commerce and unification."

"Very well, you will provide safe untraceable passage for me, Tarian, and Hu back to the Entente immediately, and I will set up a meeting with the High Council as to how we will proceed with the reconstruction of the Eastern Hemisphere."

"Agreed. You will leave tomorrow morning at ten."

She eyed him. If he was being truly honest then why couldn't she leave now? Inhaling deeply and exhaling slowly she accepted this arrangement, assuming he might have to coordinate their leave. She wasn't sure how his traceable barrier worked, but for right now she'd give him the benefit of the doubt. It'd give her a chance to think as well. She had only just woken up a couple hours ago.

"And as for this." Lautaro cradled the box that protected the precious liquid inside in the palms of his hands, offering it to Audrey.

She accepted the box and inspected it. She knew the little case could not be broken without a spell.

"You know what that is, and you know where I found it," he said.

"Yes. And you know if you touch it, it will kill you, mortal." She said the last word as an insult.

"I do know this." He took the box back. He strolled over to the bookshelf and set the cube with the golden ichor on a top shelf next to a bound manuscript entitled *The Net, Isaac Newton*. "For safe keeping." He winked at her. "Good night, Chancellor Gualtiero. Sleep well."

"Goodnight," she said with a smile that didn't reach her silver blue eyes.

The locking system clinked in place verifying her doubts. Men who lock up their guests, don't negotiate. Besides, the Guardians' mission was never to be a world leader or protector. They'd always been the keepers of North America, but she knew Lautaro would attempt conquering the Wastelands of the Eastern hemisphere. What would this mean for the future? And of what use was golden ichor to him? And how had he snuck into the highly guarded and monitored Cavern System to retrieve it? Her mind twisted and spun with questions.

She shook her head. "Focus, Audrey. Concentrate on getting the hell out of here." She paced. She wanted to summon Piper but didn't know how to do it. "Meditation!" She sat crossed legged on the floor attempting to erase all thoughts except one. *Piper, come here.*

After sitting still for at least ten minutes, she opened her eyes but saw no change and no Piper. Then a bird hit her window. For a second she dismissed the noise figuring the poor thing knocked out and fell to its death, but then she saw it again, a cinnamon colored hawk. She scrambled to her feet and scurried to the window. She slid her hands up and down the panes of glass until she found the lock. She pinched it between her fingers, but it wouldn't budge not even with her immortal strength. The hawk remained at her eye level, swaying in the breeze.

"Hold on, Joe." She searched the room for something that would break glass but found nothing. She still had the steak knife inside her bra. She crammed it in the corner of one of the panels of glass. The corner popped out allowing just enough space for the Hawk to fly into the room.

Once inside, the Hawk morphed into Joe Prescott. His chest heaved from exhaustion.

Audrey threw her arms around him. "You're brilliant Joe, just brilliant."

"I didn't think I was going to make it. I haven't flown that far in years."

Suddenly, Audrey began to look frantically around the room. In a shaky voice she said, "But you're in here with me. That doesn't help us. I can't get out of here." Just then she heard the locking system unravel. "Hide." Joe stood still. "Hide!"

"It's okay. It's Piper."

"What?"

"She's been trying to find you, but every time she vades she ends up in the wrong place. So she took one of my feathers hoping if I found you then the feather would lead her to me. She has zero sense of direction."

"So you don't know for sure that's her opening the door." Audrey's throat tensed.

He said nothing, but before she could force him into hiding Piper stumbled through the door.

"Oh good." Piper clapped her hands together. "Either I'm

really bad at vading or this castle has been playing tricks on me." A look of sheer relief crossed her face along with a wide grin.

"We need to go now. They have trackers everywhere. Joe change back, and go find Tarian," she said frantically, but no one moved.

"It's okay. Dante has cut off the trackers for this part of the castle and the cells," Joe said.

"I don't trust it. Like you said this castle is tricky," Audrey said.

"It's still better for us to vade than run through the halls," Piper said.

Audrey threw up her arms. "We could end up inside Lautaro's bedchamber!"

"But I have a strand of his hair."

"You had a strand of my hair too, didn't you?" Audrey asked.

Piper nodded.

"And you couldn't find me. We can't chance it."

Piper's face dropped.

"Sorry." Audrey's gut turned knowing she'd hurt her friend's feelings. She quickly regained her determination and turned to Joe. "Fly to the cell, find something from the castle itself like a rock. That should help Piper."

Without another word Joe turned back into a hawk and flew out into the hall. Audrey paced the floor and Piper sat rocking back and forth on the bed running her fingers along the smooth, shiny fabric of the bedspread. The bird returned with a sparkling gray stone in its beak. Piper took the round rock and squeezed it, then rubbed it gently.

"Well?" Audrey asked impatience welling up inside her.

"Grab my arm, and hold on tight," Piper said.

Audrey did as she was told.

Before they disappeared, Piper looked at Audrey. Her lavender eyes now a piercing purple. "Don't let go!"

Audrey swallowed and gripped her tighter. Piper was right, it took all of her strength and sheer determination to hold on to her friend. The forces of nature desperately tried to rip them apart. Piper's eyes were closed, and she looked at peace, or perhaps, as if this was a natural occurrence. Piper vanished as easily as most people strolled through the park. Then they landed and there wasn't anything natural about that. Audrey hit the ground hard and had to run to prevent her legs from collapsing. Piper just teetered until she caught her balance.

"That doesn't happen inside Headquarters." Piper brushed off the dust from her pants and looked indignant. "I'm telling you the air in this castle is strange."

"You did great. I recognize this area. We're close to the cells." Not only did the area look familiar but she felt the same dampness and smelled the same musty odor that she had when they came to kill Benjamin. She scanned the area for the hawk but only quiet darkness lay in front and behind them. "This way."

Piper followed.

They moved quickly and quietly, but the short distance felt a mile long. Finally, she heard the voices of Castle Guards switching shifts. She pushed Piper into the shadows. They waited for the two guards to leave. While the new guards trudged the long row of cells inspecting the prisoners, Audrey and Piper snuck in behind them. Before the guards noticed, Piper used her magic to freeze them in place.

Audrey rushed to Tarian's cell and found an elaborate confinement system. "What do I do Tarian?" She reached her hand to the barrier separating them. Unlike Benjamin's steel bars, these had a transparent pink light between the gaps that burned hot. "How does it work?"

"Touch the guard's hand to that square."

Audrey tugged the spellbound stiff guard's arm and placed his hand on the device in front of Tarian's cell and then Hu's. The pink light disappeared but the gate didn't open. Tarian grabbed the bars and then let go. His hands burned.

"Damn," Audrey said.

"They'll cool off, then I can try to bend them," Tarian said.

"It's steel." Audrey kicked the floor frustrated but could do nothing. She inspected the guard's uniform and found a ring of objects. At astounding speed, she swiped a screen, she pulled a trigger, she flipped a switch, she pushed a button, and she spoke into a speaker.

"It's opening," Tarian yelled.

Something worked. The bars lowered and disappeared under the floor. She ran inside and kissed him, wrapping her entirety around him. He felt like home to her. It took every inch of willpower to separate from the loving alcove of his virile arms.

"I was terrified that he'd hurt you." Tarian gripped her tightly.

"I'm fine." She looked up into his chocolate eyes filled with relief and rage. She gently put her lips on his to reassure him she was safe. "I'm so sorry, Tarian. I can only imagine how worried you've been."

"I went out of my mind," his voice shook with the confession.

She smiled at him then pushed away from his strong embrace. "Get Hu and let's go."

"He hasn't moved or made a sound for hours." Tarian lowered his head and eyes.

Audrey bolted to Hu's still body. "It doesn't matter. Dead or alive we take him."

Tarian yanked his body over his shoulder and ran. At the clearing he asked, "Which way?"

Audrey shrugged as her eyes darted down the many hallways. "It's not that one, we just came down it, but other than that I don't know." Stepping in all directions she threw her arms up in frustration, then she focused on Piper. "You take Hu and get out of here. Tarian and I will find our way."

Piper took a deep uneasy breath and nodded. "Okay."

"You can do it, Piper. Go to Vixy's house and stay there."

Tarian unloaded Hu's limpness onto Piper's shoulders piggyback-style. Her knees buckled from the weight, but she steadied herself and then they both vanished.

Audrey and Tarian looked at each other then shot down a hallway. After several yards, a tawny ball of feathers brushed past them. He spread his wings forcing them to halt, then let out a piercing squawk.

"He wants us to turn around," Audrey said.

"The hawk?" Tarian asked.

"That's Joe," she said.

"Oh. Cool."

The bird bolted forward, and they followed. Soon they were back where they'd started taking a sharp right to head down another corridor. The light disappeared, and they ran in inky blackness until they saw pinpoints of light far in front of them.

"Soldiers," Audrey gasped.

Hawk saw them too. Soon they could hear the stampede. Hawk pivoted and flew back the way they'd come then curved to the left, skimming the wall and almost crashing into it. Audrey and Tarian followed. The underground maze zigzagged and forked, and they continued to follow the bird. The noise of the soldiers faded. Just as Audrey felt relief, the tunnel narrowed until only one person could fit through at a time. They slowed to a walk, but Hawk flew on. They had to stoop so as not to get stuck in the tight space. The ceiling dropped lower and lower until they had to crawl.

"Should we turn back?" Tarian questioned.

"I don't know. You're barely squeezing through."

"I know. I'm backing up," Tarian said.

Just as Audrey started to back out of the tight tunnel the hawk returned squawking passionately. "He wants us to keep going,"

"Easy for him to say, he's two feet tall." Tarian coughed. "And I can't breathe."

"I know. I noticed the change in the oxygen earlier. He knows that affects us. Remember your training Tarian. Stay calm." She crawled faster. "I see light. Keep moving."

Tarian didn't answer.

"Tarian!"

No answer.

She stopped crawling forward and began to move backwards until she bumped into Tarian. He'd passed out.

"Damn!" She snaked her body around and managed to grab hold of his armpits. She tugged, pulled, and slithered the rest of the way through the shaft until finally the ceiling rose again and she could stand. She dragged Tarian's body out into the street.

Joe returned to human form and grabbed his son. The two of them toted him for yards until enough fresh air reached Tarian's lungs, and he slowly came to.

"I'm okay," Tarian said, standing to his full six feet two height. He ran his fingers through his tousled hair and inhaled a deep breath of air that smelled of the harbor and barbecue.

Once Tarian was able to run, the three of them sprinted until they came upon the city. Although Vixy's little house was close to the church that acted as a portal to the Castle, the Castle actually existed miles away along the river. They reached the vacant streets of the city and slowed as if out for a midnight stroll.

"You fly to the house. We won't look so suspicious as a couple walking in the moonlight," Tarian said.

Joe hesitated then nodded. "Alright, but I'm coming back if you're not there in half an hour."

"Okay," Audrey and Tarian said.

They moseyed hand in hand as an undercover newlywed couple and passed no one. They stepped through the door of the little house and into the horrible silence of terror.

FORTY

ESCAPE

"Hu's dying." Jun's scar glared crimson above her canary eye. "We have to get him to Ana-Clara. Now!"

"I know, but we have to wait for Piper's return," Audrey said.

"She left seventeen hours ago," Jun pleaded.

"We step out of this house, and we're caught." Audrey reminded her.

"And the longer you're here the more Dante's and my life are in danger," Vixy said.

"We are eternally grateful and will someday repay the favor." Tarian hoped he'd be able to honor his word one day.

"I don't need any favors. I just need you to leave." Vixy's complexion grew paler with every passing minute. The circles under her eyes doubled in size and darkened to a deep purple. She was clearly prepared to risk her life to save Dante's.

Audrey's eyes flicked from Vixy to Jun until Tarian

stretched out his arm attracting everyone's attention.

"I'm getting something." Tarian turned out his wrist.

He'd given Piper a communicating bracelet. It had lain like a hunk of scrap metal on the table among Felipe's gambling wins. Felipe had passed it over when offering them their pick of weaponry and devices, when Tarian had snatched it.

"I want this," Tarian had said.

"It's just a lady bracelet," Felipe had responded.

"I know," Tarian had lied, "But I can clean it up, give it to my girlfriend."

"Okay, man," he had said with a look of bewilderment.

Tarian had recognized the bracelet as a very late model Entente mobile communicator. Tarian had retrieved it hoping since it didn't use maldito parts maybe it would be an undetectable line to the Entente. He'd cleaned it and charged it during the days he'd waited for Audrey and Hu to arrive at the house. Unfortunately, he hadn't been able to get it to work, and almost thought it useless, until Piper left at midnight to inform Margaret of their situation and bring help. He'd given her the effector ring and kept the receptor. He'd told Piper to take it to the lab to see if it could be made functional.

Everyone flocked to Tarian's side and read the message as it flashed across the white skin of his inner wrist.

In fifteen minutes, Lola will be outside with a vehicle. Be ready. She'll take you out of town where you'll be retrieved.

The words disappeared. Silence fell then everyone burst

into action gathering all weapons and supplies for a trip.

Jun prepped Hu for travel grabbing the intravenous hydration packet of blood she'd rigged up. It wasn't blood from the fridge, but no one dared question Jun. She had left the house with an empty packet and came back with a full one. No one asked questions.

Tarian stocked his vest and pants with weapons for both mortal and cursed enemies. Audrey scurried through the house making sure no evidence of their visit remained. She went to the white board to erase the Lola arrival countdown, but Vixy stopped her.

"Don't." Vixy grabbed Audrey's forearm. "It'll disappear when the time is right. Plus, if there is a change the board will know before anyone else."

"You're right. It's magic. I should know better. I'm just filling the time." Audrey paced and rubbed her fingers together. She put her hair in a ponytail then took it out then repeated and repeated.

"Stop it!" Vixy said through tight lips and clenched teeth.

Tarian placed an arm around Audrey, but she still fidgeted and twirled the hair tie around in her fingers. He knew she feared it was too late to save Hu. He feared that too.

During the remaining two minutes no one moved or spoke.

"Go! She's here." Vixy pushed Audrey toward the door.

Everyone except Vixy filed into the van with twelve-year-old Lola behind the wheel.

"Aren't you coming?" Tarian held his hand out in a gentlemanly gesture, offering her assistance up onto the tall runner.

"No! Now go, get out of here." She shoved the door shut, waved, then hustled back inside.

"All I know is I'm to drive you north out of the city. Lautaro is guarding the river. He's shut down Iranduba Bridge expecting your escape is at that point." Lola set the coordinates and put the vehicle in motion.

The vehicle joined the sea of city commuters in the evening rush hour traffic. For the first five minutes, no one said a word. Jun peered down at her brother as he lay motionless on the back seat. Everyone else stared out the windows searching for trackers, anything suspicious. After a while there seemed to be no cause for alarm. They all leaned back in their seats, except Jun, she remained tense and focused on Hu.

Tarian inched closer to the driver's seat where Lola sat, small but competent. "Why does Lautaro think we're being rescued from the south?"

"Not sure. I assume your people have somehow given that impression."

Tarian prayed that whatever Margaret had mustered up was a foolproof plan.

Night had fallen, and the scenery had gone from modern

skyscrapers to jungle-like foliage. With miles of gleaming steel, it was easy to forget Manaus sat in the middle of the Amazon basin. Through the impenetrable nighttime blackness, red and yellow lights soon shone. As they drove closer, three large tiltrotors descended through the towering trees to take over the entirety of the small road. Margaret exited one of the crafts followed by Entente Secret Service Agents.

Audrey and Tarian helped Jun load Hu into one of the crafts. It quickly rose into the sky and flew away. Thankful and relieved Audrey turned to Tarian. "Let's go!"

"Hurry!" screamed Margaret just before a round of shots hit one of the two tiltrotors. It exploded into a ball of fire.

Tarian and Audrey rushed to the other tiltrotor. Tarian turned around, expecting to see Lola following them, but she still remained in the driver's seat of the vehicle. "Get over here now, Lola!"

"No! I can't leave my family. My home is here. Bye." Lola smiled and winked a brown eye, then drove the van full speed away from the chaos.

Tarian's heart plummeted to the pit of his stomach where it stuck like a rock, but the oncoming maldito army gave him no time to ponder the decision of a young girl. The tiltrotor door shut, and he stumbled into the seat next to Audrey. The craft lifted and increased speed. It rose into the sky in a flash, escaping the shots from below only to find turbulent air above. A long line of enemy flyers headed towards them. Missiles erupted, and Tarian and Audrey braced themselves for the blast but felt nothing. One by one Lautaro's army fighters fell from the sky or retreated as the superior Entente military air force came at them. Tarian's body sunk with exhausted relief.

FORTY-ONE

THE KEY ELEMENT

The green Guardian sedan whipped into the garage of Headquarters, and Audrey couldn't exit it fast enough. She immediately doled out orders. "Margaret, get Ana-Clara and Teresa here immediately."

"Teresa is already home, but Ana-Clara wouldn't leave."

"Tell her it's an emergency. I need all the Sleepers woken up as soon as possible. Tell her I wouldn't ask this of her if I thought we had time to waste. You must convince her," Audrey's angst-filled orders shot out like rounds from an old-fashioned AK-47.

"Got it," Margaret said.

"Tell her Hu's dying," Audrey said.

"I thought he was in stable condition."

"Is he? Good, but tell her anyway. I need her here now! She'll come to help Hu … I hope."

"Okay." Margaret hurried away.

"Margaret!" Audrey hollered.

Margaret turned around.

"Set up a High Council meeting ASAP. We need to get Eleanor home."

Margaret furrowed her brow and squared her bulldog jowls in puzzlement.

"Did you hear me?" Audrey asked.

"Yes, right away."

"And, Margaret," Audrey said.

Margaret swung around once again.

"The village looks nice," Audrey said with an appreciative smile.

"Thank you," Margaret smiled back.

Dragging Tarian behind her, Audrey bee-lined to the lab hoping to find Joe. She found him measuring, mixing, and pouring elements and compounds with Patrick.

Audrey charged in and blurted out, "Lautaro had golden ichor."

Joe stopped working and turned to focus on Audrey and Tarian.

"That's impossible," Joe said.

"I saw it. We had a meeting." She shivered at the remembrance of that night. "He wants to rebuild the Wastelands with our help. He wants to globalize, not destroy us—or so he claims."

"But we're the keepers of the Entente of Nations." Joe

removed his gloves.

"I know, but we can't let him gain control of the rest of the world," Audrey said.

"Audrey, that's the President's job, not ours."

"I'd agree if Lautaro wasn't a Grand Sorcerer leading a Maldito Ministry. If he was a common man." Audrey's voice sharpened.

"We're stronger. Our air force shot his out of the sky," Tarian said.

Audrey nodded thinking inwardly about what to do first.

Joe approached her. "We must inform the President that there's a breach in the Cavern System security, since Lautaro's men were able to get a sample of the ichor."

"Maybe our Cavern System isn't the only place it exists," Tarian said.

"I highly doubt it. For as long as I've been alive it's been a myth, until miners started dying from the mysterious liquid gold. It's supposed to be the blood of the gods and their immortals, and yet, we bleed red. Believe me—back hundreds of years ago we cut ourselves silly to see if any of our veins bled gold. None did. But our fellow creatures that had lived millennia to our centuries had witnessed this mysterious blood. They told stories of its incredible powers and its lethal effects."

Joe nodded. "As far as we knew golden ichor disappeared from Earth. When we found it in the caves a few years ago, we concluded it came from space, or you could say it came from the heavens."

"Another theory is that it had always been hidden under the Earth, and the meteor shower merely uncovered it," Audrey said.

Patrick took off his gloves and joined the conversation. "Either way, it's the key ingredient in both the Death Serum and the serum that turns Sleepers into Wakers. We can't have it in the hands of our enemy."

Horrible apprehension twisted Audrey's stomach. "I know. He may not know what we use it for. He claimed it was just a bargaining chip, but I don't trust him. Our top priority must be to wake up all Sleepers, including Eleanor, so he can't turn them into Wakers and use them against us."

FORTY-TWO

SHARED PERSPECTIVE

The infirmary no longer housed brutalized Waker victims. The ten remaining Sleepers and one preta inhabited the beds now.

Audrey sat on the edge of Eleanor's bed. She ran her fingers along Eleanor's pallid cheeks. Her sunken and ailing appearance crushed Audrey's heart until it barely beat. She caressed her hair and noticed it wasn't soft like before. Pinching a few strands together felt like stiff sticks of hay. She dropped the hair and rushed to find Ana-Clara. She swallowed the bitter taste of doubt and tried to mask her worry from the Bruja Blanca.

Without turning from her shelves stocked with oddities such as the yellow stones of solidified lynx urine to cups filled with unspoken water, Ana-Clara said, "It's okay dear. I'm not going to reprimand you this time. You've been through enough already."

Audrey heaved a sigh of relief. "Can you come look at Eleanor? She doesn't look good. Her hair has changed."

"Yes, I will go to her straight away if you will bring this to Hu for me." Ana-Clara dunked a rabbit's foot into a glass of water. The water turned a mesmerizing emerald green. "Here's his last dose. He should be feeling a lot better today."

"Does he know you stuck a rabbit's foot in it?" Audrey asked.

Ana-Clara drew her eyes taut in thought. "No. I don't believe I've mentioned the moon rabbit."

"Hmm." A wicked grin fanned Audrey's face. She spun on her heels and rushed to Hu's bedside. She pushed the curtain open to find Hu lounging like a cat looking perfectly at ease while reading a book.

"My Timber Wolf, what a pleasant surprise," he purred out then added, "not that Ana-Clara's wide eyes aren't pretty but you, you are stunning."

"Always the flatterer." Audrey couldn't help but smile at his compliment. She no longer found him despicable, she now found him amusing. "I have good news. This is your last dose of …," she looked at the green concoction, "medicine."

"Wonderful." He took the glass and drank.

"Is it yummy?" Audrey watched him sip the last drop.

"Yes, as a matter of fact it's quite good. Sweet like juice."

Audrey's lip curled up on one side and she winked.

"Why?" A flash of concern swept his buttery eyes.

"Just wondered," she said, her voice unusually playful.

"What did you put in it?" Hu shot upright and grabbed at

her as if she were his annoying little sister.

"I didn't put anything in it." She tried to say it with a straight face but failed and chuckled.

Hu glared at her then tipped his nose into the air as if he didn't care what he'd been drinking for the last three days. But her smugness got the better of him, and he reached to her with both hands. "Please, don't tell me it's some grotesque animal urine."

Audrey took pity on him as his face deformed, and his mouth puckered at the thought. She answered quickly, "No, no, no. Nothing like that."

"Oh, thank the Ancestors," Hu sighed.

"She dunks a green rabbit's foot in it."

"What?" Hu shouted.

"It's better than piss water." Audrey laughed.

"Not much better." He joined in on her laughter. "Feels like old times."

"Ha." She laughed the word sharp and loud. "What? When you were a drug runner in the eighties trying to kill me, you mean those 'old times'?"

"So hurtful." He pouted his lower lip in mocking sarcasm. "You know we had fun."

"It seems we have a difference of opinion."

"Don't you remember the Fontainebleau?"

"Of course, I do."

"Miami was alive back then. It was crazy."

"Those were crazy times and very bad times," Audrey said.

"Wouldn't it be fun to go back?" Hu asked.

Audrey reflected on her days helping the DEA desperately try to catch the notorious cocaine smugglers only to discover the reason they couldn't catch the SOBs was because Hu had been glamouring the boats, and Jun killed the witnesses. But Audrey had mixed emotions about this question. She had enjoyed the chase, the thrill of the hunt, and the beaches had been spectacular, but a lot of good people had been killed during the so-called excitement.

While she still pondered, he proposed, "Let's go back. You and me."

"What?" Her stomach dropped and her skin tingled. She didn't know why.

"It'd be fun. The last time I was in Miami ... was ..." Hu paused to think. "1988. How about you?"

"Same. It's been a long time." She didn't like the turn the conversation had taken.

"This is what I mean Audrey," Hu said.

"What?" she asked, confused.

"Your Tarian. He's too young. We can reminisce. We remember how it used to be, so we understand today's world better. We can share perspective." He petted the back of her hand. "I know you care about me even though you don't want to."

"We're friends Hu, just friends." She stood but didn't leave.

He smirked. "I'm making progress. From opposite sides of the law to creature enemies to friends."

Teresa pranced into the room. "Come Audrey, Eleanor is waking up."

"I'm glad you're better," Audrey told Hu, then left with Teresa.

"Ana-Clara told me you thought she looked bad, and she did but I guess that was a good thing. Her body was draining itself you could say. Her color is back, and her eyelids are fluttering, and I knew you'd be so upset if you weren't at her bedside when she came to." Teresa overflowed with delighted energy.

"Thank you for coming to get me." She meant it for more than one reason. Audrey's heart couldn't take any more tug-of-war. She didn't like her emotions rising so close to the surface.

They walked into Eleanor's room. Ana-Clara swiped a wet washcloth across Eleanor's forehead and over her palms. Teresa wiggled and bit her lips excited for her mentor to wake up. Audrey sat cautiously on the side of her bed while Ana-Clara rotated a wand that omitted a pale blue mist.

Eleanor thrust her body up and gasped for air. As her black eyes scanned the room, she panted and wheezed, then let out a panic riddled scream, "The village! My village! It's destroyed, isn't it? You've brought me back because it's all my fault."

Teresa rushed to help Audrey calm Eleanor. Teresa had one hand gently placed on her right shoulder while Audrey held her left.

"The village is fine. We're all fine," Audrey said trying to hide her guilt with a smile.

Eleanor sank a little as she shook her head and furrowed her brows. "I wanted to rest next to my daughter and husband." Her ink eyes pleaded. They weren't soulless. They filled with despair.

Tears pooled in Audrey's eyes. She swallowed the lump of guilt before speaking. "I know, and we did honor your request, but they would've dug you up and turned you into a murderous Waker. They would've used you against the people you love, your Guardians."

"Who?" Eleanor asked.

"Lautaro and his malditos," Audrey answered.

Eleanor sat stunned into silence.

"Lautaro has a vial of golden ichor. He knows about what happened to us. I couldn't risk it. You were the last Sleeper. Now everyone is either dead or awake. We must move on from here," Audrey said. The vomit of inadequacy and disappointment crept up her esophagus, burning her throat, and reminding her how much she'd failed as the Chancellor to the Guardians of Dare.

Eleanor wilted back against her pillow and closed her eyes. She remained silent for a long while then her gaze fell on Teresa's big doe eyes. She held out her hand for the girl to hold. "You look all grown up." Eleanor smiled.

"I have so much to tell you," Teresa said.

"Did you tell Patrick you love him?" Eleanor said her smile growing wider.

Teresa's jaw dropped. "You knew!"

Eleanor only chuckled.

"I'm the worst secret keeper ever." Teresa rolled her caramel eyes.

"He likes you too," Eleanor whispered, then turned her gaze to Audrey. "And you look so tired, honey."

"I guess I am. You can have your job back," Audrey said with an exhausted sigh.

Eleanor sat up, adjusted herself, and regained her former regal grace. "Fill me in on everything. Start from the beginning after I killed Zachary and then myself. He is dead not asleep, correct?"

"Yes, when we fired missiles on the warehouse it incinerated everyone. Killing immortals is a two-part process, first Death Serum injection and second, incineration." Thus, the official meeting between Chancellors commenced.

Audrey told her everything from how they'd destroyed Zachary's offspring army, to how she figured out how to wake up Joe. She beamed when discussing Tarian's amazing skills and how the Guardians and villagers praised him as the Awakened Hunter. She described Benjamin's evolution as the last Waker, and how they'd destroyed him. She went into detail about Rain's Gate, and her trip to South America, and her meeting with Lautaro. She discussed the last Prevallers' cell, and how it had been calm since then. "So while the mortal world has been productive, and the Entente has been at peace, our creature world is unsettled. With the insurgency among the Lavender Witches and the Maldito

Ministry wanting to resurrect the Wastelands, I'm unsure about the future of the Guardians of Dare." Audrey finished her briefing.

Eleanor swung her legs around and began to stand, but her weak limbs buckled. She grabbed for Teresa, who caught her and eased her into an upright sitting position on the edge of the bed.

"Slowly my dear, slowly," Ana-Clara said.

"Yes, I can see that," Eleanor said in a low growl.

"In another day or so you'll be fine," Ana-Clara said. "You have a fighting spirit."

Eleanor smiled and sighed. "Thank you."

"Out! Everyone out!" Ana-Clara ordered. "Until tomorrow. No one's invading Eurasia today. Don't worry."

"I want to meet with the High Council," Eleanor told Audrey over Ana-Clara's orders.

"I'll arrange it," Audrey said before Ana-Clara's small but powerful hand shoved her out of the room.

FORTY-THREE

OLD AND NEW

Tarian sat next to Ana-Clara at the rosewood round table awaiting Audrey and the High Council. He shifted his weight back and forth in the chair as the minutes crawled past. The somber, cold room did nothing to soften his anxious mood. He'd been home for a week and hadn't spent one night of it with Audrey. Her time had been dedicated to coordinating defense systems with Margaret or in the infirmary at the bedside of Eleanor or Hu.

One night, he had watched her talking to Hu in the recovery room. She hadn't seen him, and she hadn't done anything inappropriate, but he sensed an evolution in their relationship. He understood why they'd become closer since being flushed through the waterway because he had felt a bond with Jun. Being in the trenches with someone definitely strengthens a relationship. He knew this, but it still stung.

Ana-Clara reached over and placed her hand on top of his forearm, startling him out of his haze of memories.

"Don't worry." Her warm reassuring smile spread like wildflowers to her amber eyes.

Tarian peered at her with suspicion. How had she known what his mind was thinking?

"Believe with your heart, not with your eyes." She leaned in to whisper.

He smiled back at this silly woman. They were the only two people in the room. She didn't need to whisper.

"She loves you. Do something about it!" She raised her voice and shoved his arm.

"Alright," Tarian said, amazed by her shifting moods, but still curious about what she knew and how she knew it. He smiled again at her and thoughtfully reached for her hand. He held it for a brief second before she snatched it away.

"Oh no you don't, clever boy."

"What?" he said with the devilish grin of a naughty child. He opened his mouth to ask her what she knew of Audrey's innermost feelings when Audrey herself walked into the room.

"Too late," Ana-Clara told him with a wink.

Audrey carried a stack of documents nearly as tall as she was topped with the trusted tablet. Joe and Margaret trailed in behind her. She placed piles of papers on the table in front of the empty chairs then sat next to Tarian to wait for the High Council to join them.

Eleanor walked in looking almost fully recovered. She wore one of her classic fastidiously tailored blackberry suits, but instead of heels her feet were tucked into flats, and her hand held a cane assisting her balance. In a couple of days, the cane would no longer be needed.

She led the four members of the High Council. Audrey had told Tarian Eleanor was meeting with the High Council in private before their official meeting, but it seemed decisions had already been fashioned and this made Tarian leery. She graciously took her seat and gave the floor over to Audrey.

"We have a lot to cover so let's get started." Audrey divided her documents into four piles. "First, the village is secure. Vice-Chancellor Margaret has done an excellent job with public relations. The past physical destruction has been repaired, and the villagers' suspicions of our kind are rapidly fading. All vendors are open and selling once again. Margaret, would you like to say something before this issue is concluded."

"Yes, thank you." Margaret teetered to stand. "I met with the village board yesterday. They were extremely delighted to learn the former Chancellor will be rejoining the Guardians. They trust Eleanor. They've met with and interacted with several awakened Sleepers and have agreed to end all petitions against our kind. The party has been named the Celebration of Hope and our precious little Hope is planning a heartfelt speech that I assure you will cohere any remaining split between villager and Guardian."

"Terrific," Audrey said.

"Thank you. That is all." Margaret took her seat.

Audrey continued, "Here is the completed proposal for

the Bar District's water passage. I have laid out as per our agreement, exactly how Rain's Gate will continue safe passage for creatures under Guardian supervision."

Tarian sat straight up in his chair.

Audrey cocked her head in his direction. "Qui, Jun, and Hu are now official Guardian ambassadors, and our liasons to these creatures."

"Border penetration is illegal. That waterway is dangerous," Tarian said.

"Mortal law does not apply here," Councilor William said.

"Did the President agree to this?" Tarian argued.

"This is creature law, Tarian," Audrey said. "These laws have existed far longer than the Entente. We have always kept these laws hidden from the mortals and will continue to do so."

"And yet when we need help, Entente military lose their lives for us." Hot patriotism ran thick in his veins as he fought this point against the woman he loved. He'd only been a Guardian for a few months, but spent years training at the EMA side-by-side with mortals.

"May I remind you young one," High Councilor George leaned in to hover over the table, "there would not be an Entente if it was not for us."

Tarian crossed his arms and pushed back into his chair. He had no vote here. He surveyed Audrey. She had had no knowledge of Rain's Gate before he found it. She had been furious to hear the High Council had not only had knowledge of border penetration, but she accepted it. What had changed? Bureaucratic bullshit, he thought.

The four High Councilors huddled while reviewing Audrey's papers. After several long minutes, Elizabeth turned to address the group. "We are all in favor of this agreement."

"Very well, let's move on." Audrey glanced at Ana-Clara. Audrey's face broke into a smile when addressing the Bruja Blanca. "Ana-Clara is now free to leave the village, and we recognize your valiant contribution to the Guardians' security. Without you, fourteen Guardians wouldn't be alive today. We'd like to extend an invitation to remain inside the village for the Celebration of Hope. We will bestow you with our Medal of Honor and recognize your exceptional contribution to the Guardians of Dare. Will you attend?"

"Surely, that would be lovely," Ana-Clara said, her blossoming face bringing light into the dreary room.

"Lastly, Grand Sorcerer Lautaro," Audrey paused but was interrupted before she could continue.

Eleanor stood and spoke with authority. "The High Council and I have discussed this matter and have a plan of action. Do you mind Audrey?"

Audrey flashed a decorous smile. "By all means, continue."

Audrey took her chair next to Tarian. He touched her arm, she didn't pull away, but she didn't turn to look at him either. She stiffened under his palm, and he knew she felt slighted. She had told him earlier that she'd gladly give up her position as Chancellor to Eleanor, since she was far better qualified to be a soldier than a leader. But he knew her too well, and she never gave in without a fight.

"Lautaro cannot be allowed to have any golden ichor in his possession. Now that we have cracked the code to his protective border, we plan to get it back," Eleanor said.

"Are you sending an army to Manaus?" Audrey asked.

"No, we are sending two Guardians."

Tarian followed the gaze of her eyes to their target, his father. He began to protest when she switched her focus to him.

"Joe and Tarian with the help of our insider friends Vixy, Dante, and Lola."

Audrey shot back to her feet. "I'm going too."

"No, Audrey. You will remain here. You are required to brief Eleanor and fulfill your promised duties to the villagers," High Councilor George barked, his voice as sharp as a shard of ice.

"I demand you leave Lola out of this. She's only a girl, and she nearly died trying to help us last time," Audrey's words whipped out of her mouth wrapping their wrath around Eleanor and the High Council members.

Before Audrey could be reprimanded for her outburst, Tarian spoke up, "My father and I will not require Lola's assistance, but as for Dante and Vixy, I hardly think it's fair of us to ask so much of them without offering something in return."

"What we offer in return, young man," Councilor George said with a snarl of his lip, "is not to report them to the Lavender

Witches."

"You wouldn't dare," Tarian's words were a venomous hiss through his clenched teeth. His rage inches away from an explosion.

"Watch it, Tarian." Dad advised from across the table.

"I suggest when all of this is over you go to the library and familiarize yourself with the Esurient Eternals and their creature law that predates your existence by a millennium. Do I make myself understood?" George squared his bloodless face to Tarian, glared at him with lucid eyes such a light shade of blue they nearly disappeared into the white of his sclera. The haunting effect silenced Tarian.

"Tarian, Joe, Audrey," Eleanor said, breaking the building tension in the room. "Let us discuss this in my," she paused, "former office."

"Yes, of course." Audrey acknowledged everyone at the round table. "Meeting adjourned."

As they all exited, Audrey fell behind and nudged Tarian. "You do realize George could've thrown your ass in jail for your insolence."

"I'd like to see him try," Tarian said, arrogantly.

"We can't solve all of the world's issues. Vixy knows the laws. Besides, you and Joe are the best, and I'm going to insist I go along as well. The three of us can't fail." She smiled warmly at him, carrying her load of papers.

His pulse lessened. He felt more in control of his anger but chose to remain silent a little longer.

Audrey tilted her head in suggestion. "Come on, walk with me to the Chancellor's office."

"Your office," Tarian said.

"For now."

He gave her a sideways glance and matched her pace. Having her by his side renewed him. The beat of his heart returned to a steady rhythm as the tender warmth of his girlfriend's smile encircled him. He followed her into the grand office where she unceremoniously dumped her cargo on the desk.

"Oh sorry, I should've helped you with those." He reached his hand out to catch the tablet as it slipped off the stack.

She rolled her eyes and sighed.

"I know you're strong and perfectly capable of handling the load. It's just the thought. Or you could propose that the High Council step out of the dark ages and use modern technology."

"Ha!" she laughed, as did he, then she stared at him.

Her eyes burned through him, making every inch of his body ache for her touch, but he didn't dare approach her, for as welcoming as she looked she was equally as terrifying. Plus, the others would stroll in at any minute to map out their dangerous, covert mission.

FORTY-FOUR

TRAITOR REVEALED

Tarian fidgeted and paced inside Vixy's secret house. She squinted menacingly at him. Jun sat in a chair behind Vixy but wasn't exempt from her wrath. Her boyfriend's life was in danger again. She'd just laid into them screaming colorful obscenities in different languages. If words could cut, their faces would be a shredded mess. It had been over an hour since Joe flew from the window's ledge of the safe house to the mystical castle by the river. Dread began to brew.

Humid air interlaced through Joe's wispy feathers as he fully expanded his wings to glide over the lush green land that separated the steel and mirrored glass of the modern city from the castle's ancient stone, wood, and iron. With a hawk's precise vision, he saw the Maldito Ministry Soldiers dutifully parading behind the parapet on the allure. Joe opened his beak and screeched.

Moments later he reached the castle balcony, but the doors were shut. Fearing he'd give himself away if he hovered around the glass, he encircled the tallest tower twice then settled on a corbel. His sharp claws dug into the crusty stone. He had a good view of the exterior of the terrace, but he wanted to peer inside to find out why Dante hadn't been able to open the doors on cue.

Joe flew high above when the doors finally opened, and the brawny Lautaro strolled onto his veranda puffing on a pipe. The hawk could be seen but remained in the sky searching the ground below for a kill. Lautaro turned to admire the bird of prey. Once the casual stare turned into a curious investigation, Joe dove. Like an arrow he dropped several stories, snatched an innocent squirrel with his sharp beak, and coasted into the forest.

Under the cover of trees, Joe spit the vermin out in disgust. He could've eaten it in his hawk form. He knew from experience that it would've tasted natural on his raptor's tongue, but his scientific mind thought of the numerous parasites and shuddered.

His mission had been compromised. His disguise probably went unnoticed by Lautaro, but he couldn't risk it. To be safe, he'd remain hidden in the treetops until nightfall and return under the shadows of the darkness.

Words materialized on the white board bound by the seeing spell. *Dante 5 minutes.*

"Thanks be to the Goddess," Vixy chanted then growled at Tarian and hissed at Jun.

After five long minutes of excruciating silence, Dante plowed through the door and hurdled the steps. Vixy jumped into his arms and kissed him with fury.

The kiss lingered uncomfortably. Thankfully, Jun coughed and cleared her throat.

Breathless, Dante spoke, "I saw your friend. I'd almost gotten Lautaro out of his room when he wanted a smoke. His damn pipes. After his smoke, he told me about the hawk. He bragged about how such a magnificent predator had visited him. I didn't let on that I too had seen the bird for fear my voice would break and give me away. Anyway, the hawk dove to catch something then took his kill into the forest. I returned several times but saw the vial of gold still on the shelf. I believe he's waiting for the night. Don't you think?"

"Yes, that's a plan we'd discussed if Lautaro had made him," Tarian said.

"No, Lautaro thinks he's a hawk not a man. We are good," Dante said.

"Did you leave the terrace doors open?" Vixy asked.

"Yes."

"Good, then your job is done. You can go home." Vixy

placed her hands on her hips and expanded her narrow chest in an attempt to look dominant while surrounded by people a foot taller and broader than her.

"No, I want to help. I know you worry for me my darling." He took her face in his hands. "I do this for me. Lautaro is an evil sorcerer. He killed my uncle and my friend's sister, and I know many more stories of his brutality."

"You know I'll die if he hurts you." Pain crossed her face.

"And I for you. You put your life in danger far more than I do mine." Dante smiled.

"When are ya gonna go back?" Jun asked.

"Now. My shift doesn't end until eight o'clock. I'm on lunch break."

"Shouldn't Jun and I accompany you, as guards? You could get us uniforms," Tarian said.

"No, that would be far more risky. Your hawk has proven he can fly into the castle. He'll grab the box, and I'll let you know when he's flown away," Dante said.

"Okay." Tarian agreed, but he hated the waiting. He wanted to do something, be useful.

Jun paced the rug, shaking her head. "Why did we even come?" A tuft of her silky black hair fell over her eyes. She flipped it away with a vicious slap.

"As back up, in case Dante needs you," Vixy said.

The final shade of darkness drifted down to the branch where Joe perched. The forest blended together as one black canvas with darker strokes of coal where the tree trunks stood and the dirt floor lie. The moon was as thin as an apple peel in the starless sky. Only ice chips of light glinted off the river this eve.

Joe shoved off of the sturdy branch that had held him all day to soar to the castle's towering heights. Swooping down with grace and speed, Joe sailed through the open doors into the room and wrapped his talons around the transparent box. His wings spanned the length of the bookshelf fluttering and casting gusts that disturbed the manuscripts and other delicate items Lautaro collected.

With his prize in hand, he turned to fly out only to find himself caught. Lautaro and an Apostólo stood in front of the now closed balcony doors. Two Castle Guards manned the shut doors to the hallway. He was as trapped as the golden ichor in its pristine crystal cube.

He gouged out the eyes of a guard with the bladed point of his talons and nearly dropped the ichor. The others attempted to net the wild hawk, but the powerful wings with their slippery black tipped feathers proved too elusive.

Lautaro threw up his arms in a grand swirling motion, calling the element of wind. The air swirled, sucking Joe into its tornado. He flapped against the current until exhaustion set in.

He'd almost given up when the wind sucked from the room. The entrance door swung open. Dante had risked all to save Joe's life and shown himself for what he truly was, a traitor.

Joe didn't hesitate. He took the brave boy's offer and soared out of the room and down the hall like a bolt of lightning. As he flew away, he heard Dante's screams. The Apóstolo's dagger had reached its target. The heart-wrenching cry of agony made Joe determined to get out, not only to protect his fellow Guardians, but also to honor the young life sacrificed for their mission.

He snaked and twisted through the endless hall. The ends of his wings grazed the stone wall, and he pulled them to his side to blaze the remaining few feet like a bullet shot from a gun. Erupting into the keep and on a desperate search for the inner bailey, he gathered speed, risking his own neck if he didn't pull up fast enough as he approached the wall. He made the turn, but a bullet marked him. Luckily, he'd already flown several stories high and was able to dart through a loophole. He spiraled through the hole followed by a bullet that curved. It had to be spellbound, and who knew what evil magic it possessed. Spinning, zigzagging, and bobbing it clipped his talon. Blood spewed like spray paint, but he didn't let go of his prize.

He dove low to fly through the forest, knowing Lautaro's aircrafts would soon be on the hunt. Hovering close to ground he sailed out of the South American barrier, over the Gulf of Mexico, and across the Entente border wall. As he flew, he prayed for Tarian's safety, but he didn't look back. He only needed to get to a military base, then he could contact Piper. She could vade Tarian to safety.

Tarian wore a path in the rug with his pacing. "Something's wrong. It's almost ten. I can't wait any longer!"

Suddenly the white board wrote in loud, squeaky strokes: *DON'T SHOOT!*

Someone hit the front door with a thud. Vixy raced down the stairs to find a Castle Guard carrying a dying Dante in his arms. Blood slashed crosswise on his face and dotted his arms, as Dante lay limp across his chest.

"Oh the Goddess! Oh the Goddess!" Vixy hyperventilated. "Get him upstairs."

The man trudged the steps gasping for breath. Sweat poured over the man's face from his perspiration-soaked hair.

Tarian thrust his arms under Dante's body relieving the exhausted man and placed him on the sofa. "He's breathing," Tarian yelled. "He's alive, but barely."

"You!" Vixy turned to Jun and spoke as if a demon had taken over her body. "You fix him." When Jun didn't respond, she screamed, "Now!"

"I can't," Jun said.

"Yes, yes, yes. Give him your blood. Make him undead. Do it!" Vixy rushed to Jun and clawed at her shirt. Her lavender eyes went deep purple with desperation.

"I can't." Jun's voice wavered and tears welled in her eyes. "I'm sorry. We aren't made creatures. I'm cursed by my ancestors. I'm a preta, a hungry ghost, not a vampire."

Vixy ran in circles then stopped and tore chunks of her ink black hair out. "Fine," she stated a little too calmly. She vanished. Several painstaking seconds later, she returned with Lola clinging to her side. She shoved Lola in Dante's direction. "Fix it Lola. Please, help him," with these words Vixy broke down into sobs.

"You're a vampire?" Tarian asked.

"Yes," the young girl answered.

Tarian smiled a little as he thought how worried he and Audrey had been for this twelve-year-old. How Audrey had adamantly sworn that she'd defy the High Council if they called upon Lola's help again. And she was a child of the night, stronger and far more resistant to death than Vixy or Dante.

Lola knelt next to the sofa. The fabric squished from Dante's blood that had soaked it through. With big brown eyes, Lola glanced up at Vixy and whispered, "I'll try."

Vixy handed her a knife from the kitchen drawer. Lola ran the blade across her wrist. She let the blood drip into his mouth then she dropped her wrist onto his mouth forcing his lips to seal around her delicate skin.

"Drink," pleaded Vixy.

At first the blood pooled around the seal, bubbling and gurgling to escape. Then Dante jerked and sucked. Lola's face winced as he yanked her arm with the force of the feeding.

Tarian and Jun watched in silent awe, but neither Dante nor Lola looked well. Lola's skin paled, and her limbs wilted while Dante's persistent sucking slowed, and he eventually released her arm. His eyes rolled back, and he seized up.

Vixy paced in circles again. Suddenly, she stopped and leveled her gaze on Tarian and Jun. "Get out!" she yelled.

"No, they can't leave. Lautaro's men are everywhere," the man who had rescued Dante said, but Vixy paid him no attention.

"Leave now," Vixy ordered in a tenacious, measured grumble.

"I'm so sorry, Vixy," Tarian said. He'd honor her wishes.

"But he's going to live now," Jun added.

"He might live. Might! The process has only just begun. And if he survives, he'll hate me for doing this to him." Vixy closed her eyes standing stick still. She continued speaking with closed eyes, "He's not a man anymore. He's not human. He'll hate me forever." Her lids flew open, and the balls of her bloodshot scleras bulged. "I should've let him die. I was selfish—weak. I wish I never saved your life Tarian Prescott. I hate you! I hate you." She pounded on his chest until Jun pulled her off.

"We're leaving, and we're deeply sorry." Jun put an arm around Tarian. "C'mon. We'll find our way."

Tarian had never in his entire lifetime felt more helpless, more dirty, than at that moment. With watery eyes, he looked at Lola. He tried with all his heart and soul to convey to her his sorrow and his wish for the best for her, but he said nothing. She reminded him of Chloe, innocent but shrewd. He wanted to wrap her in his arms and thank her and apologize. Instead, he bowed his head.

He turned to read the white board. It was blank. His eyes fell again to Lola. She smiled and that was how he left her.

Once outside, they heard the shuffling of Maldito Ministry Soldiers in the streets. They ducked into an alleyway and hid behind a large trash container.

"We have to stay here until they leave," Jun whispered.

"Okay," Tarian agreed. "I can hear for miles. I'll know when it's safe to lose our cover."

As the minutes turned to hours, Tarian's knees ached from crouching. Jun looked to him every ten minutes with yellow, questioning eyes, and he shook his head each time, except this last time. He stared back at her in surprise. Astonished he finally heard nothing. They stood, stretched their stiff legs and cracked their tight necks.

"C'mon," Jun said, "We have a long walk outta the city."

"I know. I remember," his voice dry and hoarse.

They'd walked for hours and passed under the gates of Manaus long ago, when a silhouetted figure appeared in the distance. Tarian and Jun halted and grabbed their weapons. He glanced at Jun to gauge her reaction. She looked just as puzzled as he was. The figure hadn't been there a second ago. Had the bright, intense sunlight played tricks on his perfect sight?

"Tarian?" said the figure shadowed by the backlight of the sunrise.

"Piper?" Tarian asked.

"Yes!" She squealed and disappeared only to reappear inches away from his face.

He stumbled backward.

"Oh, sorry. I guess I went a little too far."

"How did you find us?" Tarian asked.

Piper held out her hand to reveal a tiny strand of his hair, hardly visible in the thin morning light. "I'm getting better at this."

"Never mind that, get us the hell outta here," Jun said.

"Okay, here goes." Piper gathered them close. "Hold on tight. I'm still new to travelling with company, and I've never taken two people before." And with a beaming smile, she gripped them tightly and nodded.

FORTY-FIVE

HOME

Tarian felt like a billiard ball struck by a cue stick as he traveled with Piper. He bounced and the blood in his veins jumped. Acid burned his empty stomach. So, when the journey finally ended and his eyes fixed on the interior of the Guardian library, he didn't dare move his feet. He waited for the nausea to pass before taking a step. Jun teetered and grabbed a chair.

Piper skipped unfazed to her post behind the desk and smiled. "You guys alright?" She asked. "You look a little pale."

Jun blew the black strands out of her face. "Is my head connected to my neck or my stomach?" She smirked. "I think I'm gonna hurl." She turned to Tarian and laughed. "Payback's a bitch."

"Oh no. No puking. Piper, get some water please." Tarian owed her one from Angel Falls, but he didn't think he could clean up someone's vomit.

Piper reappeared with a glass of water in hand. She handed

it to Jun who sipped it slowly.

Jun's avocado face returned to its normal pale honey color, and the sallowness around her eyes receded.

"You look fine." Tarian slapped her on the back.

"Too bad, I really wanted to see ya clean up my puke," Jun said with an overly toothy smile.

"You would," Tarian said, then his mind raced back to reality. "Piper where's my dad? You said he made it to the Entente."

"Yes, he made it to the tip. I'd guess he's left Key West by now. Should be home soon. Probably on a tiltrotor."

"But he's okay?"

"Yes, he took a shot in the foot and shoulder, but of course those healed quickly. I've seen your dad fly. He can maneuver like a target missile, and he's just as fast," Piper said, full of the jitters and all smiles, the short lavender tips of her golden hair vibrating with excited energy.

"I'm goin' to the Inn. It's been real." Jun waved and waltzed out of the library.

Tarian left too. It was late, but he guessed Audrey would be working, not sleeping. He meandered the maze of halls and stairs feeling as nervous as a schoolboy with a crush on his teacher. The door opened ajar. He tapped it little by little until it opened all the way.

Audrey sat in her chair. She leaned back with her arms crossed, and a grin spread wide across her angular face. Her hair was pulled back in its usual ponytail with an acute line of bangs across her forehead. "What are you doing?"

"Hi."

"Hi."

"We did it. I'm back in one piece. We got the ichor." He stepped forward, arms splayed.

"I know. I've already spoken with Joe."

He just stood still and awkwardly silent, opposing thoughts raced through his mind. He wanted to tell her all about Dante and Lola, and the horror he'd witnessed, and the state of agony in which they left Vixy, but at the same time, he just wanted to take her in his arms and kiss her.

She strolled around the desk never turning her eyes away from his. As she moved closer, his breath quickened, and his heart raced. She kissed him. He embraced her tightly as if he could never let her go.

With her body snug in his arms, she looked up at him. "It's going to be all right. You did it. You saved us again."

He looked down at her and wanted to tell her how much he loved her. He wanted to ask to move in to her apartment. He wanted to blurt out plans for their future together, but he only bit his inner cheeks and smiled. "What am I going to do with myself without any Wakers to hunt?"

"I can think of something you can do." She kissed him again.

He melted into her, but she pushed him away.

"But first we have to go to your mom's."

"What? You can't do that to me." He grinned and drew her closer.

"Sorry, but we're already late for your surprise." She wiggled out of his arms and took him by the hand. "Come on."

"Surprise? I'm not exactly ready for company," he said.

She took in the sight of him—sweaty hair, smudged face, and dirty clothes. "They'll understand you've been in the field." She sprayed him with the perfume sitting on her desk.

"Sweat and flowers."

His sarcasm made her laugh. She grabbed his arm, and he let her lead him as his feet flopped heavily against the ground in protest.

Voices and laughter seeped through his mother's closed door. He stepped into the foyer not to a party but to a gathering. Charlie had come home from college, Patrick and Teresa held hands as they talked with him. Tarian must've missed the revelation of their relationship. Eleanor and Mom stood engrossed in a deep conversation until her eye caught his.

"Tarian." Carolyn walked over and wrapped him in her arms.

"Hi, Mom." He kissed her cheek.

All smiles, his mom said, "I've got a birthday cake for

Teresa, better late than never. Seventeen! I can't believe it! Now that everyone is home, we can finally celebrate."

"Where's Chloe?" He followed his mom's line of sight and found what kept Chloe preoccupied.

"Look who's here, Tarian!" Chloe hollered in delight.

Tarian smiled at his baby sister. She was always ten times louder than her size.

"What up my man?" Gabe, his old friend from the Entente Military Academy, hugged him, slapping him brotherly on the back.

"Gabe! Maria! It's great to see you." Tarian beamed at his two best friends. He'd missed them. He hadn't even spoken to them in the last few months. Hunting Wakers had consumed him.

"You look like crap," Maria said.

Tarian laughed.

"Give me a hug anyway," Maria ordered and embraced him tightly. "I hear that crazy girl from the library is throwing a party." Maria cocked a brow.

"You heard correct," Audrey said. "Ain't no party like a Guardian party."

Maria gave her a look and shook her head.

"Well then, I'll get us some drinks." Audrey retreated into the kitchen for punch.

"I'm glad you both are here. You can come with me tomorrow. I have a special errand to run before the celebration." A sneaky expression slid across Tarian's face pulling his lips into clever curl.

Gabe had opened his mouth to ask questions, but just then Joe walked through the door. Everyone rushed to great him, but his wife got to him first.

Carolyn kissed Joe. "Welcome home."

Tarian's heart swelled with love. His dad's homecoming confirmed his decision.

FORTY-SIX

GUARDIAN PARTY

"Tarian," Chef Richard's loud voice boomed from across the tavern. He approached and gave him a big hug. "I met your nice friends from the EMA. What can I get you?"

"Hi Chef Richard, just a drink for now."

"Certainly, the drink of the day is a pumpkin mead with a twist. We'll all eat at the celebration. Oh what a spread I've dished out. Mmm Mmm! It'll be a day your taste buds will remember. All is right in the world again. I even have the finest steak tartare for that strange, spiky haired, sister/brother duo."

"Sounds terrific." Tarian sat down with his friends.

"Where's Audrey?" Maria asked.

"She'll meet us there," Tarian said curtly.

"Don't be nervous," Maria said.

"Is it that obvious?"

"Kind of," Gabe said.

"I just need a drink."

As if on cue, Chef Richard approached the table with three pints in hand. He plopped them on the table then slid each of them an overflowing mug. He smiled. "Enjoy. I've got a lot of work to do. See you later." Chef Richard retreated into the kitchen.

Tarian gulped the orange, frothy liquid. Gabe and Maria gave him a sideways glance.

"It's good. The Chef said it's the drink of the day. Try it."

Gabe swigged it and nodded. "That's good."

Maria sipped.

They reminisced about their days together at the academy, finished their drinks, and headed out of Headquarters and onto the cobbled street of the village. The air buzzed with excitement and crackled with energy raising the fine hairs on Tarian's arms. All vendors propped their doors open allowing the many customers to flow in and out. Peppy music drifted along the air lifting the steps of all who walked along. Laughter floated out of the mouths of friends happy to be out and about again shopping, eating, and gathering together without the fear of a Waker attack. The experience infused Tarian's spirit with light and exuberance. He had his friends and his home back.

The magical and colorful decorations for the celebration danced under the giant glimmering white tents erected in the vast grassy area at the end of the street. Piper had captured the theme of hope perfectly. His eyes wove through the crowd in search of Audrey.

Piper popped up and threw her arms around Gabe and

Maria.

The look of sheer surprise on their faces made Tarian laugh. "Piper, lady and gentleman."

She bowed playfully.

"Hi, how've you been?" they said.

"I've been terrific! You both look fabulous. It's going to be a great night. Here try this." Piper grabbed two toothpicks with what looked like bacon wrapped chocolate off of a tray carried by a man dressed in bright yellow and shoved them in their faces. She proceeded to hand another one to Tarian and grabbed a fourth for herself. With her mouth full, she said, "Aren't they amazing? Eat, eat, and find your table. The ceremony will start soon. Bye." She vanished leaving them tingling from her rush of energy.

Tarian smiled at his friends. "She loves party planning."

"I see." Maria chewed her appetizer.

Audrey walked on to a decorated platform with Hu, Jun, Qui, and Ana-Clara. Hu held one of her hands in both of his as they talked in what looked like an intimate conversation.

Tarian's eyes narrowed, his shoulders lifted, and his fists balled, but his smile remained in place as he tried to smother the jealous demon awakened by Hu's presence.

Maria's forehead wrinkled. She drew her lips together then she nudged Tarian out of his tunnel vision. "Who's the guy?"

He looked away from the annoying display of affection. "That's Hu."

"So what's their deal?" Gabe asked.

Tarian rolled his eyes. He didn't want to explain anything right now. The story was too long and convoluted, so he kept it simple. "Everyone on the stage is being honored tonight. None of them are Guardians or villagers, and they are being acknowledged for their outstanding contribution to us. Kind of like the party we had last spring after," he hesitated. "After we destroyed Zachary and his plan. But this party is far more lavish because we're also celebrating the return of our village. You wouldn't have recognized this place a month ago. No shops were open. Boarded up windows. Bashed out street lamps—"

"But what about the dude?" Maria cocked an eyebrow.

Tarian met her determined dark eyes with his softer ones, and she looked straight through him. He sighed. "He's a preta."

"A what?" Gabe asked.

"A preta. All you need to know is he's a creature not a human. Anyway, his creature ways cause him to, ah, basically," Tarian looked to the sky, stumbled some more, then said, "cause him to lust after her, but he's managed to control it. It's chemical. He saved her life so I'm grateful to him."

"Man, that's harsh," Gabe said.

"You have some freaky kinds, don't you?" Maria shook her head.

"Yep, welcome to the freak show." Tarian pulled a chair out and offered it to Maria.

Before he took his seat at their designated front row table, Hu bellowed, "Tarian!"

Everyone glanced in his direction.

Hu and Audrey motioned for him to join them.

"I guess I have to sit up there, but here comes everyone." Tarian's entire family and Patrick strolled toward them. Tarian gave a quick reintroduction then left with Teresa to join the others on stage.

Tarian went down the line receiving hugs from Ana-Clara, Qui, and Jun. Hu gave him a forceful, brotherly pat on the back and Audrey tucked his hand in hers. He sat wedged between them.

"You're looking much better," Tarian said to Hu. "I honestly didn't expect you to make it."

"Sorry, but I did." Hu laughed.

Tarian nodded and half joked. "Too bad."

"Well, it's all thanks to your sister and AC and the Guardian's advanced medical facility. A little magic, a little medicine, and poof, here I am. Good as new." Hu's lips curled into a wicked grin.

Tarian saw Hu's canary eyes drift in Audrey's direction. He leaned forward in his chair to block Hu's view of her. It was childish, he knew, but he couldn't stop himself.

Hu snickered, "Your girlfriend looks beautiful tonight."

Tarian's body temperature rose as his mind searched for a clever retort, but anger stole his wit. Luckily Audrey stood, walked to the podium, and began the announcements. Soon this would be over.

"Welcome Guardians, villagers, and honored guests. We

are happy to have our delightful village back and our Eleanor," she paused as the audience roared with applause. "It's been a difficult time, but with the combined efforts of all here today, we succeeded. I thank you, dear friends, for not losing faith even when you lost your dear loved ones. We have all lost too much in the past months, but tonight is a celebration of life and what we as a whole can accomplish. It takes a village, right?"

A faint chuckle circled the room at Audrey's attempt at humor. Like her predecessor Eleanor, Audrey lacked comic timing. One by one Audrey acknowledged the victims. When she finally got to Hope's name, she turned in the young girl's direction. "The Celebration of Hope has two meanings. Our beloved Hope, a survivor, a fighter, has something she'd like to say to all of you tonight." Audrey handed the microphone over to now thirteen-year-old Hope.

"Hi, everyone. I just wanted to say that I know all the wounds haven't entirely healed. I hear the gossip still tinged with judgment and prejudice, and I stand up here tonight to ask for it to stop. You all know and love my parents' bakery. Whether it's the cinnamon apple pie or the blueberry muffins. Well, let me tell you, that if mom forgets to add just one ingredient, they don't taste as good. It takes all the ingredients. We're all the ingredients. The Guardians add a little spice, the villagers add a little sweetness, Eleanor is the flour that bonds us together, Teresa mixes the batter, Audrey puts the pan in the oven, and Tarian watches over it with fork in hand to stab any evil taste testers," she paused, and everyone laughed at her analogy. "Of course, I could go on name by name, but we'd be here all night." She glanced down at a table. "Thomas, get up here." She waited for Thomas to hobble up the stage stairs with his one leg and crutches. "Thomas and I've been through the worst of this battle, and we've helped plan this party with Piper tonight, so we demand that all of us ingredients stick together, unite as one. The Wakers are dead, now we must bury the sadness that they left behind. Stick it in the oven and broil it!"

"Eat it and poop it out!" Thomas yelled out, engrossed in the moment.

"Thomas!" Hope scolded, then giggled along with the crowd. "Well, you get the idea." She left the stage escorting Thomas to the table as everyone gave her a standing ovation.

Audrey stood up again and announced, "Now to introduce my hero."

Tarian's stomach lurched because he knew she wasn't talking about him. *Did she really just introduce Hu as her hero?*

"Ana-Clara."

A chill of relief flooded Tarian's body.

"The incredible Bruja Blanca. She worked, with the help of our own Teresa, to bring back our beloved Guardians. Thank you." Audrey placed the Medal of Honor around her neck.

Ana-Clara's large eyes swept the crowd. "I'm glad I came here and met all of you. I haven't traveled in many years. I will return after the celebration and probably not travel again, too many people to help back home. I will miss you, Teresa." She glanced and nodded at Teresa who smiled warmly in return. "I feel a lot of love in this tent, but I still sense some unrest. Please, listen to the young people and let it go. I know it's hard but only through love can progress blossom." Ana-Clara sat back into her seat.

"Lastly, we're indebted to the Jones family, Hu, Jun, and Qui." Audrey placed the medals around all three of their necks. Jun and Qui stepped aside but Hu remained. He stood so close to Audrey barely a whisper could slide between them. "Would you like to say something?"

"Yes, I want to thank you and Tarian for not leaving me to die in the castle and to Ana-Clara and Teresa for healing me. AC, I bet you never thought you'd be bringing *me* back to the living," he laughed and Ana-Clara shook her head. "Life is strange, but love is even stranger." He grabbed Audrey's hand.

Tarian's spine iced over as he stiffened in his chair on the platform in front of his friends and family. He feared the words about to spill from Hu's mouth. Regret fermented inside him about the fight brewing if Hu's words didn't drastically change direction.

"There are many races, creatures and mortals alike. You in the village are the lucky few in the world to inhabit and know them. Only if we are united can we have peace." He turned to gaze into Audrey's silvery eyes. "I give you your forest, my Timber Wolf." The decorated tent morphed into a mystical forest. It smelled of lush evergreen trees and twinkled with stardust and fireflies. The crisp and cool air livened with energy. Everyone gasped at its beauty. Hu released Audrey's hand and smiled, then he turned to the crowd and shouted, "Let's celebrate!"

With that, the band Piper had hired from the local Blonde Dog Pub began to play a popular modern dance song. Soon everyone hopped out of their seats and danced.

Hu strutted over to Tarian and patted him so hard on the back that Tarian's sturdy torso pushed forward a little.

"Nice speech," Tarian said without a smile.

"What can I say? I may be a hungry ghost, but I've always known how to throw a great party." Hu's lips curled upwards and his eyes narrowed.

"Yes, you can. Speaking of that, when do you go back to the Bar District?"

"What? You don't want me to stay?"

Tarian didn't take the bait but he couldn't resist a slight smile.

"You're a lucky man, First Born."

Tarian cringed at the horrendous nickname.

"She loves you. Don't screw it up." Hu gave Tarian a brotherly – or more accurately, an evil step-brotherly – pat on the back. Then he morphed into his Tiger persona and leaped off the stage. The big cat slinked through the crowd but no one feared him. With all the other spectacular decorations they figured the giant cat was part of the magical illusion.

Tarian laughed as he noticed the tiger gently rub his silky fur against every pretty girl in his path. Each one petted him. He turned around and gave Tarian a wink.

Tarian remained alone on the stage high above the dance floor, but it was no longer a wooden platform, it was now an earthy hill. He browsed the crowd. Teresa danced arm in arm with Patrick, his mom and dad swayed happily, and Gabe and Maria skillfully matched step in their dance moves. Audrey spoke with Piper and Margaret on the other side of the forested floor. Tarian came down from the mound and wove his way through the crowd.

"Can I have this dance, my lady?" Tarian asked with a mocking old-fashioned bow and kiss of the back of the hand.

Audrey's face lit up as the liquid silver in her eyes shined. "But of course, dear sir."

After dancing to two songs, he led her away from the crowd. They strolled the gleaming midnight streets of the village. She stumbled a few times as her high heels dug into the grooves of the stone. He withheld a sarcastic comment as he swept her off her feet and into his arms. She didn't protest, instead she nuzzled her head into the crook of his neck. Her red clover scent comforted his heart and lifted his courage. He walked on with her in his arms past the bakery, the toy store, and the picnic accessory shop, then he stopped in front of Café de la Nouvelle Natuche. He set her onto her high-heeled feet as gently as he could.

She looked up and saw their location and laughed. "Our place." She kissed him. Her lips a soft, short caress, then she pulled away to look up into his toasty chocolate eyes. Her head slowly fell as he bent down on one knee. She jolted back marginally.

Tarian froze with Audrey's motion. *She's upset. She doesn't want this.* Imperceptibly he pushed on the toes of his bent leg slightly rising.

Audrey stepped into him running her hands through his styled thick chestnut brown hair tousling it up the way she liked it.

Without further hesitation for fear his nerves would soon overwhelm him, he whipped the tiny blue velvet box out of his pocket. It was warm from his body heat. He opened it and presented it to her. He smiled, but his eyes flickered nervously. "I want to spend eternity with you."

"I want that too." Her voice cracked, but her determined tone and steadfast stare did not waver.

"Will you marry me?"

Tears streamed down her smiling face.

His heart leapt from his chest as he waited for her to answer.

She forced the word, "Yes," past the huge lump in her throat. She took the ring from the box and slid it onto her ring finger.

It was a new and shiny piece of jewelry that Tarian had purchased with the help of Gabe and Maria. His father had a collection of fine rings far more lavish than the one he chose, but he didn't want anything from the past. Their love was new and young. He wanted a ring to represent the future, their future.

"It's perfect, Tarian." Audrey cupped his face with her hands and brought it toward hers. Her tender kiss planted briefly on his lips but intertwined through his entire body.

He took her into his arms and pressed his lips hard against hers capturing all of her. He never wanted to let her go.

FORTY-SEVEN

THE FOLLOWING SUMMER

Piper slept alone in her apartment. In a dream, she drifted. No, not exactly. It wasn't a dream, nor was it vading. She relaxed and allowed whatever force held her to control her. Like the time-hop of sleep, she opened her eyes and felt as if only seconds had passed, and yet, from the scenery, she knew she was far from the village.

She stepped out of the mist that carried her and into the bedroom of a little girl. The girl panted with exhaustion. Long silvery gold hair as fine as silk framed her face in perfect lines. Her skin paled next to her distressed eyes, big and pinned to her cherub face like two giant amethyst gemstones. She sat cross-legged on top of a flowery bedspread in a pink nightgown trimmed in lace, both were clean but stained and ripped. She'd been waiting for Piper.

"Did you summon me?" Piper whispered, for it was nighttime and the tiny room's door was shut. Piper assumed the house held more rooms with more people sleeping inside of it. But when she peered out the window the sun rose. Had she drifted all through the night?

"I did." The child regained steady breathing.

"Are you okay?"

"I'll be fine."

"How old are you?"

"Three or so."

Piper thought that she appeared to be a lot older but didn't question it. "You're beautiful."

Her angel lips curled shyly. "You are, too."

"I'm Piper."

"I know."

"What's your name?"

"I'm Nichola Lycott."

Shock waves of horror shuddered through Piper. She looked over both shoulders fearing Gregory Lycott hid in the shadowy corners of the room. Vivid images of soulless eyes and the carnage of babies filled her mind. *Where was he?* Her head snapped back and forth.

Nichola remained seated and content. "We're alone."

"Why have you brought me here?" Panic laced the question.

"I need you. It took me a long time to find you," she paused. "They're after me. My father can no longer hide me." Terror grew in the little girl's voice too.

"Who's after you?"

"I don't know. But someone spies on us. And I feel something horrible will happen soon. Dad says I'm special. I'm supposed to help the immortals and stay away from Lavender Witches because they kill people like us."

"Us?" Piper softened and took a step toward the sweet girl. "You have the eyes." Piper's fingers brushed the curtain of hair away from her face.

"I know. I'm like you, tainted."

"Tainted?"

"We're not pure. I have the blood of a Lavender Witch and Guardian Immortal."

Piper froze. No one in this century was born of Guardian blood except Tarian. Piper's misgivings showed on her face. Gregory Lycott was a deceitful traitor, Zachary's right-hand man. When the Guardians destroyed Zachary's warehouse of immortal offspring where he'd been breeding his immortal army, everyone inside had been destroyed, but Gregory's body was never found. The Guardians knew he'd escaped and wondered when he'd show his treacherous face again. He must have been raising this innocent child and feeding her lies this whole time.

Nichola slammed her fist on the bed in soundless violence. "It's true!"

A thumping and banging noise came from the other side of the door as if Gregory had stumbled into the kitchen for a midnight snack or breakfast. The exact time was still a mystery.

"You must go." Nichola jumped off the bed and tugged

Piper to her feet. "Dad will check on me after he has his coffee."

"I don't understand why you brought me here in the first place."

"Get the others and search me out in the Wastelands. And don't hurt Daddy," Nichola spoke as an adult, wise and calm. She yanked strands of her hair out and handed them to Piper. "Come back soon. We want to go home."

Her words were a warning and a threat, and Piper fully believed this child capable of wrathful destruction.

Nichola brought her hands into her chest in prayer position, then thrust them outwards, palms up, arms outstretched and open. Her body shook as if it took great effort to cast Piper away. Like miniscule grains of sand into the cool mist, Piper drifted back over the ocean, back to sleep inside Guardian Headquarters.

Piper shot up in bed, eyes wide. The bedsheets sodden with sweat. It felt like a dream, but she knew it wasn't. She remembered everything. She looked down at her hand as it uncurled and saw a tinsel strand of golden hair. Carefully she placed the hair inside a tiny locket then secured it around her neck for safekeeping.

FIRST BORN TRILOGY

WHO HELPED AND WHAT HAPPENED?

First Born has been a unique journey along a very bumpy road. One I began several years ago. Book 1, *First Born,* was first self-published in December of 2015 with *First Awakened* launching soon after in March of 2016. The third and last book in the trilogy manifested slowly and in pieces that proved difficult to organize. Also, another book idea took root in my head. It was loud and wouldn't yield so the *First Born* trilogy got placed on the back burner. I wrote *Dog Girl,* my debut young adult contemporary romance. *Dog Girl* found an agent and a publisher. If you're interested it's out in the world under my pen name, Gabi Justice.

Meanwhile, the third book, *Last Chance,* began to come together. Before releasing *Last Chance,* I decided to query a few independent publishing houses that accepted self-published books. One loved it and offered to publish in 2022. So, in 2019, *First Born* and *First Awakened* were shelved and the waiting game began. Then the pandemic hit. The said publishing house went out of business. It was difficult and discouraging but all three books were complete, never published with said publisher, and I had my rights back, so what was I to do—relaunch the trilogy myself!

I'd learned a few things since 2015. The wild ride had brought me knowledge and industry friends. I am forever grateful to those who have helped shape the *First Born Trilogy.*

A big thank you to my SCBWI critique group: Jill Watson, Andrea Tripke, and Ann Marie Meyers for reading lengthy, monthly experts of *Last Chance* and other stories. Thank you to my friends at the Tampa Writer's Alliance critique group—over twenty-five fellow writers who thickened my skin. Special thanks to my agent Sharon Belcastro for constantly believing in me. You may not have played a key role in these books but within my writing marathon you take the lead.

Thank you to Allison Newell, Tarian Prescott's first fan; to Sandy McCain who helped edit my first drafts; Jim Robertson for my eye-catching covers; to Diane and Jenny at BookRhythm for the fabulous support and promotion. I will be forever thankful to have sat next to Tasha Vincent at the On Point Book Fair in Tampa. Your editorial input lifted my writing to a greater level. Thank you, April Schlee for your keen proofreading eye. Thank you to my insightful friends and beta readers Mark Charest and Darrel Polsley for finding those pesky typos and errors that slipped past, for letting me know when something was out of place, and for your constant encouragement and input. To Emcat designs for former book covers and beautiful map designs. To Marina Charalambides for bringing the characters to life with your drawings. Also, to the beta readers who probably wondered if this trilogy was ever going to be completely published: Mattea Carberry, Valerie Senske, Susan VanNort, Julie Carrigan, Mimi Daniels, and the Book Gremlins.

Since this journey has been a long and winding path, I've probably forgotten to mention someone. If I have, I'm truly sorry. Every little bit counts and I'm grateful.

Lastly, a giant thanks to my readers and fans that have written reviews, joined my newsletter, and parties, all in support of Tarian and Audrey. You have brought my characters and world to life.

JANELLE GABAY

Janelle lives with her husband, three dogs, and a cat in Florida. Two of her three children are out of college and in the workforce. The third is close behind. They are her pride and joy. She was born in Nebraska and grew up in the Philippines, Virginia, Alabama, Maine, and Florida as an Air Force Brat. *First Born* is her debut novel. She spends her time writing, taking care of her animals, going to hockey games or tennis matches, and traveling with her family. She is a graduate from the University of South Florida.

You can visit her online at www.janellegabaybooks.com
Twitter @JanelleGabay
Instagram @janellegabaybooks
janellegabaybooks@gmail.com
Follow on Goodreads
Facebook page Author Janelle Gabay @authorjanellegabay

www.ingramcontent.com/pod-product-compliance
Lightning Source LLC
Chambersburg PA
CBHW021548110726
47902CB00004B/1073